P9-CBG-542

THE SCENT OF MURDER

THE SCENT OF MURDER

BARBARA BLOCK

KENSINGTON BOOKS

http://www.kensingtonbooks.com

Although the city of Syracuse is real, as are some of the place names I've mentioned, this is a work of fiction. Its geography is imaginary. Indeed, all the characters portrayed in this book are fictional and any resemblance to real people or incidents is purely coincidental.

KENSINGTON BOOKS are published by

Kensington Publishing Corp.
850 Third Avenue
New York, NY 10022

Library of Congress Card Catalog Number: 96-80067
ISBN 1-57566-195-0

First Printing: August, 1997
10 9 8 7 6 5 4 3 2 1

Printed in the United States of America

ACKNOWLEDGMENTS

I'd like to thank Kathy Veerbeck for her technical assistance. I would also like to thank my editor, John Scognamiglio, for his suggestions and unfailing kindness, and my son, Larry Block, for taking the time to read my manuscript and offer suggestions.

For Linda Kleinman,
who tells me stories from my past.
Thanks for your friendship.

THE SCENT OF MURDER

Chapter 1

It was the middle of October, and I was up on the ladder tacking a crepe paper skeleton to the wall behind the fish tanks when the girl walked in. For some reason, that's what I'd come to think of her as—the girl. She looked about fifteen, and she'd been in Noah's Ark three times in the past week and a half. She'd run her hand over the leashes, stopped and studied the fish tanks, and become absorbed reading the labels on the bags of cat food, but as soon as I'd start walking towards her, she'd bolt.

I had the impression she was working up her nerve to approach me, which was funny, considering the way she looked. I mean, you'd figure that anyone sporting Kool-Aid blue hair, heavy black eye makeup, white lipstick, and a nose ring big enough to fit Ferdinand the Bull, wouldn't be afraid of anything. Or maybe she was actually a shy, retiring soul who was getting into Halloween mode a couple of weeks early, and I was being uncharitable—a not uncommon occurrence, I've been informed, by the person that works for me.

In either case the girl had something new with her today: a large albino ferret lay draped over her left shoulder. It looked as if she'd decorated her oversized camo jacket with an ermine pelt. I watched her out of the corner of my eye as she strode over to the far shelves and paused to read the label on the flea and tick defoggers. After a minute of doing that, she turned and headed towards me. Her pace was slow, she kept stopping and pretending interest in this and that, and I'd managed to finish with the skeleton by the time she reached the ladder.

I nodded towards the ferret, as I climbed down the last rung. "He's a big boy."

A ghost of a smile flitted across the girl's face. "He weighs almost three pounds."

"I like the halter he has on." It had multi-colored stones pasted on the thick, blue nylon cloth. "Where'd you buy it?"

She pulled the zipper on her jacket up and down with her free hand. "I made it." The expression on her face gave me the impression she wasn't used to getting a lot of compliments.

"You did a good job."

She stroked the ferret's back. "My mother hates him. She says he smells bad."

"A lot of people feel that way."

"Do you?"

"No. I like ferrets."

"He's my best friend," she blurted out. She must not have intended to say that, because she looked embarrassed and changed the subject. "I thought this store was in a house."

"It was, but the house burned down awhile back." Now it was my turn to change the subject. I didn't like to talk about the fire. The scars on my calves were enough of a remembrance. "I moved the business here."

"Bummer." The girl shifted the ferret to her other shoulder.

"That's one way of putting it," I said, suppressing the vision of the flames licking at my legs.

The girl grimaced. Whether it was out of sympathy or boredom, I couldn't tell. "But you are Robin Light?" she asked. "You do own this place?"

"Yes. I own Noah's Ark."

She frowned. "Somehow I expected you to look . . ." she hesitated.

"What?"

"I don't know. Different."

"Different how?"

"I thought your hair would be redder. I thought you'd look more put together."

I didn't know who this girl was, but she was definitely beginning to get on my nerves. Okay, so maybe my hair was getting a little brownish—red does fade out when you get older—and maybe my clothes—jeans, a black tee shirt, and an old flannel shirt—weren't a fashion statement, but, given that I was cleaning out cages and feeding animals, the outfit seemed appropriate. More appropriate, I wanted to say than hers. Instead, I did my customer smile and asked if I could help her.

"Maybe." She began petting the ferret. He raised his head, twitched his nose a couple of times, then put his head back down, obviously exhausted by the effort.

I reached over and scratched him under the chin. "I used to have an albino once. His name was Snow."

"What happened to him?"

"I had to give him away. My other ferrets kept attacking him."

"That's what happened with this one. My friend gave him to me because his other ferrets were biting this one's tail."

I was about to say something about how it was interesting that animals seem to instinctively dislike what Victorians called "sports of nature" and how people do too, but I looked at the girl and decided it might be more politic to keep quiet instead. Contrary to what some people say, I do not have a terminal case of foot-in-the-mouth disease.

She ruffled the ferret's fur. "Poor Mr. Bones."

"Mr. Bones?"

"You know. White. Death. Bones. Get it?"

"It's not that difficult," I snapped. I'd just given up smoking three days ago. It was not doing wonders for my disposition.

The girl scrunched up her face as if I'd just slapped her. Jesus. One moment, she was Tank Girl, the next, she was Little Orphan Annie. I wished she'd get her act straight. "So what can I do for you?" I repeated, trying to keep my growing irritation out of my voice. I had a long list of things to do before Tim, my employee, came in and I could go home. Playing Twenty Questions wasn't one of the things on the list.

"I want to leave Mr. Bones with you for awhile."

"I'm sorry, but we don't board animals. We don't have the space." I reached in my pocket for a square of bubble gum. It wasn't a Camel, but it was going to have to do. "Why don't you try one of the vets," I advised, as I unwrapped the gum and popped it in my mouth. Its sickly sweet aroma filled the air. "I hear Grace out in Liverpool is good with exotics and I know he boards animals. Why don't you call him?''

The girl's glance strayed to the door, then traveled back to my face. "I don't have a car. I can't get out there.''

Zsa Zsa, my cocker spaniel, came out from under the counter where she'd been sleeping and rubbed against my leg. ''Maybe one of your friends can take you.'' I bent down and petted my dog. She had a mat on one of her ears. That was the trouble with cocker spaniels. They always needed to be groomed. The girl didn't move. I straightened up. ''I'm sorry, but I really can't help you,'' I repeated.

''You have to,'' the girl insisted.

''Actually, I don't.'' And I turned to go. My patience had run out.

''But Murphy said you would.''

I stopped dead. Suddenly the room seemed unnaturally bright. ''Murphy?'' I could hear my voice crack on the name. ''Murphy is dead.'' He'd O.D.'d on cocaine and left me as chief suspect in a murder case awhile back. It was something I hadn't been able to forgive or forget.

She gave me a look of contempt. "I know that. But he told me if I ever had any problems, I should come to you. Well I have a problem, and I'm coming to you.''

How classically Murphy, I reflected, shaking my head in wonder. Even when he was dead, the son of a bitch was still causing trouble. A nerve twitched behind my left eye. I rubbed my temples. ''How do you know him?''

The girl didn't answer. She was too busy looking at something over my shoulder. I turned and followed her gaze. She was staring out the front window. Two men were standing on the pavement in front of the store, talking to each other in the late afternoon gloom. I looked back at the girl. She seemed to have shrunk into herself. Her jacket highlighted her pallor.

"Who are they?" I asked.

She didn't answer my question. Instead, she touched a shaking hand to the base of her throat. "Is there another way out of here?"

I pointed to the door on my left. "Through there. What kind of trouble are you in?"

"Enough." And before I knew what was happening, she leaned over and put the ferret on my shoulder. "Be good, Mr. Bones," she whispered. Her eyes were glazed with tears.

"Wait," I cried. But it was too late. By the time I'd gotten the word out of my mouth, she was through the door to the back.

I was just about to follow her, when the front door banged open and the two men I'd just seen standing outside lumbered in. They were both in their early thirties. Dressed in Windbreakers, jeans, sweatshirts, and sneakers, they both looked like high school jocks who'd never forgotten their moment of glory on the field.

"Where's the girl who was in here?" the taller of the two demanded, as his eyes swept the store.

Zsa Zsa ran out from behind the counter and began barking at him, something she did when she didn't like someone. Usually I've found her judgement coincides with mine.

I blew a bubble and popped it, before I replied. "Why do you want to know?"

He glared at me. "This is why."

I blew and popped another bubble as he strode over, reached into his Windbreaker, took out a cheap plastic card carrier, opened it, and handed it to me.

"Detective, huh?" I said, after I'd read the card inside. Not that I was surprised. It was hard to miss the handcuffs peeking out of his side pocket. Camouflage was obviously not his forte.

"That's right. Now where is she?"

I didn't answer immediately. Maybe it was her mention of Murphy, maybe it was that she looked so small and the detectives looked so large, or maybe it was because she seemed like a lost soul. But something about the girl made me want to give her some extra time.

"Where is she?" the detective repeated.

I looked around the store. "She's not here."

"I can see that."

I blew another bubble. "Well she could have been hiding behind the rabbits."

His eyebrows came together as he beetled his brow. "I heard about you."

"Something good I trust," I replied, even though I knew it wasn't. I didn't need the expression on his face to tell me that. I'd been involved in solving three homicide cases since my husband's death and was not particularly liked downtown.

Before he could answer, his partner walked up and pointed to the door behind me. "Where does that go?"

"To the storeroom."

"Is there another way out?"

I nodded. I wasn't going to lie for the girl, either.

The two men exchanged glances and headed towards the door.

"Be careful of the boa constrictor," I called, as they opened it. "I think he's out of his cage." It was a juvenile thing to do, but the therapist I used to go to told me I should cultivate my inner child.

They didn't answer. A moment later, I heard the side door slam. They were probably running through the alley towards Devon Street, which is where the girl had most likely gone—unless, of course, she'd gone in the back door of Phil's Grocery and out the front. Or, if she were smart, she would have cut through the backyards and run towards Geddes Street. There were more people and stores there, making it easier to hide. But not for her, I realized. With her blue hair, she'd stand out anywhere. Mr. Bones began sniffing at my neck. His stiff whiskers tickled my skin.

I held the ferret up. "So what did your mistress do?" I asked. But he didn't answer. I guess this wasn't the day for questions. I put the animal back on my shoulder. He just lay there. This was one very mellow ferret. Most of the ones I've known would be racing up and down my arm and trying to burrow beneath my shirt, by now.

I was blowing another bubble and trying to figure out what the hell was going on, when the detectives walked back in through the front door, bringing the late afternoon October darkness with them.

"Do you know where she went?" the taller one asked. He must have been the designated talker for the group.

I popped the bubble. "No."

"Are you sure?"

"Yes."

He walked over and planted himself in front of me. Zsa Zsa scooted back out from behind the counter and barked at him again. She had a small dog's piercing sound. It was very annoying. I could tell, from the expression on his face, that the detective thought so too.

"Can't you shut her up?" he demanded.

"Probably." And I shushed Zsa Zsa. She tossed her ears and pranced back behind the counter.

"What did the girl want?" the detective asked.

I told him the truth. "To board the ferret." And I pointed to Mr. Bones.

"What else did she say?" I could see that the animal didn't interest him.

"Nothing." I didn't see any reason to drag Murphy into the conversation. "What do you want her for?"

Instead of answering, the detective took out a business card and gave it to me. He'd penciled in his name at the bottom. Paul Marvin. I guess money was tight at the Syracuse Police Department. "When you get bored, do you reverse your names?" I asked.

He pressed his lips together. He probably got that comment all the time. "Call me when she comes back," he said.

"What makes you think she will?"

"The rat." And he pointed to Mr. Bones.

"Ferrets aren't rodents." Everyone always says that, and it annoys the hell out of me. "They belong to the mink family."

"Ask me if I care."

"Do you?"

His jaw tightened, and he turned away.

"I guess you're not interested in taxonomic niceties."

Before Marvin could reply, his partner came up and told him they had to get going. I blew another bubble as I watched them leave and thought about what had just happened. It was all a big puzzle and there didn't seem to be much I could do at the moment to solve it, but that didn't prevent me from thinking about it, while I fixed up a home for the ferret in an old aquarium. It wasn't the best place to keep him, but since I didn't have a ferret cage around, it would have to do for the moment.

Who was this girl? I wondered, as I put the aquarium on top of the counter. How had she known Murphy? And what the hell did she want from me? That's what I wanted to know. Every once in awhile, I'd stop what I was doing and go stand in front of the ferret and ask him, but he was too busy sleeping to reply.

Chapter 2

Pickles, the store cat, was draped across the cash register, meowing for her dinner when the phone rang.

I picked up the receiver and did my standard, "Hello, Noah's Ark."

No one replied.

"Hello," I repeated. Still no answer. Just breathing on the other end. "May I help you?" Silence. I was about to hang up when I heard a soft "perhaps". The voice was a woman's. It was nasal, with a slight trace of a Bronx accent. "Can I ask whom I'm speaking with?"

"Robin Light. The proprietor." I glanced at the clock. It was almost five. Tim would be here soon.

There was a minuscule pause, then the woman continued. "I'm calling about my daughter."

"Okay." While I waited for more information, I tucked the phone between my chin and shoulder, got a can of tuna from underneath the counter, opened it, and set it on the counter. Pickles gave a last meow and began eating.

"Her name is Amy, Amy Richmond."

"I'm sorry, but it doesn't ring a bell. Is she a customer of ours?"

"She might be. I'm not sure."

"Do you want to buy something for her?"

"Not really."

"Well, does she have a question she wants to ask?"

"I don't know."

I stopped myself from asking what the hell she did want. First maxim in retail: Never insult the customer. While I was figuring out what to say next, my glance fell on Mr. Bones. Suddenly I had a pretty good idea why this woman was calling. "This daughter of yours, does she happen to have blue hair?"

"Then she *was* there."

"About an hour ago."

"Is she all right?" The anxiety the woman must have been holding in check welled up.

"Not exactly." And I told her about the police.

I heard a sharp intake of breath on the other side of the line. I could imagine this woman standing there, clutching the receiver. A few seconds later she said, "They didn't catch her, did they?"

"Not as far as I know."

"Did she say where she was going?"

"No. She just wanted to know if I'd keep her ferret."

"Are you sure she didn't mention any place?"

"I'm positive. We just talked about the ferret."

The woman sighed. "Listen," she continued, "if she comes back, tell her she has to call me. Tell her it's very important."

"And who are you?"

"I told you. Her mother."

"I know. But what's your name."

Was it my imagination, or did she pause for a few seconds before answering. "I'm Gerri Richmond." Then she hung up before I could ask her what she wanted me to do with Mr. Bones.

Cute. I got out the phone book and paged through to the Rs. It didn't take me too long to spot a listing for a Dennis and Gerri Richmond. I was just writing down the number when Tim came in. He'd been working in the store since it opened. Luckily for me, he'd agreed to stay on after Murphy died. Tim's knowledge of lizards and snakes—Noah's Ark's *specialité,* as they say in France—had proved invaluable. Watching him walk towards me, so pale and thin in his black leather jacket, I realized he could have been Amy's soul mate. Although he'd taken out his nose ring and let his hair grow back (shaving it every four days had been a drag, he'd told me,) he'd recently, for reasons he either couldn't or wouldn't tell me, gotten his tongue pierced.

"What's up?" he asked, after he'd stowed his black leather backpack behind the counter.

"You're not going to believe this." And I told him about Gerri Richmond's phone call and her daughter's visit.

Tim whistled when I came to the part about Murphy. "She used his name?"

"Yes."

He shook his head. "Ain't that a blast from the past."

"You could say that."

"So what are you going to do?"

"What makes you think I'm going to do anything?"

He shot me a how-stupid-do-you-think-I-am look. "Because I've known you for a long time. That's why."

"Okay," I conceded. "I'm thinking of returning the ferret to Amy's mother."

"And maybe getting a little conversation about Murphy going, while you're there?"

I conceded it was a possibility.

He reached for the phone and handed it to me. I guess he must have been as curious as I was, although he'd never admit it. I dialed her number. The line was busy. I hung up and tried again five minutes later. Still busy. "At least she's home," I announced.

"And?" Tim asked. Monosyllabic comments were part of the new, hip, Zen-like persona Tim had recently donned. I wished he'd undon it, because talking to him was getting to be a real pain in the ass. But when I'd expressed that opinion, Tim had just said "yes" and turned and left the room. I guess when you're terminally hip, you don't have to do polite.

"Maybe I'll just run up to Gerri Richmond's house after I'm finished with the dog food deliveries and drop the ferret off," I continued. Given the conversation I'd just had with her daughter, I had a feeling she wouldn't be pleased to see Mr. Bones, but that was too bad.

"Good luck." And Tim gave Zsa Zsa a pat and went into the back to look in on the baby boas we'd gotten yesterday.

I took Mr. Bones out of his tank and put him in my backpack. He didn't seem to mind much, since he curled up and went back to sleep. Then I called for Zsa Zsa and left the store. The windshield of my checker cab was flecked with leaves from the honey locust tree I'd parked under. It had been a long, hot, exceptionally dry summer, and many of the trees had been late shedding their leaves this fall. I brushed them off and got in. Zsa Zsa hopped in after me and curled up in the passenger seat. I couldn't have put her in the back even if I'd wanted to, because it was full of fifty pound sacks of dog food. A couple of months ago, I'd come up with the idea of free home delivery to boost sales. And it had worked. Over the past six months we'd increased our sales of pet food by twenty five percent.

The only thing I hadn't factored in was that someone would have to carry those fifty pound bags up people's stairs and that one of those someones would be me. By the time I'd dropped off my last load, my back was aching and the burn scars on my legs were itching and stinging. All I wanted to do was go home, pour myself a Scotch, and lay down, but I turned the cab onto Genesee and headed for Amy's mother's place instead.

Her house was located about twenty minutes away in one of those instant, pricey developments—the kind that look as if someone sprinkled it out of a bottle, then added water. This one was called Elysian Fields. As I drove through the stone pillars marking its entrance, I decided the place didn't seem like heaven to me, but I suppose we all have our own visions of that. Gerri Richmond's house was located in a cul de sac at the end of a narrow road called Sunkist Lane. Three carefully landscaped houses had been set down at equal intervals and even though one was a colonial, the second was plantation manor, and the third Tudor, they all had the insubstantial look of stage sets—here today, gone tomorrow.

I checked the numbers by the halo of white light shed by the mercury street lamp. One twenty one was the colonial on the left. It had the fancy door and windows that telegraph money. So did the Saab, Mercedes, and Caddie Coupe de-Ville in the driveway. As I pulled in behind the Caddie, I half expected one of the neighbors to come out and ask me why I was littering up the place with my car. But no one did. I told Zsa Zsa to stay, got out, and hurried to the door. A gust of wind insinuated itself through the fabric of my denim jacket, proclaiming the winter to come.

I rang the bell. The door chimes played the first couple of bars of "Für Elise." Beethoven would have been so pleased, I thought, as a woman opened the door.

"Yes?" she said. Even with the light at her back, she looked as if she'd gone one dance too many with her plastic surgeon. Her features were all perfect. Too perfect. Her face, like the house she lived in, gave no hint of comfort or warmth. She unconsciously brushed a strand of ash blonde hair off her forehead. Her light blue, cashmere turtleneck matched the color of her eyes. Her black silk pants fit as though they'd been made to order—which they probably had.

"Hello," I said, as I wondered what she thought about the way her daughter looked. "I'm Robin Light. We spoke earlier."

An emotion I couldn't read passed across her face. Then she recovered and asked me what I wanted.

"I've brought back your daughter's ferret."

"Really?" She didn't look happy.

I stepped inside without waiting to be invited. The foyer was one of those two-story jobs that decorating magazines call "stunning" and I call pretentious. I wondered what Amy called it, as I studied the faux marble floor. "She left it at the pet store. I thought you would want it."

"I'm sorry. You should have called first."

I smiled. "I tried, but your line was busy and, since I was in the neighborhood, I thought I'd drop by and save you a trip."

She touched the base of her throat lightly with her left hand: a gesture, I couldn't help reflecting, very much like the one her daughter had made earlier. "That's very nice of you, but this isn't a good time."

I nodded towards my backpack. "Mr. Bones is in here. Let me give him to you and I'll be on my way."

But before she could answer, a heavyset, fortyish-looking man came out from the room down the hall. He was dressed in an expensively tailored blue suit, but the cultured impression he must have been seeking to convey was offset by his bulbous nose, thick red lips, and double chin.

"You're not Charlie," he barked, when he saw me.

"No. I'm not." The man obviously had keen powers of observation. "Who's Charlie?"

"My stepson," Gerri Richmond explained.

"Did he send you?" the man asked.

"No," I told him. "I've come about Amy."

He marched over, clamped his hands on my shoulders, and peered into my face. "You mean you've seen her?"

I took a step back. (I don't like being touched by people I don't know.) "She was in my store this afternoon."

He flushed and faced Gerri Richmond. "Did you know this?"

She glared at him. "I don't have to tell you anything."

"Have you told the police? Because if you haven't, that's called aiding and abetting."

"My daughter has nothing to do with Dennis's disappearance, and you know it," Gerri Richmond cried.

"That's not what the police think."

She pointed a finger at him. "Brad, why don't you stop putting on a show. It's not convincing anybody. You don't care about your brother. You haven't spoken to him in five years. In fact, you're probably the one behind this whole thing."

"You're one to talk," the man spat back. "You goddamned slut. If it wasn't for you and that freak of a daughter of yours, I'd . . ."

I never got to hear the rest of the sentence, because Gerri Richmond raised her hand and slapped him across the face.

He slapped her back. The force of the blow sent her reeling against the wall.

"Get out," she screamed, as she brought her hand up to her cheek. "Get out now."

"My pleasure." He smiled, nastily. "Enjoy what you have, because you're not going to have it for long." Then he turned and headed for the door.

"I'm sorry you had to see that," she said as the door slammed.

"It's okay. I've seen worse. Who was that?"

"My brother-in-law, Brad Richmond." Gerri Richmond gave a strangled little laugh. "Aren't families wonderful?" And she rubbed the side of her face. The skin where Brad Richmond had hit her was strawberry red. A phone started ringing somewhere in the house. "Excuse me," she said. "I have to get that."

And she was gone, leaving me standing alone in the drafty hall to ponder what I'd seen.

Chapter 3

After a minute or so, I got bored and wandered into the first room on the left. It was the den. The place had "decorator" stamped all over it. It was Southwestern decor from the pale peach and blue upholstery to the bleached wood to the steer's skull on the fireplace mantel, as well as the collection of bad Indian pottery sitting on the beveled glass shelf on the far wall. I walked over to the fireplace and lightly ran my hand over the rough stones. The floor of the fire box was immaculate, just like the room. I was willing to bet that it had never been used, either. The thought depressed me. I was trying to figure out why, when Gerri Richmond's voice floated in on the air. She sounded angry.

"I don't care," she was saying to someone. Her Bronx accent had reasserted itself. Then her voice fell back down, and I couldn't hear her anymore.

I looked at my watch. All of three minutes had passed. Somehow it felt like ten. I peeked in my backpack. Mr.

Bones opened his eyes, yawned, and went back to sleep. Watching him made me want to go to sleep, too. I made another circuit of the room instead, then sat down on the sofa, and put the backpack next to me. It was one of those soft, oversized sofas—the kind that doesn't want to let you get back up—and I had to reach to pick up the copy of the *Herald Journal* that was sitting on the coffee table. Usually I'm religious about reading the paper but it's been so busy at the store the past three weeks, I'd been lining the bird cages with it instead. This edition had been written three days ago on October fourteenth. I was scanning the front page, when a column midway down caught my eye.

"A week ago," it began, "Dennis Richmond, part owner of the Syracuse Casket Company, told his secretary he was going out to lunch. He never came back. Yesterday his daughter, Amy Richmond, disappeared as well. The police are investigating both incidents, though foul play is not suspected at this time. Her uncle, Brad Richmond, co-owner of the Syracuse Casket Company, states he is worried that the stress of recent events has proved too great and that the fifteen-year-old has run away from home. She is undergoing medical care at the present time. If you have any information concerning either disappearance, you are asked to call the police at 555–5299."

Two small, grainy photos accompanied the article. The one of Amy looked as if it were a yearbook head shot. I was willing to bet she'd been in seventh, maybe eighth grade, at the most, when it had been taken. In the picture, she had shoulder length hair, glasses, and a serious demeanor. I bit my thumb. She sure had changed a lot in a couple of years. As I gazed at her face, I wondered what had made her go from Miss Studious to the Queen of Punk. And then, once again, I wondered where I'd seen her before. There was something so familiar about her, but no matter how hard I concentrated, I couldn't place her and, after a moment, I gave up trying and turned to Dennis Richmond's picture. He had an elongated face, close-set eyes, and a long thin nose that twisted slightly off to one side. The only thing that linked him to his brother was a surprisingly fleshy mouth.

"Since you've read the article, I guess you can understand why this isn't a good time for you to be here," Gerri Richmond said, taking the paper out of my hand.

I jumped. I'd been so engrossed, I hadn't heard her come up. Either that, or she moved very quietly.

She gestured towards my backpack. "I'm sorry, but I can't have that animal in the house. Especially now. You should have called before you came up." She picked an imaginary piece of lint off her black silk pants with trembling hands. "If it weren't for that thing, Amy might still be here."

"I don't follow."

"I told Amy not to bring it into the house. But she did it anyway. One of her lowlife friends gave it to her. We got into a terrible fight." Gerri Richmond began twisting her diamond ring around her finger. It was a good sized diamond, a little larger than the dictates of good taste demanded. "We were going to make a new start when she came home from the hospital, only it didn't work out that way." She sighed. "I should never have listened to her therapist," she murmured to herself.

"Sometimes they just make things worse," I volunteered, thinking of mine.

But Gerri Richmond didn't want to chat about therapists or anything else. Instead of answering, she glanced at her watch, making sure that I noticed what she was doing. "Listen," she told me, "I'm sorry, but you really have to go. I have things I have to do."

I stood up. "Can I ask you something?"

"What?"

"How did you get my number?"

"I thought I told you. I found it." Gerri Richmond brushed a lock of hair out of her eyes. "It was written on a scrap of paper that was lying on Amy's nightstand."

The phone started ringing again. "Aren't you going to get that?" I asked.

She waved a hand in the direction she'd come from before. "The answering machine will."

I was close enough to smell her perfume. It was Le Dix. I'd worn that when I was married to Murphy and working at the paper. Now I couldn't afford it anymore. The fact bothered me, even though it shouldn't have.

She gestured towards the door. "If you don't mind."

"Just one more thing." I took a deep breath and asked the question that had brought me up here. "Does the name Murphy mean anything to you?"

Gerri Richmond's face folded in on herself. "Why should it?"

"Because your daughter mentioned it when she came to see me."

"I don't understand."

"She told me he told her to see me if she were ever in trouble."

"Look, I don't know Amy's friends. She never brings any of them home, which is probably just as well because . . ."

I interrupted. "He wasn't one of your daughter's friends. He was my age."

She wet her lower lip with the tip of her tongue. "I already told you, I never heard of the man."

I studied her face. "You're sure?"

She returned my gaze. "Absolutely." And she rose.

She was lying. I don't know how I knew it, but I did. I wondered why she was, as I stood up. I snuck a look at her as she walked me to the door. It occurred to me that for someone whose husband and child were both missing, she seemed remarkably composed. Or maybe she was just good at hiding her feelings. I wondered which it was, as I walked back to the cab.

Tim was starting to close up by the time I returned to the store.

"Did you go and see the girl's mother?" he asked.

"Yes?"

"And?" He abandoned doing cool.

"She didn't say much, except that she didn't want the ferret back." I pulled Mr. Bones out of my backpack and scratched him under the chin.

"What about Murphy?"

"She claims she never heard of him."

"Do you believe her?"

I shook my head. "No. No I don't." I thought about the way Gerri Richmond's face had blanked out when I'd mentioned his name. "She knew him all right. The question is how?" I didn't spell it out, but then I didn't have to. Tim knew I was wondering if Gerri Richmond and Murphy had gone to bed together. God only knows, he'd gone to bed with everyone else: a fact everybody but me had evidently known about. I still don't know which bothers me more: my willful blindness or his conduct.

"Even if he had, that still doesn't explain the girl's coming in," Tim pointed out.

"No. You're right. It doesn't."

Tim nodded towards the ferret. "What are you going to do with him?"

"Keep him. Hopefully Amy will come back for him soon."

"And if she doesn't?"

"I'll worry about it then." And I told Tim I'd finish locking up. He left a few minutes later.

I fed Mr. Bones and played with him for awhile, then I put him back in his aquarium and went home. It was almost ten when I pulled into my driveway. By now I was exhausted. I gave Zsa Zsa the shortest walk I could get away with and went inside my house. James came running out to greet me—which was odd—because I could have sworn he hadn't been in the house when I left. But then, maybe he had been and I just hadn't noticed. It had been that kind of week. I checked the machine to see if George had called. He hadn't.

Oh well, I thought, as I went into the living room and poured myself a double shot of Scotch. There wasn't any reason he should have—but still, it would have been nice if he had. We had a funny relationship, George Samson and I. I contemplated it, while I went back in the kitchen and opened a can of cat food for James. George had been Murphy's best friend. Then, when Murphy had died, we'd become friends—sort of. The "sort of" had become more so, and then we'd ended up sleeping together. Which we were still doing. Which I liked. The sex was good. It was the relationship part I was having trouble with, but then that was the part I always had trouble with. Maybe, I decided, as I sipped my Scotch, we just shouldn't talk at all. Maybe we should just screw. I stretched, finished my drink, and went upstairs. It was time to take a bath and go to bed. Tomorrow was time enough to figure out what, if anything, I was going to do about Amy and her ferret.

But as I went up the stairs, I began to get increasingly nervous. It was dark on the landing and it shouldn't have been, because I kept the light on. I told myself the bulb had probably blown. Nevertheless, I found myself reaching for the box cutter I carried in my pocket. I had it out and the blade opened by the time I reached my bedroom. That light was off, too. The problem was: I couldn't remember whether I'd left it on or off. My heart was pounding as I tried to decide whether or not I was being paranoid. After all, the front door was locked when I came in. I'd used my key to open it. And nothing had been messed up downstairs. No. Things were okay. I was just getting twitchy in my old age.

I was reaching for the switch when I heard: "You sure as hell took long enough getting up the stairs."

By the time my heartbeat had returned to normal, my eyes had adjusted to the dark. George was sitting up in my bed, wearing a grin and a bed sheet. I felt like killing him.

"You son of a bitch," I hissed.

"I told you, you should get a security system in here." George had picked up his knowledge of breaking and entering during the seven years he'd worked as a cop. He patted the empty space next to him. "Why don't you put that box cutter away and come on over here?"

"What if I come over and keep the blade out?"

"We can do that too, if you want."

Chapter 4

I must have dozed off. When I woke up, George was standing by the bed staring out the window. "I may have to go down to New York tomorrow or the next day," he told me, when I asked him if anything was wrong.

"Family stuff?"

"What else?"

I sighed. About once every three months, George would get a phone call and head off for the city. When he came back, he'd be in a bad mood for days.

I leaned on my elbow. "Who's in trouble this time?"

"One of my cousins."

"The one who drives a taxi?"

"No. The one who owns a funeral home."

"What happened?"

"The asshole was running a bookie service out of it."

"So what do they want you to do?"

"Fix things up," he growled.

"Why do you keep going down there? It just makes you crazy."

"Because it's my family," he snapped. "I have to go."

And that, I knew, was going to be the end of the conversation. I got up and led him back to bed. I was rubbing his back when the phone rang.

George reached under the bed for it. "It's for you," he said, and handed me the receiver.

"Who is it?" I mouthed.

He shrugged. "Some girl."

The some girl turned out to be Amy. "You have to come here right away," she cried. She sounded far away. I had to strain to understand what she was saying.

"Why? Where are you?"

"Just come down. Please."

"What happened?"

"I'm at Lincoln Square," Amy cried. Her voice rose. "Building 213. Apartment 2F. It's the first one to the left of the stairs." Then she hung up. Boy, this was turning out to be a good night.

"What was that all about?" George asked, as he replaced the receiver.

"Good question." And I explained about Amy.

George made a fist and rubbed the edge of it across his lips. "Amy, huh?"

"That's what I just said."

"What's her last name?"

"Richmond. Why? Do you know her?"

He grunted. "What's her mother's name?"

"Gerri. Why?"

"Just curious."

But I didn't buy that. George was never "just curious." I

studied his face, but it was difficult to read his expression in the dark. "Why don't you just tell me what's going on?"

He carefully made a pleat in the blanket. "Why should anything be going on?"

"Don't do this."

"What?"

"Play games."

He shifted his position. "Don't be ridiculous."

"Look at me," I commanded.

He snorted. "What is this? Police interrogation technique 209?"

"Funny, man." I took his face in my hands and turned it towards me. "Tell me what's going on."

George remained silent.

"This is something bad, isn't it?" For some reason my heart was hammering in my chest.

"That depends on your perspective."

"How about from mine?"

He adjusted the pillow before replying. "You're not going to like it."

"I want to hear," I insisted.

"All right." As I looked at George, it occurred to me that he was wearing the same expression of detached pity the policeman wore who'd told me Murphy was dead. "But don't say I didn't warn you." He took a deep breath. I realized I was holding mine. "Amy is Murphy's daughter."

Suddenly the room felt very cold.

"I'm sorry," George said, putting his arm around me. "I really am."

I didn't say anything. I couldn't. All I could think of was how I'd wanted a baby and how Murphy had always said no. The time wasn't right. He wasn't settled enough. The business wasn't doing well. One excuse after another.

"Are you all right?" George asked.

"I'm fine," I lied. I rubbed my arms. They were covered with goose bumps.

George looked at the blinds in the window for what seemed like a long time. I spent it watching the changing geography of his shoulder muscles and thinking about how Murphy had banged his finger with the hammer when he'd put the blinds up.

"Tell me," I finally said.

"What?"

"Everything."

"There isn't that much to tell." George stroked my arm. I stiffened and moved away.

Zsa Zsa jumped on the bed. I pulled her into my lap and buried my face in her neck. The smell of her fur calmed me. She turned and licked a strand of my hair.

"You should have told me," I said, after a minute had gone by.

George bit his lip. "For Christ sake, Robin, he was my friend, you weren't. It wasn't my business."

"And afterward . . ."

"And afterward, there didn't seem much point. I never thought . . ."

"I'd find out?"

"Exactly."

"Well I have."

"Look, I was trying to do the right thing."

"You didn't."

George tightened his left hand into a fist and released it. "I admit I made a mistake. I'm sorry."

"Not as sorry as I am."

He bit the inside of his cheek. "I guess I can understand how you feel."

A surge of anger ran through me. "Can you?" I spat. "Can you really?"

"If it'll make you feel any better, Murphy didn't plan it. It just happened."

"It? It?" I could hear my voice rising. I felt feverish.

"Calm down."

"How could you lie to me like this?"

George raised his hands. "Don't put this off on me," he snapped.

"Then who the hell should I put it off on?"

"You. Murphy."

I swallowed. George was right. The anger inside me vanished as suddenly as it had come, leaving a hollow place behind.

"Look . . . I'm sorry. I shouldn't have said that."

"It's okay."

"Let's just drop the subject."

"No. I want you to tell me what happened."

"Fine."

I could hear the branches of the blue spruce brushing against the bedroom window, as I stroked Zsa Zsa's back. George pulled the covers up and leaned back against the headboard. His voice was as cold and impersonal as an accountant's reciting a column of figures, when he started talking.

"It's not real complicated. Murphy told me he picked Gerri Richmond up in the park one day over by the boathouse. They went to her apartment. It wasn't anything that special. They got it on maybe a dozen times at the most. Then they stopped seeing each other. No big deal. Murphy forgot about her. But a couple of months later, Richmond called up and told him she was pregnant. 'But not to worry,' she said. 'I'm marrying someone else. Someone older. Someone rich.' She'd just called to let him know. I think it hit Murphy really hard."

I shook my head. I'd gotten pregnant early on in our relationship. Murphy had offered to marry me. But I'd been young. I hadn't wanted the responsibility. I'd opted for a quick trip to Puerto Rico, instead. I don't think he'd ever forgiven me. Funny, but given the kind of guy he was, you wouldn't think it would have bothered him as much as it did.

"Are you okay?" George asked. "You have an odd expression on your face."

"I'm fine," I told him. "Go on."

"Murphy said he made it a point to stay in touch. Gerri was nice about it. She let him play friend of the family and take the kid out from time to time. When Gerri and her husband moved up to Syracuse, Murphy did too."

I'd always wanted to go back to Manhattan after we'd gotten up here, but Murphy never had. Now I knew why. I was tearing at my cuticle with my front teeth, when something occurred to me. "How'd he know Gerri Richmond was telling the truth about the baby being his kid?"

George shrugged. "Why would she lie? It wasn't as if she were asking him for anything."

"True." And I closed my eyes and conjured up Amy. I had to concede there was some similarity to Murphy in the lower half of her face—especially around the jawline and the mouth. That's probably why I'd thought she'd looked familiar when she walked in the store. But mostly the girl looked like her mother. "Does Amy know?"

"No. As far as she's concerned, Dennis is her real father. Like I said, Murphy was just a family friend."

"Cute."

George covered my hand with his. I moved my hand away.

I didn't want to be touched. "Robin, he really did want to tell you. He just didn't know how."

Maybe he had. Maybe he hadn't. I'd never really know. It didn't really matter, anyway. It was one of those questions—like, is there a God—that you can debate endlessly. The truth is, Murphy and I had lived together in a private world of half-truths. I thought it was all right, but it wasn't. There were penalties to be paid, and I was still paying them.

Suddenly I wanted a drink very, very badly. George watched me get out of bed. He didn't say anything when I put on a shirt and walked into the hallway. Zsa Zsa followed me, as I padded downstairs. I went into the kitchen, poured myself a double shot of Scotch from the bottle sitting on the counter, and gulped it down. The liquor burnt my throat and warmed my veins. I poured myself a third shot and lifted the glass.

"To the man who continues to make my life miserable, even though he's dead, and to myself for allowing him to do it to me." Zsa Zsa wagged her tail while I drank it down. Then I gave her a dog biscuit and headed back upstairs to my bedroom. George was still sitting up in bed. His arms were crossed over his chest.

"Do you want to talk some more?" he asked, when I came in.

"No. I can't think of a thing I want to say." I picked my jeans off the rug.

"What are you doing?"

"Getting dressed." And I put them on and began looking for my socks. They were stuffed in my boots.

George's eyes narrowed. He leaned forward slightly. The streetlight coming in through the blinds highlighted the planes on his face. He looked as if he were carved out of ebony. "I can see that. Do you mind telling me where you're going?"

"To Lincoln Square. Hopefully Amy will still be there." I glanced at the clock on the nightstand. Only twenty minutes had passed since her phone call. I was surprised. It felt as if an hour had gone by. At least.

George smoothed down a crease in the blanket. "I was wondering what you were going to do about that?"

I rammed my left foot into my boot and laced it up with vicious little tugs. "What can I do?"

"I'll go, if you want me to," George offered. It was, I knew, his way of doing penance, but I didn't want to let him.

"No. I will."

He looked at me sadly. "Are you sure?"

"Positive. Just lock up when you leave." I was halfway out the door when I turned. "Good luck with your cousin."

He managed a thin smile. "Thanks."

I walked down the stairs, got my jacket, and left. A cold front must have moved into the area since I'd been inside, because the temperature had dropped at least ten degrees, if not more. The air smelled of damp and spice and rot. As I cut across the lawn, I kicked at the pile of leaves that I'd raked up a couple of weeks ago and never gotten around to bagging. Too bad I wasn't doing that to Gerri Richmond, I thought, as I watched the leaves scatter. No wonder she had looked at me the way she had when she'd opened the door. I wondered what she thought when she saw me standing there. She must have been shocked. Good. But as I got in the cab, my thoughts turned to her daughter.

I had a feeling Amy was up to her neck in something really bad and, lucky me, I was going to get to find out what it was. I put the key in the ignition and turned. The cab wheezed twice and started. Aside from an occasional pedestrian walking along with their collar turned up, no one was out. No surprise there. Except in the summer, when people hang out, most folks are home by ten o'clock at the latest. Even the dope dealers rubbing their arms and stamping their feet in front of the pay phone by Fat Boy's Bar and Grill looked as if they would have preferred to be sitting in front of the TV. But then, the entrepreneurial life never is easy. God knows, I should know, I decided, as I turned the corner onto Fayette. The streets were empty, and I drove through the city rapidly. It took me about ten minutes to get to Lincoln Square.

It was a new development, one the mayor and the Common Council were touting as an example of the revitalization of Syracuse. And it was true that, from the outside, the condos and town houses looked nicely designed, the grounds were tastefully landscaped with evergreens and maples and laurel hedges. But whenever I drove by it, the place appeared deserted. That was probably because it was located in the middle of nowhere, on the way to nothing, in what had once been an industrial park, before Syracuse started losing their factories to the South.

I made a left at the sign that said, "Lincoln Square. The Best of The Best" and followed the road to the first parking lot. It was half-empty. The developers must be losing a bundle, I thought, as I looked around. But then, they probably weren't worried. They'd just do what they usually did: refinance their debt, leaving the taxpayers to foot the bill. And the people that ran this city wondered why everyone was moving out. By now I had a clear view of the buildings from where I was standing. Amy was nowhere in sight. Hopefully, she was waiting inside the lobby of 213. I started towards it. The sign on the building made identification easy. Everything was quiet as I walked down the path. The only noise I heard was the hum of the streetlights. The branches of the maples and the evergreens dipped and swayed in the wind.

It was obvious from the moment I opened the building door and stepped into the small vestibule that Amy wasn't inside. I sighed. Maybe she was in the apartment. Or maybe she'd gotten tired of waiting and left. I went over to the intercom panel and ran my finger down the buttons until I found 2F. When I read the name next to it, my finger froze. Dennis Richmond. Shit. According to the newspaper article I'd just read in his wife's apartment, Dennis Richmond had gone missing ten days ago. So what the hell was Amy doing here at her father's apartment? In fact, now that I thought about it, the article hadn't mentioned this apartment at all. I'd gotten the distinct impression that Dennis Richmond had been living at home with his delightful wife in his tastefully decorated home. Well, I guess I'd find out soon enough.

I pushed the buzzer.

I didn't get a reply. I didn't get one when I tried buzzing a second or a third time either.

Amy had probably gone. I should probably have done the same. But I knew I wouldn't until I made sure that Amy was all right. I owed Murphy that much. Why I didn't know, but that was the way I felt, so I pushed the buzzer for 4B. A moment later I heard a fuzzy, "yes" coming through the speaker.

I scanned the names on the wall again. "This is Millicent Chammers in 3A," I told him. "I'm sorry, but I forget my key."

"Who?" a guy asked.

"Chammers," I yelled, banking on the fact that the static would disguise my voice.

"Jesus." His voice was heavy with sleep. "Do you know what time it is?"

"Sorry," I replied, doing contrite.

"I have to get up at five in the morning." A moment later the buzzer sounded. I pushed the door open and went inside. The lobby was small. The carpeting was beige, the walls were cream. They were hung with the kind of paintings they sell in stores for sixty dollars a pop. There were no chairs or tables. Obviously sitting and waiting were not encouraged activities.

I took the elevator to the second floor and got out. Dennis Richmond's apartment was at the very end of the hallway.

It seemed like a long walk. When I got there I rang the door bell.

No one responded. The only noise I heard was the blare of the television next door.

I tried again.

Nothing.

At this point most people would have left, but I'm not most people. I can't seem to let things go—even when it's in my best interest to.

So I turned the doorknob.

The door swung open.

I took my box cutter out of my pocket and stepped inside.

"Amy. Mr. Richmond." My voice seemed unnaturally loud in the room's silence. I heard a footstep overhead and jumped. Someone was walking across the floor. Then somewhere on the other side of the wall a toilet flushed. I wondered if either neighbor had heard anything, as I looked around.

The apartment had the generic feel of a motel room. It consisted of a large room with a small galley of a kitchen off to the left. To the right was a door that, I was willing to wager, led to the bedroom. It was a box of a place slapped together by people who didn't care out of cheap materials that would disintegrate over the passage of time. But whoever had been here before me had hastened the process considerably. Two big gouges in the walls marked where someone had ripped out the supports for the shelves. I headed over toward the window, taking care to step over the CDs scattered on the carpet, like so many colorful tiles, hoping, as I did, that Amy and Dennis Richmond had left before this had happened. A second later, I saw the sole of a man's shoe protruding from behind the sofa.

That numb, empty feeling that trouble sometimes brings settled over me, as I walked around to get a better look. Dennis Richmond was lying on the floor. He looked just like his picture in the newspaper—except for a couple of differences. Like the big red blotch on his chest and the slash marks on his hands. If I had to bet, I'd say someone had stabbed him in the chest and he'd tried to defend himself.

I stared down at him. He stared back at me with unblinking eyes. The whites were already flattening out from fluid loss. I shifted my weight from one leg to the other. Well, at least the poor guy would have a fancy coffin for his funeral. It stood to reason, given the business he owned. If I remem-

Chapter 5

The lights were on. I could see most of the living and dining area from where I was standing, and what I was seeing didn't look good. The dining chairs were tipped over, the black leather sofa was bleeding white tuffs of cotton wadding, and the chrome coffee table had been upended. Leaving seemed like a good idea, but then I thought about Amy's phon call, and I moved the box cutter blade up and took anoth step in instead. One thing was for certain, I thought bitter The girl definitely took after her father. Murphy had alw managed to drag me into whatever mess he'd gotten hims into. It looked as if his daughter was busy doing the sa thing.

My feet sank into the carpet. Once upon a time, it been white. Now it was dingy with what looked like mo of ground-in dirt. The place smelled of aftershave incense and barbecue sauce and an undercurrent of thing dark and salty and fetid that I knew but couldn't bered correctly, according to the newspaper article I'd read at his wife's house, Richmond had disappeared a week, or a week and a half ago. I forgot which. It looked as if he hadn't gotten far.

As I squatted down and touched one of his fingers, I wondered if he'd been holed up here during that time. His skin was still warm to the touch. He hadn't been killed that long ago, maybe three hours at the outside. A couple of years ago, this sight would have been enough to send me running out the door. Unfortunately, dead people don't scare me anymore. Now I feel as if I'm looking at a house with no one home. Maybe I've seen too many bodies. I was about to get up, when I noticed a slight demarcation on Dennis Richmond's wrist where his watch should have been. Whoever had killed him must have taken it, I decided, as I stood up and looked towards the bedroom. The door leading to it was half closed.

A vision of Amy splayed out on the floor rose before my eyes. *Please let her be all right,* I prayed, as I willed the thought away. Then that picture was replaced by one of a man standing behind the door, knife in hand, waiting for me to come through. Which wasn't much better. My palms were sweating. I wiped them on the back of my jeans pockets, as I moved towards the door. Getting there seemed to take forever. The lamp lying on its side, the ripped copy of *Time* magazine, the Kit Kat wrapper lying atop the telephone book all took on a dreadful clarity. I could hear my watch ticking each second away. I kept wishing I had a gun instead of a box cutter, as I drew nearer to the bedroom. Finally, I was there. I raised my leg and slammed my foot into the door. As it thudded against the wall, I ran in. No one was on the other side. I quickly moved over to the bathroom and checked it out. It was empty. No killer and no Amy.

I let out the breath I didn't know I'd been holding, retracted the box cutter's blade, and considered the havoc that had been Dennis Richmond's bedroom. Everything that had been in the closet was now on the floor. The dresser drawers had been pulled out, their contents dumped. Dennis Richmond's shirts, socks, and underwear lay scattered like the leaves on the trees outside. The mattress had been turned on its side. The bedding was wadded up on top of it.

I picked up one of Richmond's shirts. It was a narrow blue and white stripe with French cuffs. It looked expensive and probably was. I dropped it back where I'd found it, crossed over to the box spring, and began going through the pile of Kleenexes, pens, little pieces of silver gum wrappers, and loose pills on it. All I learned was that Dennis Richmond had been on Prozac, but so what? So were half the people in America. Next, I smoothed out the crumpled up squares of white, pink, and yellow pieces of paper. Two were Post-it® notes. They contained shopping lists. The other five pieces of paper were receipts. Three were from local restaurants, another from the Biden Jewelry store. Richmond had had his watch repaired. The last two were dry cleaning stubs for seven shirts and a jacket. I put everything back the way I'd found it, got up, and glanced around again.

What was whoever had done this looking for? Drugs? Money? The place was too thoroughly ransacked for this to have been a casual robbery gone bad, unless of course whoever had done this had been flying on Angel Dust or Meth. And then I got to thinking about Amy.

How did she fit into all this?

What the hell had she been doing up here?

I could think of a couple of answers without trying real hard, and I didn't like either of them.

I reached into my pocket for a cigarette before I remembered I wasn't smoking. I put a stick of gum into my mouth instead and began to chew. More questions surfaced. Had Amy called me from here? Or had she made the call from somewhere else?

And why hadn't she waited for me to arrive? Had someone scared her off? Or had she gotten cold feet? I tore at a ragged cuticle with my teeth. Maybe she'd gone back to her mother's house. It was a long shot, but I decided to call and make sure. It took me a minute to locate the phone. I finally found it under the chair. I pulled it over by the cord, picked up the receiver with the hem of my shirt, and used a pencil to punch the numbers in. After four rings, the answering machine clicked on. I hung up without leaving a message. If Amy were there, she wasn't answering. I returned the receiver to its cradle and went back into the living room. I could hear water running through the pipes in the next apartment. Another question popped into my mind. Why hadn't the people next door called the police? What had happened here hadn't happened silently.

I stood near the overturned sofa and contemplated Dennis Richmond again. His skin was losing its pink hue and turning grey. His thick helmet of hair was oddly neat, as if it had been shellacked in place. He was dressed in his street clothes—dark grey slacks and a pale blue button down shirt. Had he just come in, or was he going out? It was impossible to tell. I squatted down and went through his pockets, even though I knew I should leave. I could have saved myself the trouble, though, because they were empty. So maybe this was a robbery after all. I straightened up and tucked the lock of hair that was falling over my eye behind my ear and thought about how I was going to phone this into the police.

Anonymously seemed best. As I said, the police and I aren't on friendly terms, and I had no intention of staying, so I could pay my lawyer an exorbitant sum of money to spend the rest of the night with me down at the Public Safety Building, while I explained why I happened to be here—especially since I couldn't find Amy. Which meant I had no one to corroborate my story. I sighed, gave the apartment one last look, and shut the door on my way out. The tinny laughter of late night talk shows drifted out of the apartments I passed, as I walked down the hall. The elevator came quickly. It was empty. So was the lobby. And for that I was grateful.

The temperature had fallen another couple of degrees. I shivered and hurried towards my car, taking a shortcut over the lawn. I was almost to my cab when I heard a faint hissing noise. My mouth went dry. I turned towards it. At first, all I saw were the painted white lines and the rows of cars standing sentinel. Then a few seconds later, Amy materialized from between two minivans and drifted towards me. She looked wraith-like under the vapor tail of the sodium lights.

"Did you see my father?" she whispered. Her voice was harsh.

"Yes." The dull throbbing pain that had started behind my eyes got worse. I felt as if I was being sucked down a rabbit hole.

"Someone stabbed him," Amy said. Now that I was looking at her again, I realized she had Murphy's eyes.

"I know." I took a step in her direction. She was grasping the Coptic cross hanging around her neck, as if it were her key to salvation. I was almost next to her now. She was wearing the same clothes she had worn when I saw her this afternoon. It felt as if it had been an eternity ago. I caught gusts of dope and incense and sweat and fear coming from her. "Did you do it?"

"No." Her voice trembled with indignation. "Of course not."

"Why were you up there?"

"I wanted to tell him something."

"And did you?"

"What?"

"Tell him?"

"No. He was dead. I just saw . . ." She swallowed. "What I saw, and ran."

"Why didn't you call the police?"

"Because I can't." She scratched her wrist. I noticed her bracelet. It seemed to be made up of finger and knuckle bones. Something told me they weren't plastic.

"You can't, or you won't?"

Amy stopped scratching and stuffed her hands in her jeans pockets. "Can't. Won't. What difference does it make?"

"A lot."

"Not to me. Nobody will believe I found him that way."

"Why?"

"They thought I had something to do with his disappearance before. What are they going to think now?" She wiped her nose with the back of her hand and leaned towards me. "Everyone thinks I'm crazy," she confided.

Maybe they were right. I remembered what the article in the *Herald* had said about her being under a doctor's care. It hadn't said for what. A gust of wind sent the leaves flying. I rubbed my arms. My denim jacket wasn't warm enough for a night like this. "Why did you call me?"

"I freaked," she confessed. "I didn't know what else to do."

"Let me tell you." And I repeated my suggestion about calling the cops.

"No," Amy replied. "I already told you, I can't do that." She set her mouth in a stubborn line.

I studied her for a moment. Suddenly I felt incredibly tired. "Fine. If that's the way you want to play it." I turned towards my cab. It had been a long day, an even longer night, and I wasn't in the mood to deal with crap. All I wanted to do was call the homicide in and leave.

"Where are you going?" Amy cried.

"Out of here."

"You can't," she wailed.

"Just watch me."

"But Murphy said you'd help me." She sounded like a little girl who'd just been told she wasn't going to the circus.

The hairs on the nape of my neck rose at the mention of Murphy's name. I couldn't help myself. I turned back. "When did he tell you that?"

Amy raked her hand through her hair. "About two weeks before he died. We'd gone to a movie, and I was telling him about how my father was always yelling at me for everything and about how he and my mom were always fighting. And he said, not to worry, that he'd always be there for me and, if he wasn't, you would be."

"How nice of him," I said, sarcastically.

"He was a nice guy," Amy replied. The glimmer of a smile playing around the corners of Amy's mouth made me feel small and mean. "He was always buying me stupid little stuff."

I don't know why I felt like crying. Maybe I should just

have "sentimental idiot" tattooed on my forehead. "I can't help you, if you won't tell me what's going on."

She grasped the cross again and looked straight at me. "I don't know."

Unlike her mother, the kid was a lousy liar. "I think you do."

She twisted her heel in the dirt. "I don't. Really."

I tried another tack. "What did you want to talk to your father about?"

"Stuff."

"What kind of stuff?" I asked through gritted teeth, controlling an impulse to throttle her.

Suddenly Amy startled. Her eyes widened. "What's that?" she hissed.

"What?" I glanced around. I didn't see or hear anything. Then I heard it too. A car was coming towards us.

Before I could ask Amy what was going on, she ran over to my cab and crouched down behind it. A minute later a Jeep came into view. I experienced a frisson of fear, as its headlights swept over the parking lot. But it kept going. It followed the road to the complex's upper level and disappeared.

Amy reemerged. "I've got to get out of here," she told me. Her voice was shaking. She sounded close to tears.

I took a step towards her.

"Why? What are you afraid of?"

I should have seen it coming, but I didn't. Instead of answering, Amy whirled around and ran for the copse of trees beyond the parking lot. I ran after her, but the ground was uneven. I tripped over a rock and fell. By the time I got up, she had disappeared.

Great. I was dealing with a punk Houdini. I blew on my scraped palm to ease the pain. Amy's taking off was the perfect end to the perfect day. I started walking back towards my car. My headache was worse. No big surprise there. All I wanted to do was to go home, have a drink, and go to sleep. Unfortunately, I still had to phone Richmond's death in to the cops.

I took my cell phone out of my glove compartment. Then I put it back. It just wasn't worth the risk of putting this call through on an unsecured line. A minute later, I found a pay phone at the corner of Rainbow Boulevard and West Street, dropped my quarter in the slot, and dialed. As I drove back to my house, I kept on thinking about Amy and Murphy and Dennis Richmond.

I was still thinking about them, when I pulled into my driveway and walked across the lawn to my front door.

Which is probably why I didn't see the man standing by the spruce tree until he stepped out in front of me.

Chapter 6

The guy startled me. He was about five foot eleven, a little on the plump side, but maybe that was because of the bulky down parka he was wearing. His hair was dark and he had a long, full beard that made him look as if he'd been up in the mountains too long. I instinctively reached for my box cutter as he came towards me. He stopped when he was about five feet away and I stayed my hand.

"I'm looking for Amy," he told me. His breath made clouds of smoke in the air. He smelled as if he'd taken a bath in pine-scented air freshner.

I should have known. "You and everyone else." I could feel my jaw beginning to tighten.

"I heard she might be here."

"Who told you that?"

"She did."

"Well you heard wrong. Now how about leaving." Annoyed was too mild a word for what I was feeling. Enough was enough. This guy could have been the Prince of Fucking Darkness, for all I cared. I just wanted him off my property.

"Are you sure she's not here?"

"Positive. Who the hell are you anyway?"

He grinned. "Her boyfriend. Toon Town."

I couldn't help it. I had to ask. "Toon Town?"

"Yeah. I watch a lot of cartoons."

Well, that was certainly reassuring. I took a second look at him. "You're a little old for Amy, aren't you?" It was hard to judge by the light of the street lamp, but the guy seemed as if he were in his early twenties, although that could have been the effect of the beard.

He shuffled his feet. His grin grew wider. "Girls used to be married by the time they were thirteen."

"That was a long time ago."

"She's old enough to know what she likes."

"No, she's not."

He stared at me. His eyes were a light, bleached-out greyish blue. His pupils were dilated. I realized he was on something. Great. Not only did Amy have bad taste in hair: she had bad taste in men, as well. Someone should really talk to her.

Toon Town made a wet noise with his mouth. "So you're not gonna tell me where she is? I got something real important to discuss with her."

"And I already told you: I don't know where she is. Now if you'll excuse me." Zsa Zsa had begun to bark and scratch at the other side of the door. Our conversation must have woken her up.

He nodded towards the door. "You got a dog in there?"

I nodded.

"I like dogs." He grinned again. Everytime I saw his smile, I liked it less. "Now you remember," and he pointed a finger at me, "you see Amy, you tell her Toon Town is lookin' for her." Then he mumbled something to himself and walked away.

The man had an odd gait. He'd take six or seven steps forward and a small one to the side, then continue on. Everytime he stepped to the side, he'd make a fist and raise it into the air and shake his head, as if he were violently disagreeing with what someone standing next to him was saying. Obviously whatever Toon Town had taken hadn't agreed with him. Finally he reached his car, a lime green Geo Tracker. I hadn't seen it when I'd pulled in, because it was parked behind my neighbor's conversion van.

Just for the hell of it, I made a note of the license number, as he drove away. Then I went inside my house. "A fine watchdog you are," I told Zsa Zsa as she clawed my legs with her front paws.

I picked her up, and she licked my face. I laughed and took her out for a quick pee. Then I went upstairs. George had left a note on my pillow, telling me he'd give me a call when he got back into town. I put it on my nightstand, threw my clothes on the floor, and crawled into bed. A few seconds later I was in La La Land. I thought I'd dream about Murphy. But I didn't. I dreamt about smoking a cigarette instead. I was sitting under a palm tree watching a boat bobbing out on the water. I had a rum and Coke in my left hand and a Camel in my right. I was just about to take a puff when the alarm rang.

Jesus. I leaned over and slammed the off button down with the side of my fist. Then I put my head back down on the pillow, closed my eyes, and tried to pick up where I'd left off. But it was too late. The dream was gone. I groaned. How long had it been? Four days. And I had to stay off of them for twenty-seven more days. My God. Why had I made the bet with George? What had I been thinking of? This torture was definitely not worth twenty-five dollars. What had I been looking to prove? That I had willpower? Who cared? But I knew I wouldn't give in. My pride wouldn't let me.

"I can do this," I told Zsa Zsa.

She didn't bother lifting her head off the pillow to reply. I guess she wasn't that confident. Oh well. It was too late to brood about it now. I brooded about it anyway, while I took a shower and got dressed. Then because—as per usual I didn't have any food in the house—I stopped at Nice 'N' Easy on the way to work and picked up coffee, three glazed doughnuts, and the *Post Standard.* A picture of Richmond stared back at me from the front page. He looked a lot better than he had when I saw him last. I scanned the article as I waited in line to pay. It didn't tell me much I didn't already know. "Police spokesperson, Millicent Rafferty," it said, "reported an anonymous phone call which led officers to Mr. Richmond's apartment, where his body was found. Foul play is suspected." No shit. "Several leads are currently being pursued."

I just hoped that none of them led to me. Then the article recapped Richmond's life and gave some background info about the grieving family. That was it. Nothing else about the apartment. Or Amy. I gave the clerk five bucks and tried not to look at the packs of cigarettes, while I waited for my change. Then I went to work.

I got to the store a little before ten. I'd just opened up and was starting to clean out Amy's ferret's cage when a man strode in. He was wearing a wrinkled double-breasted charcoal grey suit, a red tie, and a light blue shirt. His hair was rumpled, and he had the kind of circles under his eyes you get from not sleeping for a couple of nights.

"I'm Charlie Richmond," he announced, when he got up to the counter. "Dennis Richmond's son."

My stomach clenched. I wondered if he knew about last night's expedition. I took a sip of coffee and waited to see what was coming.

He nodded at the copy of the *Post Standard* Mr. Bones was burrowing under. "So you've seen this morning's paper. You know about my father."

I relaxed a little. At least Charlie didn't know I was the one who'd found his father's body. I nodded. "I'm sorry," I murmured. The expression had always struck me as inadequate, but I'd never been able to come up with a better one.

"Me too." Now that I had a chance to look at him, I realized Charlie Richmond had his father's mouth—red and fleshy—and his chin. His face was rounder, though, and his features were more symmetrical. He pointed to the ferret. "Is that Mr. Bones?"

I nodded. "Your mother doesn't seem to want him." And I put out my hand to keep the ferret from falling off the counter. Depth perception doesn't seem to be one of their strengths.

"Stepmother," Charlie corrected. "No. She doesn't like the ferret at all. She wanted Amy to get rid of it. They got into a huge argument over it."

"Is that unusual?"

"No. Amy was always fighting with Gerri and my dad. It made things very unpleasant."

"I can imagine," I murmurmed, having come from a similiar household myself.

Charlie nodded in the ferret's direction. "So Amy just left him here?"

"She was in a hurry." I picked Mr. Bones up and put him

on my shoulder. He immediately ran down my arm and stuck his head up my sleeve. His nails scratched my skin as he worked his way in. They needed to be clipped.

Charlie Richmond leaned forward and fixed me with an earnest gaze. "I have to find her."

I pulled the ferret out from my sleeve and returned him to his cage. "When she comes back, I'll tell her you asked for her."

Richmond fidgeted with his tie. "You know the police are looking for her?"

"They were in here already."

"Well, now they have an APB out on her. Gerri says they think she had something to do with my father's death."

I thought about last night. "Maybe she does."

"No she doesn't." Richmond's voice rose, indignantly.

"How can you be so sure?"

"Because I know her. Look," Richmond said, "the girl's a goddamned vegetarian for Christ sake. She's practically a Buddhist. She wouldn't kill a fly. Literally. She used to take them out of the house. I'm sorry, but there is no way in hell that kid would kill my father."

"Sometimes even Buddhists lose control," I pointed out.

"Not like that."

"Okay. Let's suppose for the moment that what you say is true." I took out a stick of gum, put it in my mouth, and tried not to think about how much I wanted to hold a cigarette in my hand. Maybe if I just held it and didn't light it. "But why do you care?"

"I want to help her. She needs someone in her corner."

"What about her mother?"

Charlie Richmond bit the inside of his cheek. "My stepmother and Amy don't get along too well. As you've probably noticed.'' He was silent for a moment, as he watched Mr. Bones attack the fur mouse I'd hung up for him.

''It's kind of hard to miss, but what does all of this have to do with me?''

''Simple. I want to hire you to find her.''

I raised an eyebrow. ''Me?''

''I've read about you. You've done this kind of work before, and you've seen Amy. You know what she's like.''

I chose my next words with care. ''I've seen her briefly—twice—but we haven't had time for a heart-to-heart.''

''That's better than nothing.''

I drummed my fingers on the counter. ''Maybe so, but you still haven't explained why you're so interested in all of this.''

''I guess from the outside it would seem kind of odd.''

''You could say that.''

Charlie Richmond frowned. A deep furrow bisected his forehead. ''Amy and I . . . we grew up together. We weren't close . . . but we liked each other. We covered for each other when Gerri and my dad were on the warpath. They didn't do anything terrible,'' he quickly explained, catching my look. ''But they weren't very nice to us, either. You could say we were just your typical dysfunctional, blended American family.'' He gave a bitter little smile and began fiddling with his tie again.

''And? . . .'' I prodded, when he didn't say anything else.

''She's like the family scapegoat. She always gets blamed for everything. It's not fair.''

I folded my arms across my chest. ''Is she crazy?''

''No.''

''Then why does everyone say she is?''

"She had a bad acid trip and went into a depression, so my mother put her in Cedar View."

"Expensive place," I commented. Cedar View was where the upper and upper middle class kids went when they needed to detox.

"My family can afford it." Charlie Richmond tugged on his collar to loosen it. "At least when she's there, you know where she is. She's not running around on the streets."

"Okay. Now what happened when Amy came out?"

"Gerri told me she and my stepfather had a big fight, and Amy stormed out of the house."

I interrupted. "According to the newspaper article I read, I thought Amy left after your father disappeared?"

Charlie frowned. "Gerri said she came back the day before Dad disappeared. She and Dad had another fight at breakfast."

"What about?"

"I don't know. Gerri didn't hear. Dennis told her they'd discuss it over dinner, but he never came home."

"And Amy took off the next day. I can see why the police would want to talk to her." Charlie looked unhappy. "Did your stepmother report Amy's other disappearances?"

"No. There was no point. She's been doing this kind of stuff for the past year, year and a half. I think everyone has given up on her. It's just easier. There are only so many times you can go driving through the streets at three o'clock in the morning." He ran his hand through his hair absentmindedly. It was thinner than his father's. "God, all of this has been so awful. I don't know what to think anymore. All I know is that Amy needs help. Will you look for her?"

I said yes. I'd been planning to do it anyway. Working for Charlie Richmond might make the task easier.

"Good." He smiled his tight little smile. "How much do you charge?"

"Nothing. I don't have a license." Even if I had, I wouldn't have taken money from him. Despite what he'd said, I wasn't sure enough of his motives to want to be beholden to him. "If things work out you can make a donation to the Humane Society."

"No problem."

"I didn't think it would be. But there is something else."

Charlie Richmond cocked his head and waited.

"When I find Amy, I'm going to tell her that you want to meet with her. But if she doesn't want to, I'm not going to force her, and I'm not going to tell you where she is."

Richmond's face flushed. "Don't you trust me?"

"I don't know you."

He smacked the counter with the flat of his hand. The ferret squeaked in alarm. "What the hell do you think I'm going to do?" he demanded.

I gripped the edge of the counter and leaned forward. "Look, if you don't like my conditions, go find someone else."

I watched Richmond make tiny opening and closing motions with his lips, while he decided what to do. "I guess I can live with them," he finally conceded.

"Good." I reached for the notebook and pen sitting by the side of the register. "I want you to tell me everything you can about Amy."

"Everything?" He didn't sound happy at the idea, but then I had the impression he wasn't happy about most things.

I shrugged. "It's up to you. Only I think it's fair to warn

you that the more I know about her, the easier she'll be to find."

Charlie Richmond talked for the next half an hour. Once he got started, he had a lot to say. Most of it had to do with drugs and alcohol. It seemed as if Amy had been keeping close company with both of them.

Chapter 7

I was reading over my notes from my interview with Charles Richmond when Manuel walked in the door. He was wearing a black Raiders baseball hat, a faded black and red checked shirt, and black, baggy pants. Real baggy. As in the crotch of his pants hung down to just above his knees. He was not a thing of sartorial beauty. Except, perhaps, to himself.

"You got a minute?" he asked, as he pimp-rolled his way over to the counter.

I sighed and closed my notebook. "What do you want?"

"Who says I want anything?"

"Because you always do."

"For your information I was gonna do you a favor. See, I got someone over on Oak Street that wants to sell his pit vipers . . ."

"And you thought you'd give me first crack?"

He pulled his pants up. "Yeah. Exactly."

"Manuel, do you want a lift to the North Side?"

He put on an injured look. "I'm just trying to help you out."

"Right." In my experience the only person that ever benefitted from Manuel's favors was Manuel. I glanced at the clock on the wall. It was a little after eleven. "Shouldn't you be in school?"

"I got the day off."

And I was going to win the lottery tomorrow and retire to Maui. "What if I called your mother and asked?"

"She ain't home."

"How about your social worker?" I knew I was doing knee jerk responsible adult but I couldn't help myself. Manuel was currently on probation, after having broken into one car too many. According to the court, he was supposed to be in school.

"She's probably out."

I reached for the phone. "Let's find out."

He shrugged. "Go ahead."

"I should." But I put my hand down. What was the point? Nothing was going to happen if I made the call. There wasn't enough money or personnel to enforce what the courts mandated. I knew it and, more importantly, so did Manuel.

He grinned. He had a nice smile. It would be even nicer if his mother had the money to send him to an orthodontist. "I knew you wouldn't. You and me are buds, right?"

"I wouldn't go that far," I told him. But Manuel just kept on grinning because he knew I was lying. He and I had a history. We'd gotten to know each other in the hospital when we were both recuperating. The same person had tried to kill us both. Manuel might be a punk, but he was my punk.

"What's that? Some kind of rat?" He pointed to Mr. Bones. I glanced over at the ferret. He was standing on his hind legs with his nose pressed to the glass, watching Manuel approach.

I laughed. "No. It's a ferret."

"It looks like a rat."

"It belongs to the mink family. Rodents have long front teeth that constantly grow. Ferrets don't."

"Whatever. I heard they bite real bad."

"Not usually. Do you want to hold him?"

"Naw." He changed the subject. "So what's happening?"

I told him about Amy. Actually, his coming in saved me a call. Manuel was one of my sources. Given his age, he knew a surprising number of people.

"What's she look like?" he asked, when I was done.

"She's got blue hair and a nose ring. She wears black eye makeup and white lipstick. Does a lot of drugs."

"You mean she's a burn-out."

"If that's what you want to call her. Have you seen her?"

"Maybe." A cagey look crept across his face. "Do I get a finder's fee?"

"Yeah. I don't turn you in to your probation officer."

He snorted. "Okay. Be like that."

"I intend to. Now, where did you spot her?"

Manuel took off his hat and began bending in the sides of the brim.

It was a riveting performance, but it began to pall after about thirty seconds. "So?" I said, after another ten seconds or so had gone by. "Are you going to tell me or not?"

Manuel stopped what he was doing and looked up. "I can't tell you, I got to show you, 'cause you ain't gonna find this place by yourself."

"Why not?"

" 'Cause it's out of the way. You still carrying your box cutter?"

I patted my front pocket. "Why? Am I going to need it?"

"Probably not."

"Then why are you asking?"

"You just never know who's going to be there."

"There?"

"In the place."

"Great." This was not the kind of news I wanted to hear. But I wasn't surprised. The world Manuel moved in was definitely on the scummier side of the scale. It wasn't full of heavy duty drugs and guns, but it was full of edgy kids carrying box cutters and baseball bats. I watched as he went back to work on his hat brim again. "Why are you doing that?" I finally asked.

Manuel looked at me as if I were stupid. "I'm breaking it in. You got to do this when you get a new hat."

Of course. How could I not have known? We made arrangements to meet when I got off from work. Manuel hung around for a little bit longer, hoping for a lift, then drifted out the door when it was obvious he wasn't going to get one. I spent the next hour or so calling around, trying to locate a Brazilian rainbow boa for a customer. I finally found one down in Fort Myers. Unfortunately it was on the pricey side. Four hundred dollars for a baby. I tapped my pen against my front teeth. Joe had said price was no object, but I decided I'd better call him up and make sure, before I finalized the order. I didn't want to be stuck with something I'd have trouble unloading.

Next, I ordered a dozen dog sweaters in small sizes from a local woman who knits them, fed the fish, checked the pH balance in their tanks, and waited on customers. It's amazing how they always come in clumps. I wondered if someone in an MBA program had ever done a study on the phenomenon. It's true, though. Your store can be empty for the entire day, then bam! Suddenly you got eight people in there, and everybody is in a rush, and then they start to walk out because you can't wait on all of them at once.

Naturally, George had to call during one of those periods. That's another law of retailing: You never get personal calls during slow time. I offered to call him back, but he told me he was talking from a pay phone down at the Bronx County Courthouse.

"Your cousin really messed up, huh?"

"That's one way of putting it," George said. He sounded angry and sad. I could hear someone in the background yelling for him to get off the phone.

"When are you coming back?"

"As soon as I can." Then he hung up, leaving me feeling bad that I hadn't been able to talk longer.

The feeling lingered as I worked. I was wondering what his family expected George to do, when Tim walked in. The heels on his cowboy boots made a clicking sound as he crossed the floor.

"He still here?" He pointed to Mr. Bones.

"I think we're going to be stuck with him for awhile."

"One of my friends has a ferret cage he's not using. I'll bring it in later tonight."

"Great. I'm sure Mr. Bones will be most appreciative."

Tim grunted, took off his black leather jacket, and went into the back room to hang it up. It's a good thing I wasn't hungry for conversation, because with Tim I would have starved to death—although he does okay with the customers.

When I left at five, he was trying to explain to a woman and her son why their pet corn snake wasn't eating cooked chicken. Better him than me, I thought, as I whistled for Zsa Zsa. Since I've stopped smoking, my tolerance for stupidity has gone down to zero. Not that it was ever very high to begin with. On the way home, Zsa Zsa and I stopped at Burger King and got four hamburgers and two orders of fries. Zsa Zsa finished hers first and snagged some of my french fries when I wasn't paying attention. She had begun to shred the takeout bag, as I pulled into the driveway. I took it away and got out of the cab.

James was waiting at the door, meowing impatiently. For an outdoor cat, he'd certainly gotten soft in his old age. I let both of them in, glanced through the mail, and fed James half a can of cat food. Then I went upstairs and changed into a black turtleneck, dark blue jeans, and sneakers. As I passed the phone, I thought about calling Gerri Richmond and having a little chat, but decided to wait. I didn't want to do anything that would make looking for Amy any more complicated than it already was. Both Zsa Zsa and James were asleep on the sofa when I came back down. I felt like joining them, but I called Manuel and told him I was coming by to get him instead.

Manuel lived on the west side of town. The drive over took me about twenty minutes, and I spent it thinking about how odd it was that I should now be looking for the daughter I never knew Murphy had—a daughter I would have given anything to have had—and about how maybe everything in the universe does interconnect after all, a fact that argues for the existence of God. Then a nicotine fit hit me, saving me from my bout of metaphysical speculation, and I began thinking about how much I wanted a cigarette instead. I could buy a pack, smoke one, and throw the rest of them out. George wouldn't know. I spotted a grocery store at the corner of Oswego and Clark and started slowing down. At the last minute, though, my conscience got the better of me, and I sped back up. I was still muttering when I turned onto Manuel's street.

Despite the cold, he was waiting for me in front of his mom's place. Nestled in between two other nondescript houses, the yellow, run-down, two-story colonial always housed a changing parade of aunts, uncles, cousins, and family friends. The porch sagged and the postage stamp-sized front yard was filled with discarded Big Wheels, jump ropes, and balls. Two large carved pumpkins signified the holiday to come.

"It took you long enough," he groused, as he got in and slammed the cab door shut. "I'm freezing my ass off out here."

"You could have waited inside."

He muttered something under his breath.

"What did you say?"

"Nothing." He slumped down in his seat and began tapping his fingers on the door handle.

I took another look at him. He was wearing an expression I recognized all too well. "Your father kicked you out again, didn't he?"

He corrected me angrily. "Fucking Walter isn't my father."

"Sorry."

"I don't know why my mother ever married that jerk." Manuel fingered the edge of his Windbreaker. It was too thin for a night like this, but then, he was never dressed for the weather. I haven't been able to figure out whether he can't afford to, or he's too stubborn to. "I wish he'd stay drunk. He's worse when he's sober," Manuel said angrily.

"So where are you going to go?"

"I'll crash at Rabbit's. I could use a change anyway." The bravado he was trying for was betrayed by the slight trembling of his lower lip. To hide it, he turned and looked out the side window.

I patted his shoulder, but he shrugged my hand off. I sighed and started up the car. I felt bad for Manuel, but there was nothing I could do. I tried talking to him about his stepfather before, but it hadn't worked. In fact, it had just made things worse. Hoping to find some candy, he leaned over and opened up the glove compartment. There was no candy, but his face lit up when he saw the cell phone. He took it out.

"This is new," he observed.

"I got it a month ago. It's for emergencies. Now please put it back."

"Let me make one call."

"No. Now put it away."

"All right," he grumped, returning it to its place.

"So where are we going?" I asked, after a minute had gone by.

It turned out we were heading for an industrial area over by the Carousel Mall. It was drizzling as we drove through the city. The streets were quiet. The streetlights reflected off the wet roads. Crepe paper skeletons and cardboard witches leeringly marked our progress. When we got to Wolf Street, Manuel indicated I should take a right. Halfway down the block, he told me to stop.

"Are you sure this is the place?" I asked.

The building I was parked in front of was a one-story brick structure. The sidewalk in front of it was cracked. The front door had been boarded up with plywood, as had the two front windows. A weathered sign hung above the door. I managed to make out the first word, "Syracuse," but the next two were too faded to read.

"Of course I'm sure," Manuel told me. He sounded annoyed. He didn't like having his expertise questioned.

I questioned it anyway. "How do you know?"

"Because I've seen her here." Manuel started playing with the zipper of his Windbreaker. "She was at a party I went to."

"You went to a party here?"

"What's wrong with that?" he demanded.

"Nothing, I guess." I'd done stuff like this when I was his age, too. I turned off the ignition and pocketed the keys. "Who lives here, anyway?"

Manuel shrugged. That and tugging up his pants seemed to be his favorite gestures. "Different people. Right now it's two girls."

"Runaways?" I guessed.

"They're doing okay." Manuel's voice was defiant. "Anyway," he added, when I didn't say anything, "they got no other place to go."

I didn't state the obvious. Instead, I surveyed the street. The buildings—some square, some rectangular—one-, two-, and three-story structures, housed a variety of small industrial companies and warehouses. In the background, a lit up Carousel Mall loomed off to the left like a deranged blue and white spaceship ready to take off into the evening sky. Silhouettes of oil storage tanks sat off to the right.

"Nobody comes here at night," Manuel said, voicing my thoughts.

"Except for you guys."

"That's right. Except for us. And we don't count."

I took two sticks of gum out of my jacket, gave one to Manuel, and began unwrapping the other one. "So how do we get in?" I asked.

Manuel grinned. He liked being the one in charge. "I'll show you." I wondered if he'd ever been a child.

We got out of the car at almost the same time. The thud of the cab doors shutting echoed up and down the street. Manuel beckoned for me to follow him. We walked down the driveway. In the middle of the warehouse wall, someone had spray painted a smiley face with its tongue sticking out. Under it, they had written. "Going nowhere. Doing nothing." Seemed right to me.

I continued walking. The asphalt was littered with junk food wrappers and beer cans, plus the occasional brick that had fallen out of the wall. Manuel turned the corner, and I did the same. The back of the warehouse had been black-topped over. A band of weed trees had grown up around the edges. Stray strips of newspaper and plastic hung from branches, fluttering in the wind like lost souls. I turned towards the building. A large pull-up accordion-pleated metal door marked the loading dock. A smaller door, now boarded up with plywood sheeting, sat a couple of feet away. The four concrete steps leading up to it looked safe enough, though once I got closer, I could see that the metal railing fastened to them was beginning to rust through.

Manuel climbed the stairs quickly. I was right behind him. When we got to the smaller door, he bent slightly, put his hands on either side of the bottom half of the plywood, and pulled. The wood came away, revealing a door with a hole gashed into the middle of it. It looked as if someone had taken an axe to it.

Manuel grinned. "Neat, huh? When you put the plywood back, you can't see anything from the outside."

Then he stepped inside. I felt a little like Alice going into Wonderland, as I followed him through.

Chapter 8

I looked around. We were standing in a hallway that was maybe ten feet wide at the most. The place had that fusty odor places get when they're not lived in or worked in for a long time. I rubbed my arms. It felt colder in here than it did outside, but at least it wasn't pitch-black. A large metal industrial style lamp looped onto a pipe which ran across the ceiling and threw a ragged white light on the cement walls and concrete floor. It seemed as if we'd stepped into a different time, but whether it was feudal or postmodern, I couldn't tell.

I pointed to the lamp. "Who tapped into the power lines?"

Manuel shook his head. "I don't know. Come on." He motioned for me to follow him down the hall. "We have to go this way."

I trailed my hand along the wall as I walked. It felt rough to the touch. We'd taken about five steps when two girls materialized in the corridor in front of us. They were both bundled up against the cold in long black skirts, heavy sweaters, lace up boots, and patched, oversized ski parkas.

The smaller one shaded her eyes with her hand, trying to see into the gloom. "Lisa?" she asked. Her voice was childishly high. "Is that you?"

"Sorry."

The two girls froze in alarm at the sound of my voice. In another moment, I was sure they'd be gone, vanishing into the bowels of the warehouse.

Manuel stepped in front of me. "It's okay," he said, and he put up both hands, palms facing outward, to show he meant no harm.

The bigger girl took a step back. "What do you want?"

"Everything's fine." Manuel's voice was low and soothing. "Don't you remember me? I was here with Rabbit. At the party. The one last week," he added, when he didn't get a response. "I brought the Bud."

The smaller girl snapped her fingers and giggled. "Yeah. That's right. You're the one that got sick all over Jamal's shoes and passed out."

Manuel screwed up his mouth in an expression of outrage. "Hey, I just shut my eyes for a couple of minutes."

The bigger girl put her hands on her hips. "Excuse me! You were out cold. Rabbit had to drag you out of here." Her face had relaxed while she talking to Manuel, but then she glanced at me, and she started looking scared again. "What does she want?" she asked, indicating me with a nod of her head.

Manuel stamped his feet. The cold must have been getting to him. I know it was getting to me. I could feel it seeping up through the floor, through the soles of my shoes, into the bottoms of my feet. I began to wish I'd put on heavier socks. "She just wants to ask you a few questions," he said.

"About what?"

"Amy Richmond," I explained. "I'm looking for her. Manuel told me she might be here."

The girl made a minute adjustment to the pocket flap of her parka before answering. "Well Manuel is wrong. She was here, but she left."

"I see." I took a couple of steps towards the girls, then stopped and waited for a reaction. When there was none, I took a few more. As I slowly drifted towards them, I realized I was doing the same kind of thing I did when I tried to get close to a stray cat. "And when was that?" I asked, when I was within eight feet.

"A couple of days ago."

I nodded towards the corridor they were standing in front of. "So if I walk in there, I won't see her?"

"I just told you that," the girl who was doing the talking replied.

"Fine." I made conciliatory noises. I didn't want to antagonize my only source of information. "Did Amy happen to say where she was going?"

The girls exchanged glances. Now that my eyes had a chance to adjust to the light, I could see them better. They both looked to be about thirteen. They had bleached their hair blonde and plastered their faces with makeup, trying, no doubt, to look older, but the puppy fat on their bodies and the high notes in their voices betrayed them. They should have been in their houses doing their homework, watching TV, and talking on the phone to their friends—not standing here answering my questions.

"No," the bigger one said. "She didn't."

In a couple of years, the girl's expertise would grow. But right now, she was still a bad liar.

"I'm telling you the truth," she insisted, when I politely expressed my disbelief. "She left with this guy."

I thought of the man who had been waiting for me outside my house. "Is his name Toon Town?"

She gasped in amazement. Robin Light. Genius. "How'd you know?"

"I had the pleasure of meeting him last night."

"He gives me the creeps."

"He gives me the creeps, too."

I was rewarded with the shadow of a smile. "He's always bragging on how he's always spying on people. How he knows everything we do."

"Nice."

"Amy told me her mother said if she saw him around the house, she'd call the cops."

I didn't say anything, even though I could sympathize with the sentiment. Instead I put my hands in my pockets and looked around. "So how long have you guys been here?"

"A couple of weeks."

I gave an involuntary shudder. "That's a long time."

"It's not so bad," the bigger one said. "You get used to it."

"How do you stand the cold?"

"We got blankets and camping stuff."

"And anyway, we're waiting for someone," the littler one said. "Justin's taking us to Chicago."

"Melanie." The bigger one's voice was fierce. "Shut up."

I could see Melanie flinch.

"How old is Justin?" I asked.

"Old enough," the one who was talking said. Her voice had taken on a defiant edge. "Not that it's any of your business. If my parents don't care, why should you?"

"No reason at all," I replied soothingly.

"You don't believe me, do you?"

"No, I do."

The girl looked as if she were going to cry. Melanie patted her shoulder. Her friend gave her a wan smile. I wanted to hug her. The four of us stood in silence for a few seconds. Then I offered everyone a piece of gum and brought the subject back to Amy. "So what's Amy's story? How come she ran away?"

This time the girl answered. She was relieved to talk about someone else. "She didn't run away. Her father threw her out."

"Really?" Charlie had said Amy had taken off.

"They got into a big fight."

"Over what?"

"Stuff."

"What kind of stuff?"

The girl shrugged. "She didn't say."

"Do you know why she was sent to Cedar View?"

"The usual. Smoking weed, skipping school, staying out late, talking back."

I remembered something else Charlie had said. "I heard Amy had a bad acid trip."

The girl stuck her chin out. "It wasn't that bad. I've seen worse."

She probably had, too. She was probably a better judge of that kind of thing than I was. "Okay." I wiggled my fingers to get the blood flowing. "Are you sure she didn't say anything to indicate where she might be going?"

The girls exchanged another glance.

"Why are you looking for her?" asked the one that was doing all the talking.

"Her brother wants to help her."

"Right," the girl said, sarcastically. She shifted her weight from one foot to another and inspected a lock of her hair for split ends.

"You don't believe that he wants to?"

She shrugged her shoulders.

"Amy's in a lot of trouble," I added.

"You already said that."

"Look, all I want to do is talk to her. I just want to make sure she's all right."

"So you say," the girl sneered. I realized she'd listened to too many adults making too many empty promises to believe mine. I'd have to earn her trust. Unfortunately, I didn't have the time. I was trying to decide what to say next, when Melanie muttered something.

I turned to her. "I'm sorry," I told her. "I didn't hear what you said."

Melanie's hand went up to her hair. She began pulling on a lock. "Toon Town's name is Wallace Gleason," she blurted out. "He used to hang out with my cousin's friend. That's how I know."

"Melanie!" her friend yelled.

I ignored the friend and concentrated on Melanie. "Do you know where he and Amy were going?"

Melanie shook her head. "They never said."

"Do you remember anything else about him?"

"He's weird."

"Weird as in how?"

"He's got all this electronic stuff. He's always spying on

people, listening in to hear what they say. And he's got these special glasses you can see in the dark with."

"Night vision binoculars."

"Yeah. That's it. He loves all that stuff."

"Melanie, shut up!" her friend cried, before I could ask another question.

"No." Melanie's eyes narrowed. Her hands went to her hips. "I won't. I'm tired of you ordering me around. The guy *is* a total sleazebag."

The two girls glared at each other.

"Thanks," I told Melanie. "You've done the right thing."

She studied the floor instead of answering. I guess maybe she was having second thoughts. I took one of my business cards out of my wallet and put it in Melanie's hand. Given the coldness of the room, it felt surprisingly warm. "If you or your friend decide not to go to Chicago, give me a call. Maybe I can help."

"We don't need your help," the bigger girl yelled. "We can take care of ourselves. We're fine."

Her voice vibrated inside my head like a guilty memory, as I walked back down the hallway. "What's the other girl's name?" I asked.

"Cindy. Why?"

"Just curious. Do you know their last names?"

From Manuel's expression, you would have thought I was enquiring after their blood type. "I never asked."

We left the way we came in. I took a deep breath of fresh air, while Manuel fitted the plywood back in place.

"What now?" he asked, when he was done.

I considered my answer, while I surveyed the sky. It was starless. "Two things," I replied. "I'm going to see if I can find Mr. Wallace Gleason, and I'm going to have another conversation with Amy's mother."

"Tonight?"

"No. Tomorrow. How crazy do you think I am?"

Manuel didn't answer, which was probably all to the good. I dropped him off at Rabbit's house and went home. It wasn't until I walked into the kitchen that I knew something was wrong.

Chapter 9

Of course I didn't realize anything was amiss right away. I wasn't really paying strict attention. But then, who does in their own home? I fed James, glanced at the day's mail, and poured myself a shot of Scotch and drank it, after which I got a pint of Ben & Jerry's English Toffee Crunch out of the freezer and started eating. It wasn't until I was done and went over to check my answering machine for messages that I realized I had a problem. The machine was gone. It took me another second before I noticed my box was gone, too. So were my CDs. That's when it finally hit me. I'd been robbed.

"I can't believe it," I told Zsa Zsa.

She rubbed her head on my ankle. I gave her an absent-minded pat, as I surveyed the kitchen. Nothing else seemed to be missing. I shivered. At first I thought it was just a reaction to having my house broken into, but then I realized I was feeling a blast of cold air on my back. I turned. The kitchen window—the one that had been painted shut, the one I hadn't been able to pry open—was up. I immediately thought of Toon Town standing beneath the spruce tree and wondered if he could have been responsible for this, but then I dismissed the thought. He'd said he'd been looking for Amy and, given what I'd heard tonight, I had no reason to doubt his story. We'd had a fair number of break-ins in the area recently. This was probably one of those. I went into the living room to see what else was missing.

The TV and the VCR were still there. That was good. I made a circuit of the room. At first glance, nothing seemed to be gone. I walked into the dining room. Everything seemed to be in place there, too. Maybe I'd be lucky. Maybe whoever had done this had just gotten as far as the kitchen before he left. But of course I wouldn't know that until I checked out the rest of the house. Zsa Zsa ran ahead of me, as I climbed the stairs.

"And what were you doing when this happened?" I asked her. She halted on the step in front of me and wagged her tail. I scratched her rump. "You know you're supposed to protect this house, not hide under the bed." She wagged her tail again. As a guard dog, she was hopeless. Maybe I should get a tape of a Rottweiler barking and hook it into the door bell.

I paused at the door to my bedroom. The person, or persons, had been in here, too. My dresser drawers were open, as was the closet door. I checked my jewelry case. My Mexican silver jewelry was gone. So was the thirty dollars I'd left lying on my nightstand. Great. I turned and went into my study and the guest room. The rooms had been gone through, but nothing had been taken. Not that there really was anything to take—unless, of course, the thieves had a hard-on for sheets and blankets. I put a piece of gum in my mouth, went back to my bedroom, and called the police.

Two uniforms came by, twenty minutes later.

"Probably kids," the first one told me, after he'd had a look around. "They've been really busy around here recently."

The second one opened up his evidence kit and began dusting the windowsill for prints. "Not that this will help much," he said, as he worked. "These days everyone wears gloves."

"Then why bother?"

He ignored me and kept on working.

"You should get an alarm system put in," the first one said, when his partner was finished. By now both men had been in my house for about half an hour. "Here." He handed me a paper with a number on it. "When you call your insurance agent, give him this."

They left, and I dragged myself off to bed. I fell asleep the moment my head touched the pillow. I was still sleeping when the alarm rang the next morning. I turned it off and lay in bed, too exhausted to get up. In the old days, I'd have swallowed a couple of uppers. Now, of course, I don't do that anymore. I drink a pot of coffee instead. So now my brain isn't messed up—my stomach is. Which, I suppose, is an improvement of sorts.

As I studied the stain on the ceiling, and wondered where the leak in the roof was coming from and why the roofers couldn't find it, I told myself I'd get up in five minutes. I fell back to sleep instead. I don't think I would have gotten up at all, if Jamie hadn't decided to sit on my chest and nibble on my chin. By then, it was nine o'clock and I panicked. I had to go to the bank before the store opened. I dashed into the shower, put on a pair of jeans and a turtleneck, fed the cat, and left the house.

There was a line at the bank—I don't know why the branch I use doesn't have a line just for commercial transactions, but it doesn't. By the time I got out of there, put gas in the cab—which I had to do because the indicator was below empty—got my coffee, my papers, and picked out my doughnuts, it was almost ten o'clock.

I was unlocking the door to Noah's Ark, when a guy who'd sold me an iguana a month before came up and informed me he wanted it back. When I explained that I'd already sold it, he did a good imitation of a man about to go postal. It seems Iggy the Iguana had been his girlfriend's. He sold it when she'd walked out on him. Well, now they were back together, but if she discovered he'd gotten rid of it, they wouldn't be together for long. Fortunately one iguana pretty much looks like another. Well, not exactly, but close enough, if you're not paying strict attention.

"Don't worry," I told the guy, as I sent him out the door with Iggy II. "She'll never know."

"You're sure?" he asked.

"I'm positive," I lied. At this point, I would have said anything to get him to leave. I checked the clock on the wall. It was ten forty. My coffee was cold, and I hadn't even begun cleaning out the cages. This, I decided, as Manuel came sauntering in, was not going to be a good day.

"One of Rabbit's friends has a . . ." he began.

I cut him off before he could get any further. "Whatever it is, I'm not interested."

"Hey, I'm just trying to . . ."

"I mean it, Manuel."

The tone in my voice must have finally penetrated, because he grumped a "fine" and went into a sulk.

I took the phone book out from underneath the counter and pushed it towards him. "Here," I said. "If you want to do something useful, take this into my office and dial all the Gleasons in the book. See if you can find out where Toon Town lives. I expected him to argue, but he picked up the directory and pointed to the bag of doughnuts.

"Can I have one?"

I nodded.

"Two?"

"One and a half."

"Okay." He went into the back, from which he re-emerged an hour later to tell me most of the people he'd called weren't home, and the ones who were didn't know anyone called Wallace. Then he told me he was leaving.

I stopped in the middle of changing the wood shavings in the hamsters' cage. "You can stay if you want."

Manuel shook his head. "I gotta go back over to Rabbit's. I told him I'd help him do some stuff."

"What kind of stuff?"

"Nothing special."

"I hope you two aren't breaking into cars again."

Manuel's face flushed. "I'm not that stupid."

"Good." I changed the topic to a more neutral one. "Listen," I said, as he was leaving. "Ask Rabbit if he's seen Amy. Ask him to ask him friends."

Manuel nodded, as he ambled towards the door. I went back to work. About two o'clock, I called Gerri Richmond. The line was busy. The line was still busy when Tim walked in at two thirty. At two forty five I decided to take my chances and run over there. It was probably better than phoning for an appointment, anyway. I didn't want to give Gerri Richmond a chance to prepare herself. This time I wanted the advantage on my side for a change.

No one answered when I rang the bell at Gerri Richmond's house, but, given the two cars in the driveway, I figured someone was home. So I just kept my finger on the buzzer. After a minute of listening to the first bars of "Für Elise," Gerri came to the door. She didn't look pleased to see me, but then, why should she be.

"I'm busy," she snapped.

"That makes two of us." I stepped in before she had a chance to slam the door in my face.

Maybe it was the lack of makeup, but she looked more tired and older then she had the last time I'd seen her. The one thing she didn't look was grief-stricken. Maybe losing her husband was a relief instead of a tragedy. As I took another step, I noticed that her hair was pulled back in a rubber band and she was wearing sweat pants and a matching shirt in an unbecoming shade of pink.

Gerri Richmond folded her arms across her chest. "What do you want?" she demanded.

"An end to hunger and world peace, but I'll settle for talking about Amy."

"We have nothing to talk about."

"Are you so sure?" I watched the vein under Richmond's eye start twitching like a pinned worm. I don't know. Maybe she was expecting me to mention Murphy, but I was saving him for last. I mentioned her son instead. "Charlie seems to feel differently."

"What do you mean?" she stammered.

"He hired me to find her."

She opened her mouth in amazement. "I don't believe you. Why would he do that?"

I borrowed a gesture from Manuel and shrugged. "I don't know. Call him and find out."

"I will." She whirled around and headed for the phone.

As soon as she was out of sight, I went up the stairs to look for Amy's room.

I hadn't planned to but—hey, you know what they say about opportunity: If you don't open the door when it knocks, next time it might just walk on by. I figured it like this: I needed to find Amy. To do that, I needed to know as much about her as possible. Her room was a good place to start. Not that her mother would see things that way. Which was why I was taking the stairs two at a time. I figured I had five minutes at the most, before Gerri Richmond materialized at my side.

Fortunately for me, Amy's room was the second door from the left at the top of the stairs. Someone—probably Amy—had painted the walls and the ceiling a deep red. The window frames and the sashes were trimmed in lavender. If it hadn't been for the garlands of white Christmas lights festooning the moldings, I would have felt as if I'd walked into a cave. The first thing that attracted my attention was the canopy bed. Its light color marked it as coming from an earlier, happier time in Amy's life. The purple quilted spread was piled high with clothes. I gave them a quick glance and moved on to the massive, mahogany desk. Cans of glitter and spray paint, scraps of leather and fabric, beads, leather thongs, and paint brushes were heaped in the center. I wondered if Amy had been working on something when she left and, if so, what.

I poked through the stuff, but nothing presented itself. Next I picked up a book on origami that was laying off to one side and leafed through it. The figures were complex, some like the seahorse, requiring sixty-four folds. Certainly way beyond my league, but not beyond Amy's, judging from the blue paper swan that was hidden between two pages. I put the book down and opened the center drawer. I heard a snap and pulled my hand away. Then I peered in. A sprung mouse trap sat on a small notebook. Cute. Amy had booby trapped her desk. Life in this house must be delightful, I decided, as I moved the trap out of the way and picked up the notebook. It was labeled "assignments." I was about to flip through it, when I heard Gerri Richmond coming up the stairs. On impulse I slipped it into my pants pocket and closed the drawer. Then I turned to face the door.

"How dare you?" she spluttered, when she reached the entryway.

I moved away from the desk and towards her. "I'm sorry," I said. "I assumed you'd want to help me, so I decided to get a head start and save some time."

"Get out." She pointed to the door. I felt as if I were in the middle of a Victorian melodrama.

"Fine. I guess what your stepson said was true about your not liking Amy very much."

Gerri Richmond's face turned even paler. In a little while, it would match the color of her hair, and she'd fade into nothingness. "What I feel about my daughter or what my daughter feels about me is none of your business."

"It is, now that I've been hired to find her."

"Not by me." She drew herself up. "Or my son."

"I think I'll have to take his word on that."

"Be my guest." I noticed the vein under her eye was twitching again. "You have no idea what the situation is. The only thing you're going to do is to make things worse."

"Then why don't you explain it?"

But she either couldn't or wouldn't. "If you don't leave, I'm going to call the police."

"Relax. I'm going." I walked past her. The smell of Le Dix lingered in the air. "Tell me," I asked, when I was at the head of the stairs. "Don't you give a care about Amy at all?"

Gerri Richmond gave a strangled little laugh. "What would you know? How could you understand? You don't have a child."

"And you have Murphy's." The words came out before I could stop them. I could have kicked myself. This wasn't the way I'd planned to say it.

She gazed at me insolently. She was queen of the manor and I was nothing, a field hand. "I don't know what you're talking about."

I could feel my cheeks burning with shame and anger. "Oh, yes you do. Tell me, did your husband know Murphy was Amy's father, or did he think the baby was his?"

"I don't have to answer you."

An idea flashed across my mind. "Or did he just find out?"

Gerri turned and started towards Amy's bedroom. "I'm calling the police." The words bubbled behind her. "If you're here when they arrive, I'll press charges."

I left. I was surprised to find I was shaking when I got outside.

Chapter 10

As I drove out of Gerri Richmond's driveway, I wondered if what I'd said back at her house had been right. I gnawed at my thumbnail, as I turned onto East Genesee. Had Dennis suddenly found out about who Amy's real father was, after all these years? It seemed unlikely. How would he find out? Who would tell him? But if he had . . . I pictured the scene.

Dennis threatening divorce. Which meant no more nice house for Gerri, no more fancy car, no more cashmere sweaters. She didn't strike me as the type of lady who would take that well. The question was: What was she willing to do to hold on to what she had? After all, if Dennis was gone, so was her problem. Did she know about his apartment too? Had she hired someone to go over there and stab him? End of discussion. End of messy domestic drama. She sure hadn't looked as if she were engulfed in grief over her husband's death.

I tapped the steering wheel with my fingers. It was an

attractive picture, but it probably wasn't a true one, and I reluctantly put it aside and headed back to the store. The fact that I hated Gerri Richmond didn't mean she was a murderer.

Tim looked up from sweeping the floor as I walked in the front door. "The guy you sold the iguana to this morning called."

Zsa Zsa came over for a pet. I bent down and scratched her rump. "And?"

"He said to tell you it worked."

"Good."

"And George phoned."

I cursed. I couldn't believe I'd missed him again.

"He said he'd try again later."

"I don't suppose he left a number?"

"Nope."

"Anything else?"

"The crickets haven't arrived."

Great. This was the second time this had happened this month. I was going to have to find a new supplier.

Something moved in Tim's shirt pocket. "Mr. Bones," he explained, when he saw me staring. "He was getting bored in the cage so I took him out." A moment later, two ears, a pair of brown eyes, and a white snout peered out at me.

I lifted him out of Tim's pocket and cradled him in my arms.

"What are you going to do with him if Amy doesn't come back?"

"Make him into a collar."

"Seriously."

"Why? You want him?"

"Maybe."

Zsa Zsa jumped up to smell him. I put the ferret down on the floor and the two animals began playing tag. Tim and I watched them for a few minutes. Then he went in the back room, and I returned Mr. Bones to his cage. I should have gone through the mail, but I found myself thumbing through Amy's assignment book instead. It didn't tell me much, outside of the fact that the words "assignment pad" were a misnomer. Instead of homework assignments, its pages were filled with intricately rendered drawings of necklaces, bracelets, and rings. They were good. The girl definitely had talent. If she ever got out of the mess she'd gotten herself into, she could have a career designing jewelry. Unfortunately, what the book didn't have were her friends' names and phone numbers. Maybe she didn't have any. Then on the last page I found the initials UB. They were underlined three times and encased in an ever expanding spiral.

I reached into my pocket, unwrapped a stick of gum, put it in my mouth, and stared at the letters. Did they stand for anything? A boyfriend? A girlfriend? A ferret? Then it hit me. The *Herald* article I'd read about Dennis Richmond's disappearance had mentioned that the business was co-owned by his brother Brad, the man I'd met at Gerri Richmond's house, the man she'd slapped when he called her daughter a freak. "B" for Brad. "U" for Uncle. UB. Could that be who Amy meant? It was certainly worth trying. I mean, it wasn't as if I had hundreds of leads to explore. I got out the phone directory, looked up the number for the Syracuse Casket Company and dialed. When the receptionist came on, I told her I wanted to speak to Brad Richmond and added it was in reference to his niece, Amy. He came on the line a moment later.

"Have you seen her again?" His voice was brusque. I

could imagine him tapping his fingers on the table. "Did she come back to your store?"

"No."

"Then what is this about? Why are you calling."

"Your nephew hired me to find her."

"Well I'm afraid I can't help you. She hasn't put in an appearance here."

I explained.

"All right." He sighed. "Let me look at my calendar." There was a short pause, and he came back on the line. "Let's get together tomorrow at three thirty out here." He hung up.

I went in the back and poured myself a cup of coffee and got to work.

I set out for the Syracuse Casket Company a little before three the next day. It was a perfect fall afternoon. The sky was a brilliant shade of Caribbean blue. The temperature was 60 degrees. The air had a damp, spicy, woodland aroma. A shower of golden beech leaves fluttered around my car, as I headed down the street towards 81 North. The sidewalks were full of men and women raking up the last leaves before the winter snow. Packs of high school boys and girls jostled each other good-naturedly. Children ran through leaf piles. Shopkeepers stood in the doorways of their stores enjoying the autumn sun. It was enough to make me almost believe in Mom, Apple Pie, and the American Dream.

I got off 81 at the Liverpool exit and turned onto Hiawatha Boulevard. Twenty minutes later, I was at the factory. It was an unremarkable long, square-shaped brick building. Somehow I was disappointed. I'd wanted it to be a strange, eerie place guarded by a grizzled, humpbacked caretaker and a one-eyed dog. Instead I was walking towards a plant that could have manufactured pipes or storm doors or cartons. Oh well. Murphy always had said I was overimaginative. I threw the piece of gum I was chewing out, went inside, gave my name to the receptionist, and sat down to wait.

The smell of freshly cut wood and varnish permeated the air. The reception area was small and plain. No attempt at decorating had been made. The walls were putty colored and the chairs were standard office issue. I was thinking that even a plant would have been nice, when the door to the office opened and a girl came out. She was five-five, maybe 120 lbs. She had brown hair that came to her chin, hazel eyes, and regular features. Her dress—a flowered print number—and jacket overwhelmed her frame. With the right clothes and makeup, she would have been attractive, but now she seemed invisible.

She came over and shook my hand. "I'm Elizabeth Walker, Mr. Richmond's secretary. Please come with me."

She turned, and I followed her back through the doorway. We moved past the office space and the Xerox room, walked down a hall that housed more offices and a couple of large conference rooms, took a left, and came to an alcove that contained a desk, phone, and filing cabinet. Beyond it was another office. The door was partially closed. Elizabeth Walker knocked.

"Yes," a voice from inside said.

"It's Dee." Her voice became animated. "Robin Light is here."

"I'm ready."

Walker ushered me in, then left, carefully shutting the door behind her.

"Please sit down," Brad Richmond said, indicating a maroon leather armchair in front of his desk.

He'd taken off his tie and jacket and rolled up his sleeves. I looked around, as I sat down. It was a working office. The place was crammed with file cabinets and metal shelving overflowing with magazines, thick books encased in red plastic, and papers. Two prints, one blue and one green, hung on the wall. They were the room's only decoration. Both were abstract. Neither was memorable. Something told me they'd been bought the same time the furniture had.

Richmond cleared his throat as I took my place. I was thinking I'd give anything for a cigarette, when he spoke. "I'd like to apologize for the other night at my sister-in-law's house. I'm sorry you had to see that."

I made a noncommittal noise. I was more interested in listening to him than in having him listen to me.

He ran his hand through his hair. It was, I realized, as thick as his brother's had been. It just wasn't grey. As I was wondering if he dyed it, he leaned back in his chair and studied me. I returned his gaze.

Eventually he must have found what he wanted, because he started talking again. "You have to understand. It's been a dreadful time around here. Between Dennis's death and Amy's disappearance. . . ." He made a vague gesture. "Anyway, I didn't want you to misinterpret what you saw the other night. That's why I agreed to talk to you."

I shifted my weight slightly. The chair was too deep to sit in comfortably. "How would you like me to interpret it?" As far as I could see, it wasn't the type of scene that left too much room for interpretation.

He pursed and unpursed his lips. "I like Amy, but you have to understand that she's done some things that are . . . well . . . to be frank . . . not very nice."

"She circled your name in her notebook. May I ask why?"

He made his fingers into a steeple and brought them to his lips. "She wanted to borrow some money from me."

"Given what you said about her earlier, I find it difficult to believe she'd turn to you for help."

He flushed. "Sometimes I let my temper get the better of me. But Amy knows she can come to me."

I wondered if that were true. "How much did she want to borrow?"

"Two hundred dollars."

"Did she say why she wanted it?"

"No."

"Did you give it to her?"

"I told her I didn't think it was wise, considering her past history."

"What did she do?"

"She called me an asshole and stalked out of my house."

"Did you tell her father about it?"

He gave a bark of a laugh. "No. I didn't feel it was any of his business."

"Amy is his daughter."

Brad Richmond grimaced. "My brother and I weren't in the habit of talking very much."

"It must be difficult to run a business that way."

Brad Richmond looked around. His expression was self-satisfied. "We manage."

"I understand there's been a lot of tension in Dennis's household as well."

"So I hear. Word gets around," he explained, even though I hadn't asked him how he knew.

I sat back. "Is there anything you can tell me about Amy that might help me find her?"

"Not really." Brad Richmond studied the green and blue prints for a moment before going on. "Amy's always been a difficult child, right from the day she was born. She wouldn't sleep through the night for two years. When she was three, she would only eat potatoes and milk. If you served her anything else, she'd have a tantrum. My brother spent an enormous amount of money on therapists, a private school. Take this rehab facility he sent her to—our health insurance doesn't cover this sort of thing you know. That was big bucks. Maybe forty, fifty thousand dollars." He picked up a pen and dropped it. "You know who I blame her problems on?"

"Who?"

"Gerri. The moment I saw her, I knew she was trouble. I advised Dennis not to marry her. But he insisted. She was the first woman he ever went out with. My brother was not what you call socially adept where women are concerned." He smiled wanly. "I probably shouldn't have said anything, but it's hard not to when you see someone you care about doing something you think is going to make them unhappy."

"And did it?"

"What?"

"Make him unhappy?"

Brad Richmond picked up a paper clip and began straightening it out. "Gerri has managed to make all of us unhappy. In one way or another." He tossed the paper clip down. "From the day she married Dennis, things between my brother and I have never been the same." He shook his head. "Such a shame. Family. It's wonderful when everyone gets along. . . . But when they don't . . ." His voice trailed off. I was beginning to wonder if I'd wandered onto the stage of an afternoon talk show, when I heard yelling.

Chapter 11

The yelling grew louder.

Richmond gripped the edge of the desk. Ragged splotches of red spread across his cheeks. "Stay here," he barked. "I'll be right back." He jumped up from his desk and hurried across his office. The door banged against the wall as he threw it open on the way out.

I couldn't resist. I waited all of three seconds before I went after him. His gait was stiff-legged with rage as he half-walked half-ran down the corridor. As I followed him, I became aware of how quiet it was. Besides the yelling, the only noise I heard was the whirring of machinery from the plant. I remember thinking it was odd no one was in the hallway and that all the office doors were closed. What was this? Showdown time at the O.K. Corral? Was everyone hunkering down behind their desks waiting for whatever was going to happen to blow over? I was less than a foot away when Richmond halted at the entrance to the second conference room. I couldn't see in, though. Richmond was blocking my view. I took a couple of steps to the left and banged into a trash can. Richmond didn't turn around. I don't think he even heard. All his attention was focused on what was going on inside the room.

From where I was standing, I was able to catch a glimpse of two men. One was Charlie Richmond. The second man looked familiar, but I couldn't put a name to him. They were both standing close to each other. They were breathing hard. Their hair was mussed. Their ties were askew. Their bodies were rigid. They were staring at each other with the all-consuming attention you either give to your lover or to your mortal enemy. In another couple of seconds the punches were going to start flying.

"Listen, you cocksucker," Charlie Richmond was screaming. "I'm going to . . ."

"What?" Brad Richmond bellowed. "You're going to do what?"

The two men sprang apart.

Charlie Richmond turned to face his uncle. His ears were red. His lips were quivering. "Good. I'm glad you're here. It saves me the trouble of calling you." He went over to the conference table, picked up a piece of paper, and waved it in the air. "This is it. The end. I want your son out of this building now."

"You're the one that's going," Brad Richmond's son sneered.

"I don't think so," Charlie Richmond said.

"This time daddy isn't here to protect you."

Charlie Richmond balled up the piece of paper he was holding and crushed it in his palm. "His death was real convenient for you, wasn't it?"

"Exactly what are you implying?"

"Even a moron like you can figure it out."

"Fuck you." Brad Richmond's son clenched his fists and began bouncing up and down on his toes. "Fuck you where you breathe."

"Stop it," Brad Richmond yelled. "Both of you shut up." He took another step inside and kicked the door shut behind him. It closed with a thud. The door must have been a fire door because, while I could still hear voices rising and falling, I couldn't make out what they were saying. Not that that kept me from trying. I was as close to the door as I could get without actually putting my ear against it when I became aware of someone at my elbow.

It was Brad Richmond's secretary. "Would you like to wait in Mr. Richmond's office?" she chirped. "I'm sure this won't take very long." Her voice sounded as if she'd dipped it in syrup. Just listening to her made my teeth ache.

I straightened up. A person of finer sensibilities would have been embarrassed at being discovered this way, but since my sensibilities are pretty base, I didn't have that problem. I just moved down the hall a little. I wanted to be able to see if anyone opened the door.

"What's going on?" I asked.

Elizabeth Walker shrugged and gave her nails a quick perusal. They were colored a deep pink. "It's just Charlie and Frank."

"They do this a lot?" Judging by her attitude—total indifference—I was willing to bet they did.

She shrugged again. "Usually they're not here at the same time."

"That's lucky."

"I guess." Elizabeth Walker was obviously not someone who cared deeply about the place she worked for. My guess was that she didn't care about much outside of herself.

"Do you know what they're fighting about?"

"No. I think it's a personal matter." She pushed a strand of hair that had fallen over her eye back into place and studied my appearance for a second. It was as if I'd finally penetrated her consciousness. "So how come you're here? You don't look like the kind of person Mr. Richmond normally sees."

"Charlie Richmond hired me to find Amy. I was hoping your boss could help me."

"She hasn't been here in awhile. I could have told you that." She glanced at her watch. It looked like a good Rolex knockoff.

"What's awhile?"

Elizabeth Walker thought for a minute. "Two months."

"Did you have talk to her?"

"She never talked to anybody. She used to just sit in her dad's office and read. I'll tell you one thing though." Elizabeth Walker paused to readjust her skirt. "She wouldn't be walking around like that if she was my kid."

"No?"

"No. All she needs are a couple of smacks to straighten her out."

I raised an eyebrow.

"Well it never hurt me," she said defensively, and she checked her watch again. "One more hour. Then I'm out of here." She smiled. It was a genuine one. The first I'd seen. "I'm gonna go home, take a nap, and have me some fun."

"Where are you going to go?"

"Dancing." Her smile grew wider. She nodded towards the door Brad Richmond had slammed behind him. "I think they're going to be in there for awhile."

"You're probably right." I started back down the hall. I

had a lot of other things to do. I could always come back if I wanted to. "This kind of stuff must make working here difficult," I said, indicating the conference room.

"Only if you pay attention to it." Elizabeth Walker had fallen into step beside me. Our pace was marked by the clicking of her heels on the floor. "And I try not to. Have you ever been to Cancun?" she asked, suddenly changing the subject.

"Yes," I replied cautiously, momentarily thrown by the change of topic.

"Did you like it?"

"It was pleasant. Why? Are you planning on going?"

"I'm thinking about it." Elizabeth Walker smiled again. "My boyfriend says it's real nice down there. It's like you're here, only cheaper."

"Then why bother to go to Mexico at all, if you feel that way? Why don't you just go down to Florida?" By now we were back in front of Brad Richmond's office.

"Because I can drink lots of margaritas and sit on the beach."

I suppose that was as good an answer as any. We spent the next five minutes chatting about the different hotels and where the best places to buy boots and silver jewelry were. I was just about to ask her when she was planning on going, when Brad Richmond and his son, Frank, came barreling around the corner. Both halted when they saw me. Both looked as if they wished I weren't there. I pretended I didn't notice, went over, and introduced myself to Frank. A cloud of Aramis washed over me. For a moment I thought I was going to sneeze, but then the impulse went away, and I studied the man standing in front of me. He was a taller, skinnier version of his father, except for one thing: He had two slightly different colored eyes. One was light and the other dark brown. Even though the colors were so similiar I hadn't noticed when I first saw him, the effect was unsettling, and I found myself staring at him without meaning to.

"It looks as if you're the only member of the Richmond family I haven't met," I told him.

"Is that so?" His voice was higher than I expected.

"Yes," I replied, still doing polite.

"You'll have to forgive us," his father interjected. He'd gotten his CEO persona back. "Perhaps we can finish our conversation at another time." He gestured to his secretary before I could answer. "Ms. Walker will show you out."

But I wasn't ready to go yet. I pretended I hadn't heard and asked Frank if he knew Amy.

He straightened his tie. "Obviously I do."

"Have you seen her recently?"

"I'll tell you what I told the police. Not since she disappeared."

"Do you have any idea where she could be?"

"He doesn't," Brad Richmond interrupted. "He already told you that."

"Your son can't talk for himself?"

"Of course he can," Brad Richmond snapped. "I was just trying to speed this up." He turned to his son. "Go on, answer her."

Frank crossed his arms over his chest. "I haven't seen Amy in maybe six, seven months," he informed me. "She stopped coming around when I stopped lending her money."

By now, Brad Richmond had his hand on the doorknob of his office door. He obviously couldn't wait for me to leave. I don't know. I seemed to have that effect on the Richmond family. Maybe it's a chemical thing.

"I hope you find her," Frank said. "But I don't think you will."

"Why's that?"

"She's probably run away down to New York."

"What gives you that idea?"

"Because she's been talking about doing it for the last year or so." Then he and his father turned and went inside Brad Richmond's office.

Elizabeth Walker escorted me to the front door and said good-bye. It was still nice outside, even though the sky had begun to grey over. The weather forecasters had called for rain this evening. It looked as if their predictions were going to be accurate. But I couldn't really complain. Due to an unusually dry summer, we needed all the rain we could get. The pumpkin and apple harvests had been off by almost forty percent, and deer were coming out of the woods to gnaw on the trees.

I took a piece of gum out of my backpack and started chewing it as I walked towards my car. Okay. What had I learned from this meeting? I pondered the information I'd gotten, as I watched a coven of crows convening in a tree over by the perimeter of the parking lot. I'd learned that Brad and Frank Richmond didn't know where Amy was either and that neither one had anything to do with her. Which was probably true. I blew a bubble and popped it. What else had I come away with? Well, I'd learned that no one in the Richmond family got along with anyone else. Not that this was big news. You could probably apply that sentence to half the families in America—including mine.

I blew another bubble. It was huge. For a moment, I saw the world through a pink haze. Then it popped, flattening out across my face. This, I remembered, as I scraped it off my lips and chin, was why I'd given up blowing bubbles. As

I got the last piece off the corner of my mouth, I wondered what Frank and Charlie had been fighting about and what had been on that piece of paper Charlie had waved around. Not that it really mattered except as a matter of idle curiosity. I watched the crows for another minute, as they wheeled and dipped and bobbed above the tree. Maybe it was my imagination, but there seemed to be more of them and fewer song birds every year. I spit my gum out and started on another piece. It wasn't a cigarette, but for now it would have to do.

I got in the cab and turned on the ignition. So where the hell was Amy? Basically I didn't know any more than I had when I came out here. The fact annoyed me, but then everything was annoying me these days. Someone could tell me they were going to Alaska, and I'd be ready to snap their head off. I started the cab up. It looked as if it was time to start looking for Toon Town. He was turning out to be the only viable lead I had, but first I needed to get something to eat.

I stopped at a convenience store and bought myself a pint of Ben and Jerry's Aztec Harvest Coffee ice cream, a Snickers bar, a bag of Oreo Cookies, and a cup of hazelnut coffee to which I add half and half and three packs of sugar. If I couldn't smoke, at least I could damn well eat what I wanted. I drank the coffee and ate the candy bar, while I drove over to the store. By the time I arrived, I was in a slightly better mood. I guess my blood sugar had been low.

Zsa Zsa came running over to greet me when I came in. As I bent down to pet her, I noticed that Amy's ferret wasn't in his cage. I was about to ask Tim what had happened to Mr. Bones when I saw him running up and down Tim's arm.

"It doesn't seem fair to keep animals like these in cages. Can you believe that he likes cantaloupe?" Tim marveled, as Mr. Bones disappeared up his sleeve. "I offered him a piece and he gobbled it down."

"Fascinating." I went into the back room to hang up my jacket and start on my ice cream.

"By the way," Tim said, as he came in. Mr. Bones was now riding on top of his head. "Amy called."

I put my spoon down.

"She wanted to know how Mr. Bones was doing. I told her he was doing fine."

"Did she say anything else?"

"She wanted to speak to you."

I groaned. My timing was always impeccable. Without fail, when I should be at place A, I was always at place B.

Tim lifted Mr. Bones off his head, cradled him in his arms, and began rubbing his belly. "She said she'd call back again."

"Did she give a time?"

"No." Tim rubbed under the ferret's chin. Mr. Bones sneezed.

"I don't suppose she happened to say where she was?"

He shook his head.

"And you didn't ask?"

"She hung up before I could."

"Terrific." This was definitely turning into a great day. The hell with the ice cream. What I needed was my cigarettes and about four shots of Scotch.

"I heard some noises in the background, though," Tim added. "It sounded like heavy metal."

"Boy, I can't tell you how helpful that is."

Tim raised an eyebrow. "I think I'll leave you and your ice cream alone."

"Good idea."

I ate the whole pint.

Chapter 12

It was a little after ten when I closed up the store and headed out to the cab. Amy hadn't called me back. Not that I'd really expected her to. The girl definitely took after her father. Murphy had done this kind of stuff—appearing then disappearing—all the time, when he was alive. It had made me nuts then and it was making me nuts now. As I turned the key in the lock, I couldn't help wondering, for what must have been the hundredth time, what Amy had wanted to talk to me about.

But at least I'd found out where Toon Town lived. Thank God for small favors. Around nine o'clock I'd hung the closed sign on the door, unearthed the phone book, and taken up where Manuel had left off. From the yellow highlighter on the page, I ascertained he'd spoken to twelve Gleasons. Not very many for the time he'd put in. He'd probably spent most of the hour and a half talking to his friends on the phone. That left me with forty-seven more to go. I was not happy. Fortunately I got lucky with number nineteen.

"Wally isn't home," a woman informed me. She sounded as if she were nursing a bad head cold.

"Do you know when he'll be back?" I asked, almost not believing my good luck.

"He's gone out to the clubs. Why?" Her voice was sharp with concern. I had the feeling I was talking to his mother.

"I just need to ask him something."

She sneezed. "You're not one of his customers, are you?"

It was too good an opportunity to pass up. I lied and told her I was.

"Because he told me he wasn't covering. He said he had the night off."

"That's not what I was told."

"Well, that's what Mr. Marco told him."

"Don Marco?" I guessed. Marco was a fairly uncommon last name in Syracuse.

"That's right."

Interesting. The Don Marco I knew ran a security outfit called Locked Up Tight. In fact, I'd had him give me a price on my store, but he'd come in way too high. I found myself drumming my fingers on the counter. I wondered if that's why I thought I'd seen Toon Town before. Maybe he'd been out to the store with Marco. Marco had brought a helper along. I tried to visualize him and couldn't.

The woman coughed and I went back to thinking about her. "So this isn't about work?" she asked.

"It is, but it isn't urgent," I reassured her. "I just need to ask him something." I gave her my name and phone number and asked her to have Wallace call me in the morning.

"Good." She sounded relieved. "I'll give him the message

when I see him, but lots of times he doesn't come home for a couple of days at a time. He stays over with his friends." She sneezed again. "I don't like it, but he's over eighteen, so what can I do? You'd probably have better luck trying at the store." She hung up.

I was humming as I went out the door. It looked as if my luck was beginning to change. The wind was gusting, as I drove down the block. Awnings snapped, tree branches danced, and wires hummed. As I turned onto Oswego Street, I almost ran into a downed tree limb. The thing was huge. Its leaves brushed the side of the cab, as I inched my way around it. I turned on the radio. The weatherman was announcing a gale alert. "Winds will be out of the north at up to fifty miles an hour, bringing rain in their stead. Snow has been reported in Watertown."

That was just what I wanted to hear. I spent the rest of the ride home avoiding rolling trash cans, plastic garbage bags, and fallen tree branches. I parked my car in the driveway and got out. The wind was whipping the piles of leaves beside the curb this way and that. The air was heavy with their scrabblings. Zsa Zsa barked at them, then tucked her tail between her legs and ran for the house. She doesn't like this kind of weather. Maybe the wind brings in too many strange smells. My other dog, Elise, loved it. She would stand at the door, head raised, sniffing the air, whining until I let her out. But Zsa Zsa prefers to curl up on the sofa, lap a little beer, and watch television on a night like this. Like her owner. Except for the beer of course. I like mine in a bottle instead of a saucer.

"You're a little late, aren't you?" Manuel asked, as I came through the door. He was leaning against the hallway wall. "I expected you home an hour ago." He righted himself, unfolded his arms, and put his hands on his hips.

At another time I would have laughed. Usually I give points for outrageousness, but the day had put me in a bad mood, and I didn't want to talk to anyone, let alone deal with Manuel. "What are you doing here?" I demanded.

"Waiting for you. Obviously."

"How the hell did you get in?"

He held up a key. "You gave this to me, remember."

I grabbed it out of his hand. "I feel like I'm living in Grand fucking Central."

He put his hands up. "Hey, Tim told me you got broken into last night. Listen, I'm sorry and all, but don't take it out on me."

I took my jacket off and threw it on the hall table. James came out of the kitchen and wound himself around my ankles. Zsa Zsa ran over and licked his face. He stiffened in outrage and hissed. I bent down and picked the cat up before he could swat Zsa Zsa in the face.

"All right. What do you want?"

Manuel looked at the floor. "I figured maybe I could crash here for the night."

"I thought you were staying at Rabbit's. What happened?"

"Oh, he got himself in . . ."

"In what? . . ."

"A situation."

I thought back to what Manuel had said this morning. "Does this situation have anything to do with the stuff you were helping him with?"

Manuel shrugged. "Yeah. Kinda."

"So where is Rabbit?"

"In Watertown."

"Watertown?"

"Just for a couple of days. Then he's coming back."

"Who's looking for him?"

"Wayne."

"Great." I knew Wayne. He was not known for his good temper. A burn-out, he operated out of the west side. His forte was stealing and reselling VCRs, boxes, and car stereos, although he wasn't above selling a gun or two, or a couple of nickel bags when he could get them. "Tell me, are you in trouble too?"

"Not really."

"Not really?"

"No."

"Then why are you here?"

He shrugged again. "Mom says Walter is still mad at me, so I can't go there. It's warm here. I figured maybe I could help you out. Make some more phone calls or something."

"I'll see."

Manuel smiled. He knew me well enough by now to know that that meant yes. He followed me into the kitchen. I poured myself a Scotch and filled up James's bowl with dried cat food.

"How do you think cat food tastes?" he asked, as James started to eat.

"Lousy." I looked at Manuel. He seemed thinner than usual. "Are you hungry?"

He shook his head, but the expression in his eyes betrayed him. I got out the milk, a box of Frosted Flakes, a bowl, and spoon and set everything down on the table.

"I told you I'm not hungry," he protested.

"I know." I pointed. "Eat anyway."

"Only if you do."

"Fine." Normally I would have been annoyed, but the truth was I needed to put something healthy in my stomach anyway. Well maybe Frosted Flakes weren't All Bran, but they were definitely higher on the nutrition scale than anything else I'd eaten today. As we ate, I told Manuel about my conversation with Toon Town's mother.

"I bet he went to Club 666," Manuel said, pouring more milk and cereal into his bowl. "This is Thursday night. On Thursday everyone goes to 666."

"Everyone?" I pushed my bowl away. I'd had enough.

"Everyone who likes to dance. On Friday it's the Iguana."

"I see." As I watched Manuel gulp down his third helping and go for his fourth, I wondered how long it had been since he'd eaten.

"You're thinking of seeing if Toon Town's there, aren't you?" Manuel asked. His eating pace had slowed.

"Yes, I am." I held out my bowl and James and Zsa Zsa both came over and started lapping up the last of the milk. Maybe Toon Town knew where Amy was, maybe he didn't. But until I talked to him, I wouldn't know. And I didn't want to wait to find out if I didn't have to. I wanted Amy off the street as soon as possible. The longer she stayed out, the greater the chance that she would get herself into some serious trouble, not that she wasn't in enough as it was.

Manuel sat back and rubbed his stomach. He'd finally had enough. "You should let me go with you. I go to the clubs all the time. I know everyone there."

Unlike me, I couldn't help reflecting. When was the last time I'd gone dancing, anyway? I think it was when I was down in the Yucatan with Murphy.

"I thought you had to be eighteen and over to get into these places."

Manuel looked at me as if I were a moron. "I got a fake ID. And anyway, I know the bouncers."

"All right," I agreed, thinking that if I left him home, he'd probably just drink all my Scotch.

"Great." Manuel bounced out of the chair. "I just got to

change. I'll be down in ten minutes,'' he announced. He was down in thirty.

I spent the time studying an old photograph of Murphy and trying to figure out why I felt responsible for his daughter. When we left, Zsa Zsa and James were asleep on the sofa. They obviously had more sense than I did.

Club 666 was located in a no man's land between Armory Square and the West side. Maybe there had been something there once, but now the only thing the area had was vacant lots. To get to it, you had to take a narrow, unmarked side road that formed a detour around 690, but judging by the number of cars parked around the club, the location wasn't a hindrance. We had to park two blocks away and walk up. It was colder down here, and Manuel and I both put up our collars and jammed our hands in our jacket pockets. By the time we got there, my eyes were teary from the wind. As we went inside, I thought I saw a couple of snow flakes trickling down under the streetlight.

A skinny, androgynous-looking guy with a platinum buzz and two nose rings was guarding the door. I gave him ten dollars for the two of us. He stamped our hands and we went inside. My mouth dropped opened when I saw what was going on. *Y.M.C.A.* was playing on the sound system. Strobe lights were flickering on the dance floor. I watched a boy in bell-bottoms and a girl in a miniskirt and see-thru blouse walk over to the bar and order rum and cokes. I felt as if I'd just gone back about twenty years.

''What is this?'' I asked Manuel. I had to shout to make myself heard over the music.

''Disco night. Come on, let's get something to drink.'' He started to elbow his way toward the bar.

Nothing like having your youth enshrined to make you feel incredibly old, I thought, as I followed him over.

"You're lucky," Manuel said, after I'd ordered a Sam Adams for myself and a soda for him.

"How's that?"

He gestured towards the dance floor. "It must have been fun to have been around then."

"It was." Up to a point. If you left out the war and the fights and the cops and the friends that fried their brains on too much meth. But the sex was great. So was the grass and the music and the feeling that the whole world was yours. But all that was too complicated to get across in thirty seconds and, frankly, I didn't even want to try. I took a sip of beer and listened to "Sunday, Sunday" instead.

God, I remembered that song. It reminded me of summer Sundays in New York. I'd loved the city then. Everyone was gone, escaped to the beach or the country. The streets were empty, canyons of white light, punctuated by bands of shade. Murphy and I would get up late and walk over to the park and watch the old men sailing the boats they'd made on the pond, while we gobbled down melting ice cream pops, licking the thick, sweet, white, half-frozen fluid off our fingers. I sighed and took another drink. We were going to go on forever.

"Do you see Toon Town?" Manuel asked, interrupting my thoughts.

"I can't see anyone from here." The dance floor was crowded and dark, and the flickering of the strobe lights gave everything a hellish cast. I picked up my beer. "I'm going to walk around and see if I can spot him."

Manuel nodded and turned away. I had the feeling he was relieved I was going.

By the time I was halfway around the circuit, my eyes had gotten used to the dark and the movement. I saw lots of people gyrating back and forth, but Wallace Gleason wasn't among them. I guessed he'd gone somewhere else. As I headed back to the bar, I noticed that Manuel was dancing with a girl wearing a midriff baring sweater, a black leather micro miniskirt, and black tights. She was way out of his league, and he looked as if he'd died and gone to heaven. Then he glanced up and saw me. His eyes pleaded with me to go away.

"Half an hour," I mouthed. Then I walked over to the bar and ordered myself another beer, consoling myself with the thought that Toon Town might still show up.

He didn't.

Twenty minutes later, the crowd started to thin out. I was slightly drunk and definitely depressed. I should have stayed home and saved my money. It was time to go. If Manuel didn't want to—tough. He could walk. But when I looked around, I couldn't find him.

He wasn't on the dance floor.

He wasn't at the bar.

I walked over and yelled into the men's room. He wasn't there.

I asked the bartender if he'd seen him. He hadn't.

I would have asked the ticket taker if he'd seen Manuel leave, only he wasn't there.

I tapped my fingers on my belt. Maybe he'd stepped outside to have a smoke. I opened the door to take a look.

Chapter 13

The rain was coming down harder now. I was thinking about how I should have brought along an umbrella, when I heard a muffled high-pitched noise. It seemed to be coming from down the block. I stepped out onto the sidewalk to see if it was Manuel. With him you never knew. Nothing was moving. Then across the street, past the cars, in the vacant lot, I thought I spotted a movement. I squinted, trying to get a better look. It was one person. No, two. It just looked like one because of the size difference. Were they hugging? No, they were fighting. As I watched, the smaller person broke free and started running towards the club. The bigger one went after him—or her. It could be either. As they ran towards the streetlight, I realized I knew who they were. It was Toon Town and one of the girls from the warehouse.

By now the two of them were in the middle of the street. Toon Town reached out and grabbed the girl. She started to yell, but he clamped his hand over her mouth and cut her off. She began kicking, but it didn't seem to bother him much. He half lifted her off the ground. It looked as if he were carrying her back to the vacant lot. I glanced around. No one else was out. God damn. I felt like kicking something myself. Here I finally find Toon Town. All I wanted to do was to talk to him and look what happens. I was going to have to do something about the girl. What was her name, anyway? Ellen? Melanie? Melonhead? Why wasn't she in Chicago? Hell, why wasn't she home, like she was supposed to be? If she were, none of this would be happening.

For a moment I thought about going back inside and having the bartender call 911, but it didn't look as if there were going to be time for that. By now the two of them were almost across the street. If I waited much longer, the girl would be back where she started.

"Put her down," I yelled, as I ran down the path onto the sidewalk.

Toon Town and the girl froze for a heartbeat. Then the tableau came to life.

"Stay out of this," Toon Town warned. His eyes shifted from side to side, as if he were looking at someone standing next to him.

I was about to tell him I wanted to, when Toon Town squealed and jerked his hand away from the girl's mouth.

"You bit me," he cried. He sounded incredulous.

Then, before he'd fully recovered, the girl twisted around and kicked his knee. I could hear the thud as she connected. He groaned and lurched to the side. She yanked her arm away. Her hair was plastered to her head, drops of water were dripping down her face. She took a couple of steps back. Then she started to run down the street. After going about fifteen feet, she made a left and crossed into a vacant lot. A moment later, she was gone.

"Why'd did you have to do that?" Toon Town whined, as he limped towards me. "You should have stayed out of my business." He was regarding me with an intensity I found unnerving. I reached in my pocket for my box cutter. "You cost me money. You gonna make it up to me?" he demanded.

"What kind of business are you doing?"

He stopped about twelve feet away from me. "What the fuck do you care?"

"I care because you have Amy."

"So?" His pupils looked liked cat's eyes in the dark. I wondered what he was on.

"So I want to speak to her."

"You and everyone else."

"She's in trouble. She needs help."

"She's doing just fine."

"Where is she?"

Toon Town rocked back and forth on the balls of his feet. He formed his right hand into a fist and began punching it into his left hand. Slap. Slap. Slap. "You think I can't take care of my own?" His voice began to rise. "You think I'm some kind of jerk-off that you can just say whatever you want to me?" A spray of spit flew out of his mouth. "You think you can come over here and ruin my business? Well I'm smarter than you are. I know more than you do. I know more than you'll ever know." And he moved towards me.

"Stay where you are," I warned.

He laughed and kept coming. "You can't dis me like that and just walk away."

"Really." I held the box cutter up and slid the blade out. I wasn't getting hurt if I didn't have to. Actually, all I wanted to do was to go inside and dry off. My sneakers were sodden, my hair was wet, and my fingers were going numb in the rain.

Toon Town snorted. "How you gonna hurt me with that thing?"

"Come and see."

"I got something in my car that could rip you open." He moved his head slightly to the left. I saw his lime-green Tracker. A man was sitting in it, but I didn't have time to identify him because a second later Toon Town was coming for me.

For somebody who'd been limping, he traveled pretty fast. I slashed at his arm. I could feel a pull as I drew the blade up. I'd connected.

Toon Town's "Jesus!" hung in the air. An imprecation? A prayer? He jumped back and clutched at his jacket sleeve. I turned and ran into the club. The doors closed behind me. Toon Town didn't follow. Which didn't surprise me. There were too many people in here. But something told me he was going to wait. I had a feeling I hadn't hurt him badly enough to send him to the hospital. I'd just hurt him enough to piss him off even more. Which gave me an idea. I began to cheer up. Things might work out after all.

I blotted the rain off my hair with the inside of my jacket and headed for the bar. I wanted something to warm me up a little before I got started. I saw Manuel immediately. He was down towards the middle drinking a beer.

"Having fun?" I growled.

He hurriedly put the Corona down. "What do you mean?" he asked, all innocence.

"Where have you been?" I demanded. "I've been looking all over for you."

"I was here."

"Well I didn't see you." I reached over and snagged his beer.

"Hey! What did you do that for?"

"Because you're not supposed to be drinking it." I took a sip. "If you were here, how come I didn't see you?"

"I was talking with my friends over in the corner."

I decided he probably had been. It was dark enough in here to miss someone if you weren't careful. "So where's the girl you were dancing with?"

"She left. She had to go home." He changed the subject. "So how come you're all wet and everything?"

I finished off Manuel's beer and order a Scotch. Then I told Manuel what had happened. It was a short story and, by the time I was finished, my Black Label was in front of me. I lifted the glass and took a sip. I could feel it warming my throat, as I swallowed. God, it was good.

"Do me a favor," I said, after I'd taken another sip. "See if Toon Town is still out there. Just look," I cautioned.

"Sure." Manuel left and came back a few minutes later. "He's standing right outside the door."

"Is he hurt?"

"There's blood on his jacket. But he's not like writhing around on the floor."

"That's too bad." I moved my fingers back and forth to restore their circulation.

Manuel watched me for a moment without saying anything. "So what are we going to do now? Wait till he goes home?"

"Not exactly." I gulped down the rest of my drink and explained. "We're going to go out through the back door, get into the cab, wait for Mr. Wallace 'Toon Town' Gleason and his friend to leave, and then we're going to follow him.

Hopefully, he'll lead us to Amy. Even if he doesn't, at least we'll know where they're staying."

Manuel grinned. "This is why I like you, man. You don't act like no grownup I know."

God, wasn't that the truth, I thought, as I threw a tip down on the bar.

Manuel tugged on my sleeve, "The back door is this way." He gestured off to the right. We walked past the bar and around the dance floor. It was less crowded now, the music softer. Couples were swaying to the sounds of "Disco Queen." The sight made me sad. I guess my mood must have shown on my face because Manuel asked me what was the matter.

"I was just thinking about how much time has gone by and how little I've done with it," I told him.

He gave me a blank look—I could have been talking about Einstein's theory of relativity—and pointed to the exit sign. "This is it," he said.

I asked him to check and see if anyone was there. Manuel opened the door and stuck his head out. "A guy's standing about twenty feet away," he announced, when he was back inside.

"What does he look like?"

"I can't tell. He's got his baseball cap pulled all the way down and his collar pulled all the way up. You want me to go outside and take a look?"

"No. That's okay." I was aiming for inconspicuous. Having Manuel popping in and out of the door like a jack-in-the-box wasn't going to do it. Given the weather, the odds were the guy was either Toon Town's friend or a drug dealer.

Manuel pulled his pants up. "So what do you want to do?"

I clicked my tongue against my teeth and thought. I'd seen a window when I'd gone to the ladies room. It was small, but I was positive I could squeeze through. I handed Manuel my car keys—an act that pained me deeply—and told him to go get it.

Manuel blinked. He couldn't believe what he was hearing. "But I don't have a license," he protested weakly.

"That never bothered you before." I pushed him out the door and headed over to the bathroom. Robin Light. Upholder of Law and Order.

I heard giggling when I stepped inside the ladies room. The sound seemed to be coming from the second stall. The door was closed. I glanced down. Two pairs of legs were entwined. A man's and a woman's. The woman had her nylons pulled down around her calves and her heels off, while the man had his pants around his ankles. His shoes were on. The door rattled. I heard a gasp and an "Oh baby."

Well, at least they wouldn't be paying attention to what I was doing, I thought, as I went over to the window and lifted the sash. Why anyone would want to screw in a toilet stall was beyond me. It might be amusing to ask them, but I didn't have the time. I wiggled through the window. My left foot hit a can when I landed, and I almost fell down. I looked around quickly, half expecting someone to come running after me. But no one did. The street was empty. I huddled against the wall trying to keep dry, as I waited for Manuel to arrive. I was picking a sliver of wood from the sill out of my jeans when he came driving up.

"You did good," I told him, as he slid over to the passenger seat.

For an instant, Manuel's smile lit up his face, then it vanished, as he tried to look tough. I turned on the heater and pulled away from the curb. I slowed down when I got to the corner. No one was at the back door. I was wondering if Toon Town and his friend had left, when I spied the Tracker down the block. It had people in it. I guess they'd just gotten tired of waiting out in the storm.

I parked and turned off the engine. The rain rat-tat-tated on the roof of the cab.

"I hate this shit," Manuel groused. "Why can't it ever be nice out?"

"Because this is Syracuse."

"The first thing I'm gonna do when I get me some money is move down South."

"You and everyone else. They should just close down the Northeast and let the forest take over."

Manuel grunted and closed his eyes. I was thinking about how much I'd like to do that, when Toon Town got out of the Geo and went into the club. A minute or two later, he came storming out. I nudged Manuel.

"Look," I told him, as Toon Town got in the car and slammed the door. I guess he'd figured out that I wasn't there.

"He's pissed," Manuel said.

"No kidding."

The car roared to life and took off. I let him get to the corner before I followed. If Toon Town had gotten on the highway, it would have been easy to tail him, but he didn't. He kept to the local streets, which meant I had to keep about half a block's distance between us. Everytime he turned, I kept thinking I was going to lose him.

Then around Coleridge, I did. I circled the block. Nothing. I turned left and went down Cleveland. Still nothing. I tried Easton.

"Look." Manuel pointed at a driveway midway down the street. "There it is."

"I think you're right." I drove past the house. Yup. It was the Geo all right. We'd found the place.

Then the front door opened and Toon Town and Amy came out.

Chapter 14

Toon Town was holding Amy by the elbow. I watched him guide her towards the Tracker. If either had turned their heads, they would have seen me, but they didn't. They were in too much of a rush. I jumped out of the cab though, as it turned out, I could have saved myself the trouble. By the time I'd taken two steps, they were inside their car. I heard the engine roar. They were taking off. I sprinted back to the cab.

"Go, go, go," Manuel yelled, as I slid in. "They're getting away."

"I can see that," I snapped. I wiped the rain out of my eyes and closed the cab door. Its thud punctuated the night.

By the time I'd completed my U-turn, Toon Town was down at the corner taking a right. I followed suit. But Easton was deserted when I got there. Toon Town and Amy must have taken one of the four streets that fed off of it. But which? That was the question.

"You think they spotted us?" Manuel asked, as I drove down Ansel Road.

I steered around a garbage can lying in the middle of the street. "Maybe." I thought about how I would give anything for a cigarette. "I don't know." When I got to the corner, I made a left onto Adams.

The swaying branches of the trees lining the streets were the only things moving. I cursed and went on to the next block. It was deserted too. The asphalt gleamed wetly under the streetlight's glow. A white cat sprinted out from under a parked car and ran across the road. Then I saw what looked like a set of taillights in the distance. Manuel sat up straighter. He'd seen them too.

"You think that's them?" he asked.

"Let's find out." I put my foot down on the gas. The cab jerked—it doesn't like surprises—jumped forward and took off.

The car I was following turned left at the next corner and so did I. I was a little under half a block away from them when I realized I'd made a mistake. I was tailing a sedan.

I pounded the steering wheel and cursed.

Manuel half turned towards me. "They had to go somewhere."

"I know." I concentrated on the road in front of me. The houses on either side of the street were dark and silent, blind to our progress. The only sound was the swish-swash of the cab's windshield wipers. As I turned onto Coleridge, Manuel took his lighter out of his pocket and began flicking it on and off.

"Can you please stop that," I snapped.

"Why?"

"Because it's annoying me."

"Fine." Manuel shifted around in his seat. The wind had

picked up again. I could hear the power lines humming. "You know, from where I was sittin' it didn't look like Toon Town was draggin' Amy to the Tracker. It looked like she was goin' of her own free will."

"True," I admitted. Maybe it was time to drop the white knight act. Amy and Toon Town could be running off to Vegas for a vacation for all I knew. I reached over and clicked on the radio. A minister was preaching salvation. "I guess if you're up at this time of the night, you probably need it," I said, as I changed the station.

Manuel yawned, by way of an answer. We drove around for another twenty minutes. Then I went over to the warehouse to see if Toon Town had ended up there. He hadn't. There were no cars in the parking lot. It was time to go home.

Manuel was sound asleep when I pulled into my driveway. He was groggy when I woke him, and I had to steady him as he went into the house. He made it as far as the living room before he collapsed on the sofa. I let him stay there because I was too tired to make him go up the stairs. He really had to patch things up with his family. I'd talk about it with him tomorrow, I decided, as I went to bed.

When my alarm went off at seven thirty, I pushed the cat off my chest, pulled the cord out of the wall, and put the pillow over my head. I would have stayed that way if Zsa Zsa hadn't started barking and licking my fingers at twenty after nine. I was tired, every muscle in my body ached. I felt as if I were ninety-eight years old, and the day hadn't even begun yet. Standing under the shower, I decided I couldn't do this anymore. I had to start getting more sleep. I used to be able to run on four hours a night. Now I needed at least six.

I got out and pulled on some clothes. Then I went downstairs, gulped down half a cup of day-old coffee, grabbed a handful of Oreo cookies, and ran out the door. I made it to the store with three minutes to spare. The only good things about the morning so far, I reflected, were that the sky wasn't grey and it wasn't raining. In Syracuse, a little blue goes a long way.

I had the key in the lock, when George pulled up to the curb in his Taurus. I watched him get out of his car. He looked as tired as I felt. He held up a Dunkin' Donuts box and a white paper bag. "Coffee and doughnuts."

"Sounds good." I opened up the store and George, Zsa Zsa, and I went inside. Pickles came running out to greet us, while Mr. Bones ran excitedly from side to side in his cage. I said hello to all the animals, opened the register, took the coffee George was offering, and sipped it. Compared to what I'd just drank back at the house, it was ambrosial. "So when'd you get back?"

"Just now. I left the Bronx at six."

"Did you get everything straightened out?"

"For the moment." George frowned. "Jesus, though, it's like patching up a sieve."

"Then why do you keep going down there?"

"Because they call me."

"Can't they call anyone else?"

"I don't think anyone else in my family wants to be bothered anymore. I guess they got tired of the phone ringing in the middle of the night."

"And you aren't? Don't you have a paper that's due soon?"

George rubbed his lower lip with his thumb. "I don't know why I just can't seem to say no. I tell myself I will, but the next time they call, back down I go. And the worst part of it is whenever I'm there, I feel like I want to kill them."

He looked so sad that I went over and gave him a hug. His lips curved up in a tiny smile. "Let's talk about your mess instead. It'll make me feel better."

I laughed and told him about Amy. He ate a doughnut, while I gave him a rundown of what had happened while he'd been away.

"It seems like you're getting to meet the whole Richmond family," he remarked when I was through.

"Yeah. Aren't I lucky?" I broke off a piece of a peanut-covered chocolate doughnut and popped it in my mouth. "I wonder if Dennis was as bad as the rest of them?"

"Oh yeah. He was a real jerk."

I did a double take. "You knew him? You never told me that."

"I didn't know-*know* him. The guy used the same gym I did." George picked up a glazed doughnut and took a bite.

"What was he like?"

"He was one of those guys who wouldn't do anything all week and then would come in and try to bench two hundred and fifty pounds." George finished the rest of the doughnut and wiped his hands off with a paper towel. "Dave, the guy that owns the place." I nodded. "Tried to tell him he was going to get himself in trouble, but he blew him off. His attitude was—I got money, so kiss my ass."

"He sounds charming."

"He was a real sweetie." George ran a finger under the collar of his crewneck sweater. "Damn thing itches," he grumped.

"Wool does. You should wear a shirt under it, the next time."

He grunted. "So what do you think the story with Amy is? You think she killed her father?"

"No."

"How do you know?"

"I don't. It's just a feeling I have. But I think she knows something, and I think she's terrified." She'd certainly acted that way in the parking lot the other night when the car had driven by.

"Of what?"

"I haven't a clue."

George puffed his cheeks out and sucked them back in. "Then why doesn't she go to the police?"

I thought back to our conversation. "Maybe she doesn't think they'll believe anything she says."

"And why's that?"

"Because she's a druggie. Because she's been in Cedar View."

"Maybe she's right." George drained the last of his coffee. "According to you, she was one of the last people to see her father alive. I know if I were investigating this case, she'd be on the top of my list."

"If I were betting, I'd pick the mother."

George laughed. "You're biased."

"No, I'm not. Well, maybe a little," I conceded. "What did Murphy see in her anyway?"

George shrugged. "She asked him. That was enough."

It was true. Saying no had never been one of Murphy's strong suits. "Actually, the whole family is peculiar. There's something off about all of them."

"Why do you say that?"

"Observation. What I really need is some information." I gave George a speculative look.

"Why are you staring at me like that?"

"I was just thinking about your cousin."

"What about him?"

"I was wondering if he knew anything about the Richmond family."

George snorted. "Why the hell should he?"

"Well, they are in the same field."

"That's really stretching it. He's a nobody, a nobody who's about to lose his license. The only thing he knows about the Richmond family is their name in the catalog they send him."

"Maybe he's heard something."

"Like what?"

"I don't know. I know you don't want to, but could you call him up and ask?"

George scowled.

"For Amy's sake. And Murphy's."

"That's a low blow."

I didn't say anything. I just watched George fiddle with his sweater cuff.

"I don't see how finding out about the Richmond family is going to help you locate Amy," he protested after a minute.

"Just call it a hunch."

George sighed. "All right."

"Thanks."

"But it's a waste of time. He won't know anything."

"Thanks anyway." I went over and gave George a kiss.

He kissed me back. Hard. Then he started nibbling on my ear. "Let's go in the back."

"Someone could walk in."

"Let them wait." He slipped his hand between my legs.

"You're right. What do I need customers for, anyway?"

"You don't, when you got me."

I could feel my resolve start to weaken, when the phone rang. George sighed. I reached over and got it. Another joy of owning a business. You can never do what you want when you want.

"It's Frank Richmond," I mouthed. George moved his ear closer to the receiver.

"Can we talk?" Richmond asked. His voice was faint, and there was static on the line. He sounded as if he were using a cell phone.

"We are."

He gave a weak laugh. "No. I meant face-to-face."

"Let me guess. It's about Amy."

"More or less." There was a longish pause on the other end of the line.

"Are you still there?" I asked.

"Sorry. Yes." I heard honking. "Nine thirty tonight?" Richmond asked. "The Garden."

"How about Pete's on Westcott," I suggested, instead. The Garden annoyed me. It was full of rich, thirty-year-olds trying to act hip.

"Fine."

"See you then." By now the static was so bad I could barely make out his words.

George took the receiver out of my hand and replaced it, while I put the closed sign on the front door. As we went into the back room, I decided I shouldn't have been so quick to condemn the couple in the bathroom last night. What George and I were about to do wasn't really much better, after all. I guess a quickie is a quickie is a quickie, no matter where you do it.

George left about half an hour later. I spent the rest of the morning thinking about how Amy had ended up the way she had and wondering what Melanie and Toon Town had been fighting about.

Around twelve thirty I called Locked Up Tight and asked

for Wallace Gleason. I figured we had a lot to discuss. Don Marcos got on the line instead.

"Is there a problem?" he asked anxiously.

"No. I just have a question for Mr. Gleason."

"I'm sorry, but Wally doesn't work for us anymore."

"I see."

There was a pause. Then Marcos said, "Can I ask what this is about?" His tone was tight.

"It's about a credit card application," I ad-libbed. "I'm calling from Marine Midland."

"Good." He sighed in relief.

"May I ask why he left and how long he worked for you?"

"Actually, I fired him."

"Would you mind telling me why?"

"With pleasure. He was taking merchandise out of the store, missing work, doing wildcat work, and using our name. That kind of thing. In my line of work I can't afford to employ unreliable people. I had to let him go."

"In your position, I would have, too," I assured him. "Can you tell me anything else?" It always amazed me that people are willing to talk so freely on the phone. Even a guy like Marcos.

"Not really. He started off good and then just slid downhill. I tried talking to him a couple of times to find out what was going on, but he didn't have much to say."

I thanked Marcos and called Toon Town's mother's house. The answering machine picked up. I left a message and hung up. Around seven, I hopped in my cab and ran over to see if anyone was in the house Manuel and I had spotted Toon Town and Amy coming out of. No one was. Somehow I didn't consider that an encouraging sign. Tim was hooking up an elaborate tunnel maze for Mr. Bones from PVC pipe when I got back.

He glanced up. "Someone was here to see you,"

"Who?"

"He didn't give his name."

"What did he look like?"

Tim proceeded to describe Toon Town.

I groaned. "What did he say?"

"Not much. He looked around, bought a tin of fish food, and asked if he could use the bathroom."

"That's it?"

"Not exactly. He said to tell you that you were going to pay for last night. What exactly did you do to the man?"

I told Tim the story.

"Amy doesn't have very nice friends, does she?" he observed, when I was done.

"It would seem not."

Chapter 15

I parked the cab in front of Pete's Bar and got out. At nine thirty, Westcott was quiet. A while back, the street might have been filled with college students, but in recent years SU's enrollment had dropped and the houses that had once held mommy and daddy's pride and joy were now filled with Section Eights—read low income—families. The neighborhood was changing. No one liked it, as the last neighborhood meeting had demonstrated, but no one knew what to do about it either. Last year, Ike, Pete's owner, had told me business was down. He was looking to sell. So far though he hadn't found a buyer.

But maybe that wasn't because of the economy. Maybe that was because of the kind of bare bones place Pete's was. The walls were a greyish-brown, as was the floor. Decoration was limited to a collection of sports memorabilia behind the bar, two SU Lacrosse posters tacked up on walls, and a stunted cactus near the window. It was a drinking man's place, the kind of place you could wreck and not feel guilty about. The reason I went there was because my friend Connie worked there now—though she wasn't there when Zsa Zsa and I walked in.

"She's got the flu," Ebsen Field told me, when I asked where she was. Tall and thin, with a beard that needed pruning, Field was a perennial grad student. Right now, he was in the Anthro Department. Before that, he'd been in Human Biology. And before that he'd been in Architecture. Next year, who knew? "Or a new boyfriend," he added, as he set a bottle of Sam Adams and a saucer down in front of me.

"Probably the latter." Connie was as free sampling men as Ebsen was sampling courses. They'd both acquired a fair amount of knowledge over the years. Neither was shy about sharing it, either.

I lifted Zsa Zsa up and put her on the stool. Ebsen poured a little of my beer in the saucer. "Here you go, toots," he said, pushing the saucer in front of the dog.

I raised an eyebrow. "Toots?"

He chortled. "Great word, isn't it?" Ebsen had an affinity for expressions from the twenties. He pointed to Zsa Zsa, who was wagging her tail and barking for more. "She just laps it up, doesn't she?"

I groaned and fed Zsa Zsa a pretzel to quiet her down, while I looked around the bar. There were ten people there, and I didn't know any of them, but then again I hadn't expected to. Five were sitting around, talking, and the other five were huddled around the foos ball table.

Ebsen leaned both elbows on the bar. "They've been playing since seven," he said, stifling a yawn, as he glanced at his watch. "Four and a half more hours, and I'm out of here."

"Then you can go home and sleep."

"No. Then I can go home and study. I've got an exam in linguistics." He straightened up and went to wait on a customer down at the other end of the bar. When he got back, I asked Ebsen to dial my house. It occurred to me I should let Manuel know I was going to be late.

He told me to bring home some food and hung up. I was just finishing my beer when Frank Richmond walked in. He looked as if he'd aged three years since the last time I'd seen him. Now there were bags under his eyes and a faint hint of jowls around the jawline.

"God, I haven't been in a place like this in years," he said, his tone making it clear he could have done without the experience. "What's that?" he asked, pointing to Zsa Zsa.

"My dog."

"I didn't think they allowed animals in places like this. I thought it was against the Health Code."

"Actually, she's really Zsa Zsa Gabor in disguise." We hadn't even started our conversation and I was already sorry that I'd come. "So you want to talk or what?" I figured there wasn't much danger of his walking out the door. After all, he wouldn't be here if he didn't want to be.

"Talk." The word came out as if it hurt him to say it. He ordered a Molson. When it came, I grabbed a bowl of popcorn and the three of us walked over to one of the tables sitting by the wall.

"So?" I said, as I watched Frank Richmond carefully fold up his black cashmere overcoat and place it on the chair next to him. "What's going on?"

He gave the coat one last pat before he spoke. "You sure don't waste any time do you?"

Zsa Zsa barked and I poured a little more beer in her saucer and pushed it towards her. "It's late and I'm tired."

Frank Richmond began tearing tiny pieces of the label off his beer. Soon the bottle was surrounded by a mound of blue and gold confetti. "I heard Charles," he gave the name an ugly twist, "hired you to find Amy."

"Who told you that?"

He took the label pieces and began making a large circle out of them. "Word gets around."

I threw a piece of popcorn to Zsa Zsa. She caught it and swallowed. I did it again. "And that's why you're here?"

"I just thought you should know that he doesn't exactly have Amy's best interests at heart."

"In what way?"

"Let's just say he wouldn't be unhappy if the police caught up with her."

"What would that accomplish?"

"These days she usually carries enough dope on her to get herself into some serious trouble."

"Why would he want to do that?"

"Because they don't like each other."

"I'd say this goes beyond dislike."

Frank leaned forward. "Charlie hates her."

I took a sip of my Sam Adams and watched the foos ball players urge each other on. Their voices filled the room. "That's not what he told me."

Frank Richmond sniggered. "I just bet it isn't."

"He told me they used to stick up for each other when they were kids. You know, kind of band together against their parents."

"Yeah, right." Frank Richmond ran his thumb around the top of his Molson. "Charlie hated Amy from the moment she was born. He was jealous as hell. They used to have to watch him all the time to make sure he didn't hurt the baby."

"That's not so unusual."

"He wasn't much better when she was older. He was always hitting her and stealing her toys. Doing stuff to make her cry. I know. I was there."

"People's relationships change as they grow up." I threw a couple more pieces of popcorn to Zsa Zsa and ate some myself. "Maybe Charlie has had a change of heart."

"Not him."

I leaned back in the chair and regarded Frank. "And you're telling me this because you like Amy so much."

"No." He scratched his inner ear with his pinky. "Actually, I don't give a shit about Amy. I just don't want to see Charles get away with anything."

"Why is that?"

"You were at the plant. You saw what happened."

"I saw two men arguing. I don't know what you were arguing about."

"It's simple." Frank swept the bits of paper back into a heap. "Charles is accusing me of stealing from the business. That paper is supposed to be the proof."

"And are you?" God, at that moment I would have given anything for a cigarette.

"No. *He* is. He's doctoring up the inventory sheets."

"Why is he doing that?"

"To divert suspicion from himself."

I took a deep breath. "This is all fascinating, but what does it have to do with Amy?"

"Nothing, really." The foos ball players were yelling, and Frank had to speak loudly to be heard over them. "I just thought you'd be interested in knowing what was going on."

"And what is going on?"

"What do you mean?"

"Well, what you're telling me doesn't really make sense."

Frank bit his lip. I watched him decide whether he was going to talk or not. "All right," he finally said. "Amy told me she was going to tell the police Charlie was supplying her with acid. I guess Charlie figured he'd better get his licks in first."

"Did he?"

"I don't know. He could have. Amy lies a lot. It's hard to say."

"Nice family."

"Yeah, isn't it." Frank gave a grimace of a smile and slumped back in his chair. "I'd love to go out to California or New Mexico. I'd love to just go anyplace and do something else for awhile."

"So why don't you?"

Frank studied the table before replying. "Because I never finished college, which means I'll never be able to get another job like the one I have." Then he got up, went to the bar, and came back with two beers. He pushed one over to me and started on the other one.

I took a sip. "Since you're being so generous, how about telling me one last thing."

"What's that?"

"Why did your father and his brother stop talking?"

Frank spun his beer bottle around. "I don't think it was any one thing. Just lots of little things over a period of time. Lots and lots of little things." He stood up suddenly, as if the realization had just hit him that he'd said too much. "I'd better go. I have to be at the plant early tomorrow morning." He put on his coat and left.

I followed a minute later. On the way home, I stopped at the new Mexican takeout place on Westcott and picked up three beef and spinach *enchilada* dinners, two sides of corn bread, and four Kahlua brownies for Manuel, Zsa Zsa, and myself. I ate my portion, watched a little TV, and went to bed, but I didn't fall asleep right away. I kept staring at the ceiling and wondering what Toon Town had meant.

The next evening I had my answer.

It was a little after ten thirty at night and I was sitting on the sofa in the living room, paging through the morning paper and listening to Manuel tell me how he was going to Atlanta, when the phone rang. The police were on the line. They were calling to tell me that my store had been broken into. They wanted me to come down immediately. I cursed, as I hung up the receiver.

"What's up?" Manuel asked.

I told him as I headed for the door. Manuel grabbed his jacket and ran after me.

"What do you mean he broke in?" Manuel asked.

"Just what I said." I spent the ride cursing Toon Town and wondering what he'd done to Noah's Ark.

"Just wait for me," I told Manuel, as I pulled up behind the patrol cars parked in front of the shop.

He grunted. I took that as a yes and hopped out of the cab.

One of the cops glanced up from his clipboard, stopped writing, and came towards me. I had to squint to read the name off his badge in the dim light. It was Harvey. "Robin Light," he said, making the words into a statement instead of a question.

I nodded. "How bad is it inside?"

Harvey pulled at the corners of his sparse mustache. "Bad enough."

"How are the animals?"

"I don't know. When I saw what I had, I turned around and came out. I've been waiting for you to take a look." He tugged on the ends of his mustache again. "Shall we go in?" he asked, nodding towards the store.

"Might as well."

We walked up the path together.

Then I opened the door.

Chapter 16

Our entrance was greeted by raucous squawks. A small cloud of green, blue, and yellow parakeets rose, flew in a circle, and settled back down on the ceiling pipes. I'd been thinking of booking a trip to Costa Rica to see this kind of stuff. Seeing it in my own place, however, was not what I'd had in mind.

Harvey took in the scene and shook his head. "It looks as if someone gave this place a pretty good going-over."

"You could say that." I gritted my teeth, took a deep breath, and told myself I needed to stay calm and assess the damages. What I wanted to do was cry.

Okay. The Macaw was still here. That was good. Especially since it was the most expensive item in the place. But everything that had been on the shelves was now on the floor. That was bad. The ferret's cage was on its side, the bottom tray had fallen off. Mr. Bones was gone. Also bad. I bit one of my cuticles. He'd probably fallen off the counter and was somewhere on the floor. I just hoped he hadn't worked his way into some crack in the floorboards and disappeared into the infrastructure of the building. Then I'd never find him. Ditto that for the hamsters and gerbils. They were gone too, their cages tipped over on their sides, bleeding cedar shavings. But at least Toon Town hadn't touched the fish tanks. I didn't want to think about what would have happened if he'd toppled those over. And then I thought about the snakes and the lizards and my heart sank.

But they were all in their cages.

It looked as if Toon Town had caused a lot of damage, but it wasn't the expensive kind. It was the kind that was just going to take a lot of effort to clean up.

"Do you have any idea who did this?" Harvey asked. He was standing by the door.

"I wish I knew." I'd been going to give him Toon Town's name, but at the last moment I decided against it. Even if the cops picked him up, they weren't going to charge him with much. But if Amy was with him and they picked her up, too, she'd be in real trouble—if Frank Richmond was to be believed—and judging from Amy's past history, the odds were he was telling the truth.

Harvey looked around the store. "Have you had a fight with anyone lately?" he enquired.

"No," I lied.

"A dissatisfied customer. Someone who felt they were cheated."

I shook my head and looked down. Something was pulling on my sneaker lace. It was Mr. Bones. I gave a sigh of relief and lifted him up. He chittered and tried to burrow into my jacket. I opened the zipper and let in him. Poor guy. He'd had a rough night. A moment later, Pickles slunk by with a dead gerbil in her mouth. Snack time. I had a feeling

I'd be seeing a lot of those in the next couple of days. She meowed a greeting and headed for the back room. I wondered how many other gerbils Pickles had already eaten.

I reached into my pocket for a stick of gum. "How did whoever did this get in?"

"Broke a window in the back. Do you want to see it?"

I backtracked towards the door. "Please."

Manuel popped out of the car when he saw me come out of the store. "What's going on?"

"Who's he?" Harvey asked.

I told him, then I filled Manuel in on what had happened as we headed towards the side of the building. Harvey stopped about thirty feet into the alley and pointed to the window that led to the back room. "The guy broke the glass and climbed in here."

I sighed and nudged a shard of glass towards the wall. It wouldn't have taken much of an effort to get in this way. Maybe I should have installed a burglar alarm after all, although in this case it wouldn't have helped much.

"The only reason I discovered the break-in," Harvey explained, as I stared at the space where the window had been, "was because I was checking the alley for someone. I noticed the broken window and went back and tried the front door. It was open a crack. Whoever did this must have forgotten to close it all the way."

I thought of the birds flying around. I'd have to duct-tape a plastic garbage bag over the window the moment I went in. Then tomorrow I'd get someone to come out and fix it. This wasn't Florida. If they got out outside, the cold would kill them.

Harvey ran a finger down the center of his nose. It was long and thin and cut the air like a hatchet. "Are you sure there isn't someone you've had a fight with recently?"

Manuel started to speak, but I interrupted before he could say anything. "I'm positive," I replied, firmly ignoring Manuel's startled expression.

"Well, if you do remember, give me a call." Harvey headed back towards the squad car.

We followed, a minute or so after.

"Why didn't you tell him about Toon Town?" Manuel hissed.

"I'll explain later."

"So you gonna let him get away with this?"

"No," I replied grimly.

"What are you going to do?"

"I'm not sure, but I'm definitely going to think of something."

By now we were back in front of the store.

"I got some friends," Manuel said, and then fell silent as Harvey came back with the crime report number. I stuffed it in my pocket.

"I may take you up on your offer," I told Manuel, after Harvey left. Then Manuel and I turned and went back inside the store.

The first thing I did was fix the window. The second thing I did was fix up a home for Mr. Bones. The third thing I did was call Tim. I wanted to prepare him for what he'd find when he arrived in the morning. After that, Manuel and I went home. I was too depressed to do any cleaning. I was too depressed to have my talk with Manuel about finding another place to stay. Instead, I had two Scotches and went to sleep.

I had to drag myself out of bed the next morning. Surprisingly, Manuel was already up and waiting to go to work. One good thing you can say about him: He is there when you really need him. In the car on the way over to the store we talked about his trying to get back in his house, and he agreed that maybe it would be a good idea to have a chat with his mom. At least I was getting somewhere with something. Not that that really helped my mood much. Thinking about what was waiting for me at the store made me want to spit. I felt even angrier when I walked in. In the light of day, the damage looked worse than it had last night.

Tim had beaten Manuel and me in. "Jesus," he said, as I walked in. "I can't believe this."

"I know."

"It's going to take us a day to get this place back together."

"At the least." I put my backpack and denim jacket on the counter and thought about where to start.

The three of us worked for the next five hours straight.

With every bag of dog food I put back on the shelf, with every can of flea and tick spray I replaced, I just got angrier and angrier.

I wanted to find Toon Town. I wanted to find him really badly.

Amy had brought him into my life, and I wanted to make sure he knew he'd better get out.

Chapter 17

I spent the rest of the day and the next one getting the store back in shape. Then I went after Toon Town. But he'd disappeared. So had Amy. They weren't at the warehouse—in fact, no one was. Maybe Justin had carried Melanie and her friend off to Chicago after all. I visited the house I'd followed Toon Town to a couple of times. No one was there, either. I peeked in the mailbox. Except for a circular from Pizza Hut, it was empty.

I knocked on the neighbors' doors hoping to get a lead. All of them said the same thing: people came and went at a variety of hours. Some of them had blue hair, some had green, some looked normal. After awhile, they'd stopped paying attention. I called Toon Town's mother. She hadn't heard from him. I called the store where he worked on the off chance he'd dropped by. He hadn't. I called Amy's family. She hadn't touched base with any of them. It looked as if I'd hit a dead end. Then around six-thirty Manuel strolled in and put the ball back in play.

"I heard something you're gonna be interested in," he told me.

I put my pen down. I'd been taking advantage of the dinner slump to decide which cat toys I wanted to order. "Yeah, what's that?"

"You know John John?"

"The kid that was busted for stealing three cars and shooting at cans with a Glock in Barry Park?"

"That's him. Well I met him downtown while I was waiting for the bus, and I did what you said."

"You went to school?"

Manuel rolled his eyes. "Funny man. Really funny. No. I asked him about Amy."

"He's seen her?" I could hear the excitement in my voice.

"She was dancing at a topless joint called Good Girls over on the Northside a couple of days ago." Manuel tugged his pants up. "You're gonna give me some money for this, right?"

"Twenty bucks."

He put on his poor-me face. "How about a little more?"

"I don't think so."

"Come on Robin, I need it."

I didn't ask what he needed the money for, because Manuel wouldn't tell me anyway. I sighed. "You can earn another ten if you bring out the dog food bags from the back."

Manuel looked at the clock. "I would, but I got someone waiting outside for me. How about you front me the money and I work for you tomorrow."

"Sorry." I shook my head. I'd learned that arrangements like that didn't work out.

Manuel frowned and tugged his pants up. "Then at least

give me five for the work I did helping you put the store back together."

"All right." It seemed only fair.

He grinned and slipped the twenty-five dollars I handed him into his pocket and headed for the door. I watched through the window as he jumped into a grey Plymouth Sundance that was parked across the street. The car roared away from the curb, and I went back to what I was doing, wishing I hadn't given Manuel the money. Whatever he and his friends were going to get up to probably wasn't going to be good.

I locked up at nine and dropped Zsa Zsa off at the house. Manuel hadn't come home yet, so I wrote him a note and took off for Good Girls. The wind smelled of snow. Driving through town, I thought about how much better I would like fall if it came before spring. Oh well. Maybe I should move down to Atlanta like everyone else and have done with it.

Once I reached North Salina, I turned down the radio, put a stick of gum in my mouth, and started looking for the bar. It wasn't hard to find. There were five topless places in a three block area, Good Girls being the fifth. Or the first, if you came at it from the opposite direction. It was certainly the smallest and seediest. It didn't advertise Monday Night Football on a giant TV screen and free late-night pizza, or bill itself as a gentleman's club, or brag about its VIP lounge, concert lighting, and onstage bachelor parties which earned Good Girls a certain amount of points, as far as I was concerned. At least it wasn't pretending to be something it wasn't.

I blew a bubble, popped it, and pulled over to the curb. When I'd lived in New York, I'd known a girl who'd danced in a place like this in Queens. She'd liked the money and the attention. Especially the money. "I make more in one night here, then I would in two weeks if I worked as a secretary," she'd told me. Finally, when she'd saved enough to go to college, she quit. Of course tuition then had been a hell of a lot cheaper. We'd celebrated by burning her pasties and G-string.

Last I heard, she'd gotten an assistantship and was working on her Ph.D. in clinical psych. I was wondering what had happened to her, as I opened the door and went inside. Looking around, I decided there was something to be said for modernizing, after all. The place was small and cramped. The walls were the color of putty just before it needs to be replaced. The space smelled of old beer, unwashed bodies, and stale tobacco. There was a bar on one end and a strip on the other where the girls danced, though none of them were dancing now, even though the music was blaring.

It was definitely a low-rent operation, the kind of place where no one would look too closely at anyone's I.D., including the dancers'. Which was what Amy needed. Although, now that I thought about it, I couldn't see even this place hiring someone with blue hair and a nose stud. Down in the City yes. Up here in Syracuse, no way. I decided to ask some questions, anyway. It couldn't hurt, and I was already here.

I was heading for the bar when I was intercepted by a man who was so fat he'd have to buy two seats for himself on a plane if he wanted to fly. "There's a ten dollar cover charge and a two drink minimum," he informed me in a gravelly voice. Even though it was cold in here, his forehead was beaded with sweat.

"I don't want to come in. I just want to talk to the manager," I told him.

"That's me." He folded his arms across his chest and regarded me with basset hound eyes.

"It's about Amy Richmond."

"Don't know her," he promptly replied.

"Maybe she uses another name." I described her.

"Still don't know her." I tried reading his face but it was like trying to read Play-Doh. I continued, anyway. "A friend of mine said he saw her here a couple of days ago."

"He must have made a mistake. Maybe he meant someplace else."

"It's possible," I conceded. Then I asked him if I could talk to the performers, anyway.

He pursed his lips and flicked a sausage-like finger in the direction of the stage and told me it was out of the question. "My money, my time," was how he put it. "Now if you don't mind, I have work to do. Are you staying or going?"

"Going."

I thought he muttered "good" under his breath, but I couldn't be sure. Then he turned and waddled away. The two men at the bar, who had been watching our conversation, continued watching me with unblinking eyes. I felt as if I was the pre-entertainment entertainment. I gave them a little more by describing Amy to them and asking if they had seen her. They both said no and turned back to their drinks. Maybe they preferred being observers to being participants.

But I wasn't ready to go home yet. I walked around to the side of the building, found the back entrance, and pulled on the door handle. It was locked. I didn't want to knock in case the manager opened it. It looked as if I were going to have to wait till the "performers" came out. I went back to the cab and pulled it up until it was blocking the alley.

Then I waited. Half an hour later the back door swung open and a woman came out.

I got out to greet her. She jumped when she saw me and clutched her bag more tightly. "What do you want?" she demanded.

"I'm looking for Amy Richmond. I was hoping you could help."

"Never heard of her." She took another step forward. I took a step with her. "Look," she said to me, "if you don't mind. I got to go home and relieve the sitter." Under the streetlights she looked all skin and bones. The skin on her face was pitted with acne scars. She had a bump in her nose where it had been broken and badly set. She looked about as sexy as a tablecloth hanging on a clothesline. I couldn't imagine anyone stuffing dollar bills in her G-string.

"How old are you?"

"Twenty." Right. I had her pegged for thirty-five. At least. "Why?"

"Just curious. Amy's fifteen."

She raised her eyebrows. They were penciled in and gave her face a hard cast. "What's that got to do with me?"

"Don't you think she needs to go home, too?"

"How would I know? I told you. My babysitter's waiting. Go ask one of the other girls. Maybe they know something."

"Listen, I know she was here. I know she danced. All I want to do is talk to her. It's very important."

"You her mother?"

"No."

"Her aunt?"

"No.

"Then what?" She moved her arm slightly. Her jacket fell open and I saw the pin. It was round and made of gold wire that had been wound into a circle. A red stone sat in the center. It reminded me of one of the sketches I'd seen in the assignment book I'd found in Amy's room. The woman followed my gaze.

I pointed to the pin. "She made that, didn't she?"

The woman took a step back. "I don't know what you're talking about."

"I've been in her room. I've seen her work. That's hers. Where is she?"

The woman tried to look angry and came off looking frightened. "I don't know. I already said that."

I leaned forward a little. "I know what you said and now I want you to listen to what I'm going to say. The police have an APB out on Amy. They want to question her about her father's death. If you're hiding her, and she did kill her father, you could be charged as an acessory after the fact."

The woman flinched. "I don't know nothing about that."

"It was in the papers. Her father's name is Dennis Richmond. Listen, I'm not going to hurt her. All I want to do is talk to her." I raised a hand. "I swear."

The woman started fiddling with the clasp of her pocketbook. "She didn't say nothing about no killing," she said, sullenly. "She just told me there was this big family fight and she ran out."

"What else did she say?"

"She told me she needed to make some money. Sometimes the prize at amateur night gets as big as two hundred dollars."

"How'd she do?"

"Not so good." Her voice took on a professional tone. She could have been an English professor critiquing a student's paper. "Her body's okay, but I told her she'd have to lose the hair. I offered to lend her one of my wigs, but she didn't want to listen."

"How'd you get the pin?"

"I felt bad for her. I've been out on the street too. I offered her ten bucks for it."

"Where was she going?"

The woman tugged on a strand of hair. "She didn't say. Last time I saw her, she was walking down North Salina."

"And you're positive you don't know where she was headed?"

"She said something about picking up her stuff."

"Did she say from where?"

"No."

"Was she alone?"

"I didn't see no one with her." I wondered where Toon Town was, as the woman glanced at her watch. "Shit," she cried. "You made me miss my bus. Now what am I going to do?"

I drove her home to Solvay. Then I went to see if Amy was at the warehouse. Maybe I'd get lucky. Maybe I'd find her. And maybe she'd know where Toon Town was.

Chapter 18

It had begun to snow, as I drove across town. The first of the season. Glittering flakes danced under the streetlights, melting away when they hit the ground. In a way, they reminded me of Amy. I could see her—I had seen her—but when I tried to grasp her, she disappeared into the air. I felt as if I were chasing a chimera. Oh, well. It was a feeling I was familiar with by now. In fact, it was a feeling I seemed to specialize in.

I turned on the radio, started on a piece of bubble gum, and told myself that this time it would be different. This time Amy and I would finally talk. For the rest of the ride, I hummed along with the oldies on Station 92.5 FM and tried to decide whether or not I was going to go to my twenty-fifth high school reunion in the spring. I mean, what would I say to everyone? I didn't have a husband. I didn't have children. I wasn't working on the paper anymore. I was running a business that was marginal at best. There were some people, though, I would like to see.

I still hadn't decided what I was going to do when I reached the warehouse. One of the boards that had been nailed over the front windows had been yanked off and was lying on the ground. As I turned into the alley, I noticed more bricks had fallen out of the wall's corner, giving it a snaggletoothed appearance. If things kept on going at this rate, the warehouse wouldn't even be habitable for people like Amy in another year or so. The strips of plastic that caught in the trees at the edge of the lot fluttered a greeting, as I parked the cab. I took the can of mace I often carry out of the glove compartment and got out. I wasn't taking any chances with Toon Town this time. On the way to the door, I accidentally kicked a beer can. The clattering reverberated through the night, underscoring its silence.

I was on the third step when I noticed the piece of plywood that covered the hole in the door was slightly off to one side. Someone hadn't refastened it properly. My pulse went up a notch. Then I told myself I was just being silly. Amy, or whoever else was inside, probably hadn't bothered replacing the wooden rectangle. Just because Manuel had taken such pains with the door didn't mean that everyone else did.

I ducked down and edged my way through. Everything seemed the same, except it was colder. But that was to be expected. Brick and cement hold the temperature. The colder it was outside, the colder it was going to get inside. My breath formed clouds of vapor, as I walked down the hall. The overhead light was swinging slightly—probably from a draft—but it gave everything a sinister cast. When I got to the end of the corridor, it angled off to the left. I followed it, trying to walk as quietly as I could. If Toon Town or Amy were in the building, I didn't want them to know I was coming.

After about four feet, I began smelling the faint odor of garbage. It got stronger as I continued on. Discarded beer cans, half eaten apples, banana peels, and cereal boxes dotted the floor, and I had to be careful where I walked. I trailed my hand along the wall. The concrete chilled my fingers. It was covered with graffiti. Fat initals, thin initials. Pictures of smiley faces. Pictures of smiley faces frowning. Pictures of smiley faces with bandanas.

If this wall were found three thousand years from now, would the archeologists give those faces significance? Would they posit a religion based on them? I was wondering if that was what the cave paintings in Spain and France were really about, when the hallway ended and I found myself standing on the edge of a large, open space. Most of it was dark, but in one corner near to where I was standing, someone had hung another light from an overhead pipe. It acted as a spotlight, illuminating everything within its circle.

My eyes were drawn to the two pup tents huddled close to each other. Then I noticed the tarps and the three sleeping bags. The charred remains of a campfire lay a little ways away. Two rats scampered away from the plate of spaghetti that sat nearby. The Boy Scouts had never envisioned camping like this, I thought, as I spotted a bundle of clothes and took a step forward. Maybe that was Amy's stuff. Then I spotted a white oval and realized my mistake. For a few seconds, I thought I was looking at a large rag doll. But I wasn't.

I was looking at a person.

I was afraid it was Amy.

I moved closer.

It wasn't. It was Melanie, the girl I'd seen running from

Toon Town. I felt relieved and then I felt awful that I felt that way.

A dark pool of liquid fanned out from beneath her chest.

Her mouth gaped open.

Her eyes stared out into the blackness.

She wasn't going to be running away from home any more.

Her parents would always know where to find her.

They could visit her grave once a month.

What a waste.

I wanted to cry, and then I wanted to punch something, only there was nothing to punch. I was taking a step towards her when I caught a whiff of something. For a few seconds, I couldn't identify the odor—then I could.

It was gas. The place smelled faintly of gas.

A pipe must be leaking somewhere.

Instinctively, I whirled around and started to run. All I could think of was the beam crashing down on my legs when my store had burned down and the time I'd spent recovering in the hospital. Not again, I thought. Not this time. I was at the entrance to the first hallway when I heard a sharp crack. A gunshot. Someone was shooting into the warehouse. I ran faster. I was gulping air. George was right, I thought: I am really out of shape. I should go to the gym.

I was three-quarters of the way down the first hallway when I felt the shock waves under my feet. I put on a burst of speed, turned the corner, sprinted down the last corridor, and threw myself through the door. I heard a whoosh as I reached the other side. I looked up. Tongues of fire were floating in the sky. I stumbled towards the cab, got in, and drove it across the grassy median to the next warehouse parking lot. The car bumped up and down, as I negotiated the ruts. Fingers of tree limbs tapped on the cab's side windows, as I reached in the glove compartment for my cell phone. I was dialing 911 as I pulled onto the other lot.

It took a little over three minutes for everyone to start arriving. You mention the words "gas leak" and people hustle. When I heard the wail of the fire trucks, I walked out front to meet them. By the time I got there, the street was cordoned off. It was full of Ni Mo emergency trucks, pumpers, and police cars. Men, hoses, and lights all seemed to meld into one blur. The only people not there were the media, and they would arrive soon enough.

I was thinking that this was definitely a five o'clock news kind of event, when a man in a yellow jacket came over and asked if I was all right.

Amazingly, I realized that I was.

My clothes were torn and dirty, but, outside of that, I was okay.

He left and was replaced by a policeman who asked for my statement. I told him what I knew, which wasn't much.

"You're sure she was dead when you saw her?" he asked, when I got to the part about seeing Melanie. "You're positive?"

I thought about the way her face had looked and nodded. "Absolutely."

"And you don't know this girl's last name or where she lived?"

"She had a friend, Cindy. But I don't know her last name either."

The cop tapped his pad with his pen. "Can you think of anyone else who might be acquainted with her?"

I gave him Justin's name, but I didn't tell him about Manuel. The less that kid had to do with the authorities the better, I decided. Then I told him about Toon Town's fight with Melanie. This had gone beyond protecting Amy. Melanie's death had changed the equation.

The cop shook his head as he wrote. He looked as if he'd been on the job long enough to have seen more than he should have or wanted to. "Was anyone else in the building?"

"Not that I know of."

He lifted his eyes. "Meaning?"

"Meaning I didn't see anyone else."

"Okay." He flipped to a new page. "You said you heard a gunshot before the explosion?"

"Yes." I watched the red lights dancing off his face.

"How can you be sure?"

"I've heard them before."

I thought he'd ask me where I had, but he didn't. Instead, he closed his notebook. "Wait here," he ordered. "I'll be right back."

I watched him thread his way through the trucks and the hoses. For a second, he was there, and then he disappeared behind a ladder truck. I knew I should wait. I knew he'd be pissed. But I didn't. I turned around and started towards my cab. I'd told him everything I knew. He had my name and address. If he wanted me bad enough, he'd come and get me. As it was, I'd have to go downtown tomorrow and talk to people, anyway. A lot of people. But before that happened I needed to try and sort things out. And call my lawyer. Have some Scotch. And smoke a cigarette. Especially, smoke a cigarette. I glanced around. No one was paying any attention to me. All attention was focused on the warehouse.

I tried not to think about Melanie, as I trotted towards my cab. Poor kid. Poor parents. Poor everyone. Did stuff like this happen when I was growing up? Maybe it had and I didn't know about it, but I didn't think so. I turned the key and the engine kicked over. It seemed very loud. I expected someone to come running over. No one did, though. All their attention was riveted on the blaze. A few seconds later, I was out on the street and driving away from the fire. Half a mile down the road, I saw a mini-mart and stopped to buy a pack of Camels. Gum just wasn't going to cut it anymore. The sales clerk stared at me, while I counted out the change. I guess I looked worse than I thought, or maybe it was because my hands had started shaking and I couldn't get them to stop and it took me forever to get my money out of my wallet. Delayed reaction, the part of my mind that had walled itself off noted with a detached, clinical interest. I lit up in the car and went home.

Zsa Zsa was wagging her tail when I opened the door. I knelt down and she licked my chin and the corners of my mouth. I hugged her. She licked my fingers. That's when I noticed my hand was smeared with blood. I got up and looked at myself in the mirror. I had a gash on my chin. It didn't look bad—nothing that required stitches—but I had a thin line of blood running down my neck. My face was smudged with soot. So was my jacket. No wonder the sales clerk had stared at me.

"Jesus, what did you get into?" Manuel asked.

I jumped. For some reason I hadn't expected him to be home.

"There was an explosion at the warehouse."

"You're kidding."

"Do I look as if I'm kidding?"

He swallowed. "No." He hiked his pants up. "What happened?"

"I'm not sure. There was a gas leak. I think someone shot into the warehouse and set it off."

"On purpose?"

"I don't think they were hunting rabbits."

"Was anyone hurt?"

"That girl Melanie was killed." I rubbed my head. My temples were beginning to throb. My legs ached. I felt as if I couldn't walk another step. I had to sit down before I fell. "Actually the blast didn't kill her. She was dead before." I stopped because I realized I was babbling.

"Who was killed?" A voice enquired from the kitchen.

I cocked my head. "Who's in there?"

Manuel took a deep breath, let it out, and said, "You're not gonna believe this. It's Amy."

Chapter 19

Manuel was right: I didn't. And then looking at the expression on his face, I did. A surge of anger ran through me. And then relief. And then anger again. And then for some reason, I started to laugh. How classic. You run all over God's creation and the answer is in your own kitchen. And then I went back to being angry and stormed into the kitchen. Amy was sitting at the table petting the cat. James's eyes were closed. His ears were back. His tail was draped over the table's edge. Next to him were the empty take-out cartons of the Chinese food I'd bought earlier. A strip of white paper from a fortune cookie lay nearby. My fortune cookie. The one I hadn't had time to eat.

She looked up when she saw me. "Who was killed?" she repeated.

"Melanie."

She paled. "You're lying," she cried. "You're just saying that because you're mad at me."

"Why should I do something like that?"

"I don't know," she whispered.

She remained perfectly still while I talked. She was even paler now, her hands showing a ghostly white against James's black fur. I had the feeling she'd fade into the wall if I took my eyes off her. She began to sob before I was finished. The sound of her crying filled the room, pushing my anger out. I went over and put my arms around her, but she froze at my touch and I moved away.

I waited until she was done before I said anything else. "You have to tell me what's going on."

She grasped her cross and looked up at me with tear-puffed eyes. "I don't know what you mean."

"Yes you do."

"I just met Melanie a couple of months ago," Amy wailed. "We talked maybe three or four times. That's all."

"Really?" I put my hands on my hips. My anger returned. "Then I don't suppose you know how come your boyfriend was fighting with her? Or how come he broke into my store?"

"I don't," she stammered.

"You know," I said. "Fuck Murphy. I should have thrown you out when you walked into my store."

Her jaw dropped.

"I would have been a lot better off. Since you came into my life, my house had been robbed, my store has been trashed, I'm an after-the-fact accessory to a homicide, I was almost blown up, and I've left the scene of another homicide—one the police are going to be here to question me about very soon. And every single one of those incidents is tied up with you in some way." I placed my palms on the kitchen table and put my face into Amy's. "Now I want an explanation, and I want it now."

"I don't know anything," Amy cried.

"Tell that to the police." I went over to the phone and dialed. "Maybe by now they'll have picked up that charming boyfriend of yours, as well."

Amy shook her head from side to side."He didn't kill Melanie. He wouldn't do anything like that."

"I'm sure they'll be interested to hear what you have to say."

Amy half rose out of her chair. "Put the phone down."

I ignored her and kept the receiver to my ear. "Yes," I said when an operator came on. "I'd like to . . ."

"Wait," Amy cried.

I turned towards her.

"You win," she said, slumping back in her chair.

I told the operator I'd made a mistake and hung up.

Amy nervously turned her bracelet made of bones around her wrist. "What do you want to know?" she asked. She seemed spent, as if her last outburst had sapped all her energy.

I leaned against a kitchen cabinet and crossed my arms over my chest. "Let's start with the fight Toon Town and Melanie had outside of Club 666 a while ago. You wouldn't happen to know what it was about would you?"

"Melanie owed him some money."

"For what?"

"Some stuff."

"Drug stuff?"

Amy looked down at the floor and nodded.

"She didn't look as if she had enough money to buy a stick of gum."

"She was going to get some from Justin."

"Justin must be a generous guy." I shifted my weight from one leg to another.

Amy didn't say anything. Her silence filled the room.

James yawned, his fangs gleamed under the kitchen light. He stretched, jumped down from the table, and sauntered into the hallway.

"What kind of drugs are we talking about?"

Amy shrugged. "The usual—Acid. Weed. Ecstasy."

"Your boyfriend deals?"

"No," Amy retorted sharply. "He was just doing Melanie a favor. But then she wouldn't pay him and he got angry 'cause he'd fronted the money."

"So he went looking for her?"

Amy nodded.

"How'd he know where to find her?"

Amy looked down at her hands and back at me. "He told me he just wanted to scare her a little, that's all."

I thought about Melanie sprawled out on the warehouse floor. "I'd say he's done a lot more than that."

Amy folded her arms over her chest. Her eyes were smudged black from her makeup. "He didn't kill her," she insisted. "He wouldn't do anything like that."

"What makes you so sure?"

"I just know." She glared at me defiantly. She'd obviously managed to convince herself that what she was saying was true. Whether it was or not was something else.

"All right." I walked around the room, ending up in back of her. "Let's change the subject for a moment."

"Fine with me."

I placed my hands on the back of her chair and leaned over. "Tell me how you found out about your father's apartment?" Amy didn't answer. "Okay. If that's the way you want it," I said, after a minute, and headed for the phone.

"Wait," she cried.

I stopped where I was.

She narrowed her eyes. "I was following him, okay? Is that what you want to hear?"

"It's a beginning. Why were you doing that?"

Amy looked down at the floor and then back up at me.

"Come on," I urged. "It can't be as bad as all that."

She picked a speck of lint off her skirt.

"Murphy thought you could trust me."

She favored me with a big smile—or it would have been a smile if her lower lip hadn't been trembling and her eyes weren't misting over. "They say confession is good for the soul."

"So I heard." I waited to hear what she had to say.

Once she began, her words spilled out one after another as though she were afraid to stop, now that she'd started. "My dad and I got into a big fight after I got back from Cedar View. I wanted him to send me down to New York—they've got this really neat high school down there that specializes in the arts—but he said he wasn't going to spend another fuckin' cent on me. He said he'd done enough. So I called him an asshole—it's not like he doesn't, didn't," she corrected herself, "have the money, 'cause he did. He just didn't want to spend it on me."

"What happened?"

"He told me to get out of the house. What else is new?"

"Tell me about it!" Manuel chimed in. He was standing in the corner. "That jerk-off my mom married is always booting me out. I think he'd be happy if I died. That way, he wouldn't have to never spend no money on me."

"Manuel," I hissed.

"Right. Sorry." He put his hand to his mouth and stopped talking. Amy continued. "I told my mom, and she went to talk to him, and they got into this big fight." Amy scratched her cheek. "It was pretty intense. They started calling each other names."

"Then what happened?"

Amy shrugged. "I don't know. I left. I just didn't want to hear it. I don't think they even noticed I was gone."

"Then what?"

"I hooked up with some friends."

"Toon Town?"

"Not at first. I just hung out."

"Where?"

"The mall. People's houses. We'd sneak in when their parents went off to work and smoke out." Amy started twisting her bracelet again. "Then I got to thinking about something I'd overheard my mom say about how she knew my dad was taking money out of the company, but she figured it was okay because she was going to make him give some to her."

"And that's why you were following him?"

She nodded. "It was easy. I found out about his apartment."

"How'd you do that?"

"I staked out the factory."

"Staked out?" I raised an eyebrow.

"Yeah. Well." Amy gave an embarrassed shrug. "I like the word."

"But you don't have a car or a license. How could you follow him?"

"Toon Town has a car."

"I would think a lime-green car would stand out a bit."

"We borrowed one of his friend's car, okay?"

"Then what? Did you go up there?"

Amy fiddled with her bracelet. "Just the night he was killed."

What she was telling me didn't make any sense, but I let it go, because I didn't want to antagonize her by calling her a liar. "Why'd you do that?"

"I wanted to talk to him about something."

"What?"

She looked away.

"Tell me," I insisted.

"I was going to ask him for money. So I could get out of here."

"Why should he give you any?"

"Because I was gonna tell him if he didn't, I was gonna tell my uncle what he was doing."

"So you were trying to blackmail him?"

She swallowed and studied her nails."Yes."

"Go on."

"When I got up to the apartment, the door was open. I went inside. I saw him lying there." She paused and swallowed. "And I ran. When I calmed down, I called you."

"Where was Toon Town during all of this?"

"He dropped me off and went to do an errand. He was supposed to meet me back there." Tessa began to cry again. "It was so awful seeing my father like that. I didn't like him, but I didn't want him to die."

I went over and put my arms around her again. This time she let me.

"I want to leave," she moaned. "I want to go somewhere else." I stroked her hair. "I don't know what to do anymore." And then the sobs took over—wracking ones that made her body shake. "I don't feel well. I want to lie down," she told me, when she could talk.

I maneuvered her into the living room and sat her down on the sofa. Then I went back into the kitchen to get her something to drink. Manuel was leaning against the counter. He didn't look too well either.

"What's up?" I asked, as I turned on the tap.

Manuel fidgeted. "I was just thinking about Melanie."

I waited.

"The warehouse . . ."

"Yes."

"Well, Rabbit tipped her to it. He thought he was doing her a favor."

"He was."

"It doesn't seem that way now." He began twisting a button on his flannel shirt.

I filled up a glass with water and turned off the tap. This evening was turning out to be endless. "Why don't you ask around and see if you can come up with her last name," I suggested. I knew the police would get it eventually, but Manuel might accomplish it faster, plus, doing something might make make him feel better. I was about to say something else when I heard the front door slam.

Manuel and I looked at each other.

We ran for the hall.

Chapter 20

"So she just disappeared?" Connelly asked me. He was wearing brown slacks, an off-white shirt, a blue tie with yellow flowers, and a too tight grey jacket that couldn't contain his expanding paunch.

"That's right." The guy must have gained thirty pounds since I'd seen him last year, and he hadn't exactly been Mr. Slim Jim then. Now he looked like the Pillsbury Dough Boy on steroids. "Manuel and I searched the neighborhood. We couldn't find her."

Connelly intertwined his fingers, turned his hands so his palms were facing me, and cracked his knuckles. "Maybe the aliens came down and beamed her up?"

"Actually, I think she went through the woods behind my house and up over the hill." Though my house is in the city, it's built into the side of an old, overgrown orchard. The area, which covers the upper part of the entire block, houses raccoons, pheasants, and a variety of song birds.

Even in the fall, when the leaves are off the trees, the thick underbrush makes it a good place to hide.

"How long did you spend looking?"

"About twenty minutes. Then your guys came." I shifted my weight from one hip to the other. The wooden chair I was sitting in was uncomfortable when I'd sat down in it four hours ago and it was more so now, but then again, I don't suppose the people that furnished this room considered comfort when they were decorating—and I use that word loosely—the interrogation rooms at the Public Safety Building.

Connelly cracked his knuckles again.

I rubbed the back of my neck. My headache hadn't gone away.

My lawyer, Joe, stifled a yawn and checked his watch. Then he straightened his tie. I knew the signs. In another five minutes or so he was going to give Connelly his "charge her or let her go" speech. Connelly knew the signs, too. He should. We'd played this game often enough, too often, by my lights. Which was why he probably started talking faster. He must have figured he wanted to get in as much as possible in the time he had left.

"All right," Connelly said. "Let's go on to something else."

I waited to see what was coming. So did Joe.

"The girl at the warehouse."

Joe jumped in. "What about her?" he demanded. If Connelly was a bulldog, slow, fat, and tenacious, Joe was a cairn terrier, small, yappy, and aggressive.

"I just want to see if your client knows her last name," Connelly snapped. "Any objections?"

"None." Joe leaned back in his chair and fingered his

tie. It was Italian, silk, and expensive—the kind you buy on Madison Avenue.

Connelly turned to me. "So, *do* you know her last name?"

"I already told you, I don't." My left foot had fallen asleep. I moved it from side to side and wiggled my toes.

"And you don't know the full name of the other girl you saw in the warehouse the first time you were there?"

"No. I just know her first name: Cindy," I repeated, for what must have been the hundredth time.

"How about this boy, Justin, the one that was supposed to take them to Chicago?"

I shook my head. "I don't know their last names. I don't know their addresses. I don't know anything about them. I would tell you if I did, but I don't."

Connelly glared at me. I ignored him and checked my watch. It was five in the morning, not a good hour for me, under the best of circumstances, and these were definitely not the best of circumstances. I'd been in my clothes for almost twenty-four hours now. During that time, I'd gone to work, talked to a stripper, seen a dead body, got caught in an explosion, found Amy, and lost her again. I needed a vacation, I needed to go someplace with a beach. Short of that, I'd settle for going home, getting out of my clothes, and going to bed.

Connelly pulled on his earlobe. Both his ears were red around the edges. I was wondering what, if anything, that meant, when he said, "Tell me about Wallace Gleason again."

I glanced at Joe. He nodded. I repeated my Toon Town story, leaving out the part where I sliced up his arm and ending with my losing the Tracker.

"And then poof!" Connelly raised his hands, spread his

fingers out, and inscribed two half circles in the air. "They were gone."

"That's right. What's your point?"

He looked at the manila folder on his desk, then looked back up at me, and cracked his knuckles again. "I don't know. It seems to me like we got a theme going here."

"Meaning?"

"Meaning the Amy disappearing theme. The girl just keeps vanishing. It's amazing."

"I think so too."

Connelly slammed his hand down on the folder. I would have jumped if I hadn't been so tired. "I want to know what the hell is going on," he yelled. His earlobes were getting redder.

"I'm telling you. It's not my fault if you don't believe me."

Connelly narrowed his eyes. "You're leaving something out. I want to know what it is."

Connelly was right. I was leaving something out. Actually I was leaving a lot of things out.

I wasn't telling him about Amy following her dad. I wasn't telling him about Amy discovering her father's body.

I wasn't telling him about my being in the apartment.

And I wasn't going to.

Ever.

I had no intention of landing myself in more trouble than I was in already.

Connelly thwacked the manila folder on the table with his palm again. I hoped he hurt his hand. "You know, you could be charged with aiding and abetting."

"Abetting who?"

"Amy. In the commission of her father's homicide, possibly even her friend's."

I rose from the chair. "That's a crock of shit, and you know it. She hasn't been charged with anything."

"Not yet." Connelly smiled. He was enjoying himself. I was about to say something else, when Joe motioned for me to sit back down. Losing charge of the show was not what he had in mind.

"At the very least, we can charge you with leaving the scene of a crime," Connelly continued. "You should have stayed at the warehouse."

Joe sat up straighter, put his hands on his knees, and leaned forward slightly. "My client was very upset. Disoriented. She wanted to clean up after what she'd been through. Since when is that a crime?"

Connelly glanced at me and snorted. "Come on," he said to Joe. "Give me a break. We're talking about a person who blew someone's brain's all over the wall a couple of years ago. I don't think what happened at the warehouse would make her blink." Connelly snorted again. "Disoriented my ass."

"Excuse me," I interjected. "Should I have just stood there and let myself get shot? Would that have been better?"

Joe shot me a look, and I shut up.

Connelly pretended he hadn't even heard me and continued talking to Joe. "You know what I think? I think she wanted to get rid of something."

"Like what?" Joe snapped. Exhaustion was making him irritable. "Come on," he continued, when Connelly didn't reply. "Admit it. You're reaching here. You don't have anything. Give it up. Let's just end this thing and go home."

Connelly swallowed. His complexion had that ashy undertone people get when they've had too little sleep. Joe's looked a little on the grey side, too. I'm sure mine probably looked the same. "I got some more questions," he insisted.

"You've been asking the same ones for the past four hours."

"Yeah, and I don't like the answers I've been getting."

Joe smoothed down his tie. "Do you have any new ones?"

Connelly did his glare.

Joe seemed unmoved. "Because unless you do . . ." His voice trailed off, and he gestured towards the door.

Connelly rubbed his nose with one of his knuckles, then he scratched his earlobe. I watched emotions wash over his face as he made up his mind and listened to the sound of footsteps in the corridor outside. "All right," he growled, after a minute had gone by. "Go on. Get out of here."

Joe stood. I followed suit. It felt good to be on my feet. "It's been fun, as always," I told Connelly, as I headed for the door.

I was passing him, when he pushed his card at me. "Take it," he ordered. "It has my beeper number. You find out Melanie's name, or Amy shows up, you call me right away."

"I will," I lied.

"If you don't, you're going to be very, very sorry." He emphasized the "very, very."

"Right." I put it in my pocket and headed for the door.

"He's not kidding," Joe said, when we got in the elevator.

"I know."

Joe didn't say anything else until we got outside. "It might be better for you if she came in."

"Well, I'll tell her that when I see her." He'd parked his Saab down the block. We started towards it.

"I'm serious, Robin."

"Me too." I studied his face under the streetlight. "You think I know where she is, don't you?"

"It doesn't matter what I believe." Joe buttoned his trench coat. It looked starched. Mine was stained and wrinkled.

But then, he had a wife to keep him all clean and tidy, and I only had myself. "What matters is what Connelly believes. He *can* have you arrested, you know."

"So you told me." I wondered what Connelly would do if he knew I'd been in Richmond's apartment. Actually, I didn't have to wonder. I knew.

But maybe being arrested wouldn't be so bad.

At least then I'd have time to sleep.

It was almost six when Joe dropped me off in front of my house. "One last thing," he said as I got out of the car.

"What?"

"Try and get picked up during the daytime for a change. I'm getting too old for this crap."

"I guess that's what happens when you marry a young wife. You don't have any extra energy." But I was talking to the air, because Joe had already taken off.

Zsa Zsa was waiting for me when I opened the door. I let her out for a quick pee, then we both went inside. Manuel was asleep on the sofa. The TV was on, the remote was in his hand.

He woke up when I removed it.

"I'm back," I told him.

"Great." He closed his eyes and turned over.

It would be so nice to be able to sleep like that, I thought, wistfully. Somewhere along the way, I seem to have lost the ability. I clicked off the lights and went upstairs to bed. An hour and a half later, I was finally dozing off when my alarm sounded. I turned it off and lay there. I thought I'd be able to make it into work, but I'd been mistaken. I felt as if I'd been tossed out of a moving truck. Short of ordering an ambulance and a wheelchair, there was no way I was getting to the store this morning. Tim was going to have to open. I called and told him. He wasn't pleased, but that was too bad. I just hung up, rolled over, and went back to sleep. I was still sleeping at two, dreaming about swimming in water so blue it seemed bottomless, when George called and woke me up.

"I called the store," he told me. "Tim said you were sick. What's the matter?"

"Nothing." I yawned. "I was too tired to get up." I noticed the stain on the ceiling had gotten worse. The leak in the roof was getting bigger. I'd have to have someone fix it before the snows came.

"How come?"

"It's a long story."

"I'm listening," George said.

But I didn't have the energy to go into it then. "Let's talk later," I suggested.

We agreed to meet at Pete's at nine thirty. Maybe by then I'd feel semi-human. I took a quick shower, dressed, and went downstairs. Manuel was talking on the phone in the kitchen. He startled when he saw me. Then he said, "Got to go," into the receiver and hung up.

"I waited up for you," he told me.

"I figured as much."

"So what happened downtown?"

"The usual. They asked questions I couldn't answer." I gave him a rundown of my conversation with Connelly. I opened the refrigerator door and closed it again. "I was right, wasn't I? You don't know Melanie's last name."

Manuel frowned. "I already told you that. I don't know her friends' last names either. It's not like I'm sending a letter to them or anything."

"Have you asked Rabbit?"

"He's not back from Watertown yet."

I opened the door of the refrigerator, leaned against it, and studied the contents. It was a depressing sight. The only things in it were a liter bottle of Pepsi and a Mounds bar Manuel had somehow missed. I took out the soda and the candy bar.

"Have you called anyone else?" I rinsed out a dirty glass.

"It's too early."

"Right." It was only almost three in the afternoon. I took a bite of the Mounds bar and put the soda back in the fridge. "So who were you talking to?" I asked more out of a desire to keep the conversation going than because I really cared.

Manuel hesitated a fraction too long before replying. "No one you know."

Now I was interested. "Would you like to try that answer again?"

Manuel tugged his pants up. "Okay," he admitted, looking away. "I was talking to TJ."

Ah. My favorite dealer. Actually, I liked TJ. He'd bought a Burmese from me last year and was saving up money for a Haitian boa. I just didn't like what he did. I gave Manuel a long hard look. "Are you trying to score?"

Manuel did injured innocence. "Hey man, I don't do that stuff no more."

I raised an eyebrow to convey disbelief.

"It's true," Manuel insisted.

And I was going to win the Lottery tomorrow, pay off all my bills, and go live in Spain. "So what were you guys talking about?"

"TJ's moving. He said he'd give me twenty bucks if I help him."

"I thought he just moved two months ago."

''Well he has to move again.''

Given TJ's lifestyle, that was a real possibility. I looked at my watch. I had to get to work. ''Listen, I'm just going to tell you this once. If I catch you doing dope in here, you're gone.''

''I wouldn't disrespect you like that.''

''I hope not.'' I turned to go. I had a nagging feeling that something else was going on, but I was going to have to find out about it later. If I didn't show up at the store soon, Tim was going to kill me or quit, which would be tantamount to the same thing.

Chapter 21

I walked into Pete's a little before ten. Since I'd last been in, someone had stuck three cardboard pumpkins and a couple of crepe paper witches on the walls in an attempt at holiday decoration. I glanced around. Three college kids were watching a rerun of *I Dream of Jeannie* on TV, Ebsen Fields was hunched over the bar reading a book, highlighter in hand, while George was hunkered on a stool, sipping a beer out of a stein. I sat Zsa Zsa and myself down next to him and apologized for being late.

"No problem. I just got here myself," he said, turning towards me. I watched his eyes widen as he took in my appearance. "Jesus, what happened to you?" he demanded, staring at the cut on my chin and the bruises on my jaw. "I thought you said you were sick."

"I am. I'm sick of getting hurt." The bruises on my jaw had gotten worse overnight, as injuries like this are wont to do, settling into a purplish-yellow color that no amount of makeup could hide. Not that I was complaining. Considering what I'd been through, it was a miracle I wasn't in the ICU. "I almost got myself blown up." I told George about last night. He listened the way he always does—intently, his eyes half closed to block out distractions.

"I'm impressed," he said, when I finished. His lips curled in an expression of disapproval. "All that in one evening. That's almost a new personal best."

I was trying to think of some smart assed comeback, when Ebsen Fields set a bottle of Sam Adams and a saucer in front of me.

"Boy, you look like shit," he observed. "What happened? Someone beat you up?"

"I was in an explosion."

"Right." Ebsen tugged on his beard. "Happens every day. I was in one last week."

"It was on the news."

"Then how come I didn't see it?" He leaned towards me. "You know, you and Connie, you're both the same. If you don't want to tell me something, that's okay. Just say so. I was only trying to be polite."

"Where is she anyway?"

"How the hell should I know?" Ebsen snapped. "I just work here. No one ever tells me anything. Now, if you'll excuse me, I have work to do." He moved back down the bar and picked up his book.

I poured some beer into the saucer and pushed it over to Zsa Zsa. "Boy, he's in a pissy mood."

George made a popping noise with his lips. "He's got a paper due the day after tomorrow." He watched Zsa Zsa drink. "Why do you think dogs like alcohol?"

I shrugged. "Probably the same reason people, birds, and elephants do: It makes them feel good."

"So all God's creatures get drunk?"

"I don't think fish and reptiles do," I replied, as I was thinking that I was glad I'd put Zsa Zsa between us. That way George wouldn't be able to smell the tobacco smoke on my clothes. So I'd had a lapse. Or two. Or three. It's not every day a building explodes when you're inside it. But George wouldn't understand. He was too much of a hard ass. Tomorrow I'd get back on track, I promised myself. I'd smoke two more cigarettes when I got home and throw the rest of the pack out. God, I wished I could have one now. I reached for a pretzel instead.

George rubbed a finger around the rim of his glass. "It's too bad about the girl," he said.

"Melanie?"

"I used to come across kids like that all the time when I was working. I always figured half wouldn't live to see their twenties."

"A lot don't."

"You're sure she was dead when you saw her?"

It was the same question Connelly had asked me, and I gave George the same answer I'd given him. "Yeah. I'm sure. She was crumpled up. She wasn't moving. I saw some blood. If she wasn't dead, she was doing a really good impersonation."

George asked another question. "And no one knew you were inside the warehouse?" I guess he couldn't help playing cop, even if he wasn't one any more. After seven years on the force, the habit was too well-ingrained. But I didn't mind going along. I could use all the help I could get.

"I don't think so. My car was parked in the back. Whoever did this would have had to have driven through the alleyway to see the cab."

"And the gunshot that set everything off came from the street?"

I nodded. "Why? What are you getting at?"

George reached over and moved the bowl of pretzels closer. "I'm just thinking out loud."

"I'm listening."

"I'm just wondering if whoever did this wanted to kill you, too."

I snapped a corner of the pretzel off. Tiny brown crumbs rained down on the bar as I played the other night's events back in my mind. "I'd say the odds are against it. I'm pretty sure I wasn't followed and, unless someone had a reason to, they wouldn't drive around to the back. No. I think I was just in the wrong place at the wrong time. As per usual."

"Well, if it was inconvenient for you, think what it was for the killer."

"True."

"Because if you hadn't come along, everyone would have assumed some nut job was squatting, there was a gas leak, and bang!—the place blew up. Very unfortunate, but these things happen all the time. Too bad. End of case. On to the next." George gave a pretzel to Zsa Zsa. She dropped it on the bar and began licking the salt off it.

I reached over and picked a burr I'd missed off her ear. "Establishing cause of death would certainly be harder, that's for sure."

"Yeah. Crispy critters don't cut up so good."

The laugher of the college kids erupted in spiked peaks, taking over the room. Ebsen Fields glared at them and went back to reading.

George took a gulp of beer. "Those kids think they own the world."

"You did, too, when you were their age."

"No I didn't. If you're black, you know you don't." He opened his mouth to say something else, changed his mind, and grabbed another pretzel. I could hear the crunch as he chewed. Watching the jutting of his jaw muscles, I realized that this was the first time I'd heard him mention what it was like to be African-American. I waited to hear what was coming next, but he went back to talking about Melanie. I guess it was a more comfortable topic. Maybe it was for me too, because I didn't bring the other back up. "Do you think Amy knows something about Melanie's death?" George asked.

I recalled Amy's ashen face when she heard the news. She'd been shocked. And scared. "Yeah, I think she does."

He traced an invisible crack on the bar with his finger. "You think Melanie's death is related to Dennis Richmond's?"

"Definitely. Don't you?"

"I'm not sure. What do you think the link between the two deaths is?"

"I'd like to say Toon Town, but I can't because I don't know if he was up in Dennis Richmond's apartment or not." I reached for a cigarette before I realized I wasn't smoking. "So even though I don't want to, I'm going to have to say Amy. She was involved with both people." I wound a lock of my hair around my finger, as I thought aloud. "So far we've got two deaths, Dennis Richmond's apartment was searched, my house has been burglarized, and my store has been vandalized, and all the above happened within a relatively short period of time. I didn't think there was a connection with everything before, but now, looking back, I do."

George ran a finger around the the rim of his glass. "Personally I think the two homicides are related, but that's all."

"What makes you say that?"

"The MOs in the break-ins are different. Let's start with Richmond. A homicide and an apparent robbery."

I interrupted. "His place was pulled apart."

"Hey," George replied. "I've seen guys pull the light sockets out of the wall looking for money." He continued. "As for your place, I think that was a straight B&E—some kids looking for a quick score—and the store we can lay at Toon Town's feet."

"So you believe in the randomness of the universe?"

George stretched. "Do you believe everything is connected?"

"I'm not sure," I replied, after thinking over my answer for a minute. "That concept has theological implications I'm not sure I'm willing to entertain right now."

George laughed, picked up a pretzel crumb, and deposited it in the ashtray. "I'll tell you one thing, though. And this I'm certain of: Amy is definitely Murphy's daughter."

"Yeah. She has his genes. Chaos follows wherever she goes. Kind of like Mary and her lamb."

George let out a sad little sigh. "Funny thing is I still miss the guy. I miss our Tuesday night pool games."

"That's because you always won."

"He was good company." A ghost of a smile flitted across George's face, and I knew he was remembering their past adventures. "We should take a couple of beers out to the cemetery and go visit him."

"Let's," I agreed. It was time. I hadn't been back since the funeral, because I hadn't been able to face it. And I switched to a less painful topic. "Did you ever get hold of your cousin?"

George took another sip of his beer before answering.

"He doesn't know anything about the Richmond family. I told you he wouldn't."

"Well, it was worth trying."

George frowned and narrowed his eyes. "I don't know how that man gets through the day." His leg began to vibrate. "He's going to end up on a slab if he's not careful."

I changed the subject again. It seemed as if I were doing a lot of that this evening. "I wonder who is going to get Dennis's half of the business, now that he's dead?"

"His wife and children, I would assume."

"Not necessarily." I recalled the scene I'd witnessed between Gerri and Brad Richmond. "His share could revert to the surviving partner."

"Why don't you ask Gerri?"

"Funny, man."

George tapped his fingers on the counter. Then he said, "So do you believe what Amy's telling you?"

"I believe she's scared. I believe she's drugged up. I believe she's running. But from who or what, I couldn't say."

"Why do you think she came back to your house?"

"I don't know. I didn't get a chance to ask her. When she heard about Melanie, she freaked. I wonder if she said anything to Manuel?" I mused.

"Wouldn't he tell you?"

"Not unless I asked. Which I'm going to do right now." I slid off the bar stool, told Zsa Zsa to stay, and went and called my house. Manuel was in.

"So?" George said when I sat back down.

"Well, the good news is that Connelly called in. They've got Melanie's last name."

George smiled. "You must be going up in his estimation."

"I don't think so. He actually wanted to know if Manuel or I had heard from Amy yet."

"So what did Manuel say?"

"He said he hadn't."

"Did you ask him if she said what she wanted?"

I nodded. "He said Amy was babbling on about how she's scared she's being watched."

"Did she say by whom?"

"No. Manuel thinks her brain's fried and she's totally whacked out."

George grimaced. "He should know."

I drew myself up. "What does that mean?"

"What do you think it means?"

"He doesn't do that much stuff," I protested.

George snorted. "What world are you living in?"

"Boy, Ebsen isn't the only one in a pissy mood."

"I just think you should get that kid out of your house."

"What do you care?" I snapped. I didn't like George's tone.

"I just don't think you're doing Manuel any favors by helping him out."

"What's this? Your tough love speech? Given your family situation, I think you're the one that needs it, not me."

George didn't answer. He didn't even look at me. His face had become a blank. His jaw muscles had formed knots. He dropped some money on the bar, stood up, and walked out.

Way to go, Robin. Zsa Zsa barked and I gave her an absent-minded pat. I would have apologized, but I knew it wouldn't do any good. You can't talk to George when he gets angry. You have to let him cool down first. Anyway, what I said was true. I just should have said it differently. Oh well. I wound a lock of hair around my finger. George and his family really weren't any of my business, anyway. At least not yet. But they were going to be, if we kept going out together. I sighed and finished my beer. The perfect ending to a perfect day.

I paid my bill and walked out the door.

Chapter 22

The temperature had fallen since I'd been inside, and my windshield was etched with whirls of frost. I used the edge of one of my maxed-out credit cards to scrape it clean—it was about all it was good for these days. Then I got in the cab and took off. But I didn't go home. My fight with George had made me restless, and I wanted something to do, so I drove over to TJ's instead. I wanted to ask him if he knew Amy or Toon Town. It was a long shot, but TJ dealt what Amy used, and there was always a chance that they were hooked up in some way. And while I was at it, I wanted to see what, if anything, Manuel was up to. George's comments had reawakened this afternoon's concerns.

TJ had recently moved to a ground floor apartment on Dell Street which he shared with three other sixteen-year-olds, none of whom turned out to be there tonight. I'd been there once before. The apartment was furnished with ripped furniture, the windows were covered with tacked-up sheets, the walls needed to be painted—but it housed a large TV, a VCR, a state-of-the-art stereo system, and the biggest bong I'd ever seen. The door was always unlocked, so I pushed it open and walked in. The smell of marijuana hit me. I took a deep breath and thought about the days when I had nothing better to do than to lay around and get stoned.

TJ was lying on the sofa in front of the TV watching *Cops,* drinking a forty, and stroking Cuddles. The Burmese was curled in a ball on his chest.

I pointed to the snake. "He's still doing well."

TJ looked in my direction and smiled. "Yeah. I'm feeding him three mice a week. He's growing real fast. How's it going?"

"Not bad. Don't feed him too much though. If you do, you'll make him sick."

TJ put Cuddles on one of the cushions and sat up. He had buzzed and bleached his hair and added a couple more earrings to his left ear since I'd seen him last. The hair cut emphasized the delicacy of his features. "I know. He threw up on me once already."

I moved a load of clothes off an armchair and onto the table and sat down. "You're definitely moving up in the world."

He put his forty down on the floor, sat forward, and leaned his elbows on his knees. "I'm trying. Give people good value for their money, and they'll always come back."

"Very commendable." The Young Republicans would have been proud of him.

"So what's up? You wanna buy something? I got some good shit."

I laughed. "No. I'm afraid those days are long gone. I'm looking for some information."

"About what?" TJ tugged on the sleeve of his flannel shirt. It looked as if it had come from the Salvation Army.

"Amy Richmond. You know her?"

TJ nodded.

"You know where I can find her?"

He shook his head. "I haven't seen her in awhile."

"That's too bad, because she's out on the street. She's involved in some bad stuff, and I'd like to bring her in before things get even worse."

"She still with that geek boyfriend of hers? Toon Town?"

I nodded.

TJ rubbed the side of his nose. "He's a deeply disturbed dude. He thinks he's James Bond."

"How do you mean?"

TJ sat back and reflectively fingered the thermal shirt he was wearing under his flannel. "Just what I said. He's always screwing around with this electronic stuff. I don't know what she sees in him. 'Ask me, she needs a few good whacks on the ass."

"Why is that?"

"Well I come from a shithole. I ain't got no choice. But Amy, she's got a nice home, nice clothes. So her old man was a douche bag. So what?" TJ laughed. "Listen to me. I sound pretty good, don't I?"

"Absolutely. Schools should hire you."

"I'd do better than DARE."

"Probably." From what I heard about that program, he would. "So where you moving to?"

"Moving?" TJ gave me an incredulous look. "Why the hell should I move? I just got here."

"Manuel said you were paying him twenty dollars to help him move."

"I ain't paying him shit." TJ sat forward and started

jabbing his finger in the air. "In fact he still owes me forty bucks. You talk to him, tell him I'll beat his ass next time I see him iffen I don't get it."

"So you didn't speak to him today?"

"I haven't spoken to him in six weeks."

The kid was dead. I got up and went home.

But Manuel wasn't there.

The house lights were on. So was the TV. A couple of cans of soda and an opened, empty pizza box from Little Caesars sat on the coffee table. I wondered who had been here, as I gathered up the debris and slam-dunked it in the garbage can in the kitchen.

"You are out of here," I said out loud.

This was it. Manuel was going. I hated to admit it, but George was right. I clomped upstairs and went to bed.

Surprisingly, I fell asleep instantly. For some reason, I dreamt about Murphy and our dog Elise. They were riding on a bus in Amsterdam when it was rerouted to Oslo, only I was supposed to meet them in Lima and no one could tell me how to get to the new stop. I woke up with my heart pounding. I watched the sky out the window. It was gunmetal grey. Thin streaks of rain hit the windowpanes—definitely not the kind of weather that made you want to get up in the morning. I dragged myself out of bed anyway and walked into Manuel's bedroom. It was empty. He hadn't come back yet. My anger from last night came back full force. But there was nothing I could do about it now, so I went back in my bedroom, turned off my alarm, and got ready for work.

Before I left, I taped a note to the hall mirror telling Manuel to phone me the instant he got in. Then I called for Zsa Zsa and went outside. It had stopped raining. The clouds had thinned a little. A few remaining tattered leaves fluttered on the branches of the cherry tree in front of my house, the rest lay on the ground in a sodden carpet. I heard honking and looked up. A flock of geese was heading south. Most had left weeks ago. I wished I were going along.

I got in my car, stopped along the way for coffee and doughnuts, and drove to the store. Around ten o'clock, after I'd finished cleaning out the bird cages, I checked in with Toon Town's mother again.

"He still hasn't come home," she told me. I could tell from the irritated tone in her voice she was getting tired of my calling. I heard kids screaming in the background. "I baby-sit a couple of times a week," she explained, even though I hadn't asked. "You should try the store."

Obviously her son hadn't told her he'd been fired.

"Wally is a good boy," his mother continued. I wanted to point out Jack the Ripper's mother had probably said the same thing, but I didn't. "He's a genius. He can fix anything." I heard shrieks. "I have to go," she said, and hung up.

As I started in on the teddy bear hamsters, I decided that a trip to Toon Town's house might be in order. At eleven thirty, I tried my home. Manuel didn't answer. Either he was asleep, or he hadn't come home yet. That didn't improve my mood. I tapped my fingers on the counter. I felt restless. I needed to do something. I could have washed the bird room floor but I decided to make some calls instead. The first was to Gerri Richmond. I was going to ask if her daughter had phoned, but she hung up on me before I could. I took care of the fish and called Brad. Elizabeth Walker came on the line and told me he was out for the day.

"That must make things nice for you," I observed.

"Yeah. I like it. It's quieter."

"So, any more fights since the last time I was there?"

She stifled a giggle. "Charlie and Frank really are a pair, aren't they?"

"They certainly are. Why do they hate each other so much?"

"I dunno. I guess they both want to be president."

I watched Mr. Bones yawn and marveled yet again at the needle sharpness of his canines. "Who do you think would be better?"

"A couple of years ago I would have said Charlie, but now I'd have to go with Frank."

"Why's that?"

"Because Charlie isn't always all there, if you know what I mean."

"I thought he worked all the time."

"He does, but that's not what I meant."

"Are you talking drugs?"

There was a long pause. "You won't tell anyone what I said will you?" She sounded panicked.

I assured her I wouldn't.

"Good." She let out her breath. "Because I really need this job. My mother always said I had a big mouth. I guess she was right." And she got off the phone.

I tried Frank Richmond next. After six rings, an answering machine clicked on and offered to take a message. I hung up and tried Charlie Richmond. Maybe he'd heard from his sister. I doubted it, but it never hurt to ask. He picked up on the third ring. Which surprised me. Given the way my luck was running, I'd expected a machine.

"Have you found her?" he asked, the moment he heard my voice on the line.

So much for my question. I told him I hadn't.

"Because my father's funeral is the day after tomorrow. It would be nice if she attended."

"I'll tell her if I see her." I took Mr. Bones out of his cage and put him down on the floor. He and Zsa Zsa began playing tag.

"I should have listened to Gerri and hired someone else," Charlie continued. "A professional. He would have located her by now."

"You're still free to," I observed.

"I might do that. I'm having trouble sleeping at night, thinking of her out there."

"That's an interesting comment." Charlie sounded as if he were reading soap opera cue cards. I lit a cigarette.

"Why do you say that?" he demanded.

"Because Frank told me you and Amy never got along. He said you two disliked each other. Intensely. He hinted that you just wanted me to find her, so you could turn her over to the police."

"Why would I want to do that?"

I told him the rest of what Frank had said.

"And you believe him?" Charlie's voice vibrated with indignation.

"I'm not sure."

"Frank has always hated me."

"Why's that?"

"Because he's jealous."

"Of you?"

"That's right. No one in the family likes him. He's always in trouble, always doing the wrong thing."

"As opposed to you?"

"Hey, at least I've tried. That's more than you can say for Frank. He's never here and when he is, he's fucking up. I've had to cover his ass, I don't want to tell you how many times. While he's been out screwing around, I've been working six, seven days a week, ten hours a day."

Not exactly the picture Elizabeth Walker had painted for me, I thought, as I shifted the receiver from my left to my right ear.

"So I wouldn't believe anything Frank says," Charlie continued. "The man is a congenital liar. Ask anyone."

"Maybe I will."

"You do that." Charlie hung up.

So much for the Richmond family.

As long as I was doing unpleasant, I decided to ring up my house again. No answer. I tried again at two and four with the same results. I tried Manuel's house. He wasn't there either. I even tried Rabbit's, but Manuel had been telling the truth about that one. Rabbit was still in Watertown. If it had been someone else, I might have begun getting nervous, but I figured Manuel was holed up at someone's house sleeping one off. Eventually he'd show up and I'd have it out with him. I was thinking about what I was going to say, when the first customers of the day walked in. I put Manuel out of my mind and got to work. When Tim came on at five thirty I got out the phone book, jotted down Toon Town's mother's address, and took off.

Mrs. Natalie Gleason lived on the north side in the shadow of St. Ann's on a block composed of tired looking, asphalt-shingled, two– and three–family dwellings. They were the kind of places that had never seen better days. When I rang the bell, the woman that answered the door was so thin she appeared almost skeletal. Her eyes were a faded blue and her scalp shone pink under her thin, dun colored hair. She had no features in common with her son at all.

"Mrs. Gleason, I'm here about Wallace," I began.

She frowned and put her hands on her hips. "You're the one that's been calling, aren't you? I recognize the voice."

I nodded.

"I already told you, he ain't here."

"Since I was driving by, I thought I'd just stop and check."

"Well, you could have saved yourself the trouble."

"I wonder if I can come in and talk?"

She studied me for a minute. "You ain't a cop, right?"

"Right." I would have lied, but I was pretty sure she'd ask for my ID.

"Then I don't have to talk to you. And don't call no more, neither. My son says all you're looking to do is cause trouble." She slammed the door shut.

Well at least I'd been right about one thing. She *had* spoken to him. As I walked back to my car, I kept an eye out for Toon Town's lime-green Geo Tracker, but I didn't see it. I looked at my watch. It was now a quarter to six. Maybe Toon Town was the home cooked dinner type, though given his mother, I couldn't imagine what the meal would be. I decided to invest a little time and find out. I spent the next hour and fifteen minutes slumped down in the seat of my cab, observing Ms. Gleason's chateau, smoking Camels, and trying to figure out what I wanted to do with the rest of my life. But I didn't come up with any answers.

Around seven, I got bored and drove over to the house where I'd last seen Toon Town and Amy. Unfortunately there was an addition since the last time I'd been here. A "For Sale" sign was planted on the front lawn. I would have preferred a plastic pink flamingo. I told myself it didn't mean anything. Whoever lived here was probably still around—sometimes it took a year or more for a house to sell—but the part of me that always looks at the glass and sees it half empty didn't believe that. I got out and rang the bell even though the house was dark and the driveway was empty. Naturally no one answered. I opened the mailbox lid. Still no mail. Now, I could have gone home and called the realtor and seen what I could find out from him or her. But that would have meant I would have had to wait until tomorrow, and I wasn't in the mood to do that.

I turned and studied the area. The houses on either side of the one I was standing in front of appeared to be empty—not atypical in a day and age when everyone works. I glanced across the street. The people in those two houses were home, but it occurred to me it didn't really matter if they were watching me or not. The "For Sale" sign gave me a perfect excuse to be prowling around. I headed down the driveway, stopping here and there to look at foundation plantings, until I reached the utility door. It was hedged on either side by several transparent garbage bags full of beer bottles and cans. Whoever lived here was a big supporter of the brewing industry.

I pushed the bags aside and inspected the lock on the door. It was a deadbolt. No way could I pick that. I went around to the back. Someone had conveniently put a deck, which now took up most of the backyard, on the rear of the house. I walked up the three steps and studied the lock on the door that led, I was willing to wager, into the kitchen. Another deadbolt. Something cold hit my nose.

I glanced up. A few snowflakes were swirling out of the sky. Maybe it was a sign from God to go home. I ignored it and took the measure of the window. From what I could see, it didn't have a latch. I took off the storm and carefully leaned it against the wall. Then I pushed up on the window. It didn't budge. I pushed harder. It gave a little. I pulled up as hard as I could. It moved about a foot—just enough space for me to wiggle through. A moment later, I was standing inside, hoping that no one had seen me and was even now dialing the police. At this point, my story about wanting to buy the house was not going to work.

I looked around. The white kitchen counters poked out of the dark like bones. I opened the refrigerator. It housed three six packs of Miller and a can of Comet. The cabinets held a box of plastic spoons, knives, and forks, a stack of paper plates, four mugs, a couple of pots, a box of cereal, and salt. Unfortunately, it looked as if my hunch had been right. Whoever was living here was in the process of moving out. I continued on into the next room. It was a combination dining/alcove/living room. The room was bare. It smelled of rug shampoo. I touched the carpet with the tips of my fingers. It was slightly damp. Someone had washed it recently.

Three packing cartons sat in the middle of the floor. I crossed over and looked in them. Two were empty and one contained an iron, a clock, a roll of toilet paper, and a bunch of coat hangers. I was putting everything back when I heard a car. I froze as the light from its headlights seeped through the blinds, tracing their shapes on the walls. Then a few seconds later, the car was gone and the wall was dark.

I straightened up and headed upstairs. The steps were covered with the same kind of carpet—probably something beige, it was impossible to tell in the dark—the downstairs was. I went up the stairs slowly, my footsteps cushioned by the pile. When I got to the landing, I stood still for a moment and waited for my eyes to become accustomed to the dark. There were four doors. I chose the closest one and stepped in. The first thing I noticed was the floor was hard. Then I saw glints of white. I was in the bathroom. I took a chance and switched on the light. The vanity lights over the mirror were so bright I blinked. An amoeba-like blob of red swam in front of my eyes. A second later it was gone and I looked around.

The bathroom was all white. The two blue towels hanging

over the rack matched the shower curtain. A bottle of Head and Shoulders sat over on the far corner of the tub. I opened the door to the medicine cabinet. It contained a couple of toothbrushes, dental floss, a can of shaving cream, a razor, a stick of deoderant, a bottle of aspirin, a comb, a brush, and a bar of soap. Nothing that couldn't be bought in Fay's. Nothing that was in any way unusual. The only thing I now knew was that two people were staying here. I closed the door and went into the first bedroom. It was empty. So was the closet.

I went on to the next room.

Aside from a couple of magazines lying in one corner and a stack of newspapers lying in the other, it was empty too. I went over and picked up the magazines. They were both high-end travel magazines. As I put them back down, I began feeling as if I'd wandered onto the stage set of a play in progress, only I didn't know which play it was. I shook my head to dispel the image and went on to the next room. At least here there was furniture. A twin bed sat in one corner. A small dresser stood along the opposite wall. The sight heartened me, because it meant the owner hadn't moved out yet. Tomorrow I'd call the realtor, tell her I was interested, and try and get a name. I opened the drawers. They were empty, of course.

I turned my attention to the desk by the closet. The middle drawer contained pens, pencils, and envelopes. I closed it and opened the two drawers on either side. Nothing. No address book. No bank statements. No credit card receipts. Did whoever live here exist? Were they real? I was beginning to get the feeling they weren't. I tried the closet next. Except for a dozen or so wire coat hangers, it was empty. They jangled as I stepped inside. An old cloth Starter jacket was hanging, forlorn and forgotten, by the far wall.

For form's sake, I took it out and went through the pockets. I found five pennies, a stick of gum, and a couple of old, discolored aspirin tablets that were beginning to dissolve around the edges. I was putting the jacket back when I heard a jingle. Okay. There was something else inside. I took the jacket out into the hall where there was more light and turned the pockets inside out. There was a hole in the left one. Ordinarily I wouldn't have bothered, but I was in a perverse mood, so I worked my fingers through it and into the lining. I fished out a couple of quarters, a dime, and a crumpled up piece of heavy paper.

I put the jacket back where I'd found it, went back to the bathroom, closed the door, and turned on the light. Then I smoothed the paper out. Once it had been white, now it was stained and grimy. The bottom half was ripped off, but it was still possible to make out the type on the card's upper half.

It contained three words. Syracuse Casket Company.

Chapter 23

I kept glancing at the card I'd found as I drove across town to the store. It was suggestive, all right, but of what? That was the question. I wouldn't know until I talked to the Starter jacket's owner, and I couldn't do that until I talked to the realtor tomorrow. Maybe I was finally on to something. God only knows, it was about time for my luck to change. I stopped at Noah's Ark, picked up Zsa Zsa, who let me know she didn't appreciate being left alone by peeing on the floor, and headed for home.

James came out to greet me when I opened the door of my house. He and Zsa Zsa did their little dance, while I thumbed through the day's mail. Even though the lights were on, the house was quiet. I noticed the note I'd taped to the mirror wasn't there. I called for Manuel, but he didn't answer. He'd come and gone. The anger I'd been holding in check since last night welled up again. When I walked into the living room, I noticed a crumpled up MacDonald's bag and a half-full cup of soda sitting on the coffee table. My note was lying beside it. I picked it up. *Sorry,* Manuel had scrawled on the bottom of the page. *I know you must be pissed. I'll explain everything tomorrow. p.s. I bought James some cat food. Salmon. He really loves it.*

I crumpled up the note and threw it back down. At least he'd had the decency to write something. I'd be really interested to hear what he had to say. I poured myself a Scotch and headed up the stairs. The door to Manuel's room was open. I looked in. The bedcovers were rumpled. He must have come in, gone to sleep, and left again. I shook my head. The longer he stayed with me, the more I sympathized with his stepfather.

I went into my room, set my glass on the night table, shucked off my clothes, and crawled into bed. Then I tossed down my shot, turned off the light, and closed my eyes. But sleep wouldn't come. I lay awake watching the cedar branches tossing in the wind and listening to Zsa Zsa making little whimpering noises in her sleep and wondering where the hell Manuel was and who had been eating pizza in my house. And then I started thinking about Toon Town and Amy and trying to figure out what a card from the Syracuse Casket Company was doing in the Starter jacket's pocket and worrying about the leak in my roof. At some point I must have drifted off though, because the next thing I knew, I heard my alarm ringing.

When I went off to work, Manuel still hadn't returned. Not that I was surprised. I really hadn't expected him to. The clarity of the sky dazzled me when I stepped outside. Its blue washed over me and I found myself smiling, as I noticed a cardinal perched on a branch of the Japanese maple across the street. As I walked to the car, I realized the air smelled of burning leaves, the way it had when I was younger. A little way down the block, two of my neighbors were standing on the sidewalk drinking coffee and watching their children play. I would have liked to have joined them, but I had too much to do, so I waved and drove by. On the way to the store, I phoned the Happy House Realty Company from the car, but none of the brokers were in, so I told the secretary which property I was interested in and asked to have an agent call me back. Around eleven thirty one did.

Monica Selles started right in with her pitch. "It's a really good buy," she said. Her voice was just a hair's breath away from being chirpy. "It's got new carpeting, a new deck, and the upstairs bathroom was redone last year. The owner is very anxious to sell."

"It appears empty. Has the owner moved out?"

"Actually, he's been renting it for the past year."

I shifted into concerned prospective buyer. "Oh. To whom? Not students I hope. They always make such an incredible mess."

"Oh, I agree. No. These were working people."

"Really? Where did they work?"

"I'm not sure. Would you like to see the house?"

I didn't, since I already had, but if I wanted any more information, I would have to. I made an appointment to meet her at the house at two o'clock and got back to work.

Tim was not pleased when I told him I was running out for an hour. He was tired of holding things down on his own, he told me. I mollified him by promising to pick up some KFC on the way back.

Monica Silles was waiting for me when I got to the house. She was a well-dressed woman somewhere in her forties who looked as if she did this for pin money. A doctor's wife, maybe. Someone who wanted something to do, but nothing too strenuous.

"Let's go inside," she suggested, brightly.

"So what's the story with the owner?" I asked, as she put the key in the lock box. "How anxious are they to sell?"

"It's a corporation, really."

I almost groaned. That meant I'd have to pay a visit to the County Clerk's Office to see who the corporation's officers were—unless, of course, Silles knew. I asked. She didn't.

"A corporation owning a home. That's unusual," I said still fishing around.

Monica Silles shrugged. "I've seen it done before. People do it for tax purposes, or when they're trying to limit their liability." She stepped inside, and I followed.

In the light, the house looked bland and boring.

Monica Silles gestured around. "As you can see the place is in move-in shape. Just get some curtains on those windows and you'll be ready to go."

I nodded. "What's the name of the corporation?"

The realtor consulted the file she was holding. "Maxwell."

I hadn't heard of it, but then there was no reason I should have.

Silles took me into the kitchen."The asking price is $65,000."

That is one thing about living in a depressed area. Real estate prices are low. You can get a really nice house in Syracuse for not much money. Of course, if you have to sell and go someplace else, you're in trouble.

I opened and closed cabinet doors and turned the water tap in the sink on and off. If you're going to pretend, go all the way. "That's a bit high for this neighborhood, don't you think?"

Silles pursed her lips. "I might be able to get them to come down a little."

We climbed the stairs and went through the three bedrooms.

A chill worked its way up my back when I opened the door to the closet in the third bedroom.

The jacket was gone.

Someone had been here since last night.

I wondered who.

I turned back to Monica Silles, who was chatting on about the benefits of this particular house. "Now, let's suppose I wanted to buy this place for an investment," I said.

Silles stopped talking. She cocked her head slightly to the side and waited to hear what I had to say.

"Would you handle the rentals, as you did for the Maxwell Company?"

"We don't do that sort of thing." Silles frowned, to show she thought her company should. "Maxwell handled the rentals themselves."

"I see." I studied the view out the window. Two squirrels were chasing each other up and down the branches of a maple tree. "Perhaps I could speak to someone at Maxwell to see what their rental experience was like. You know, kind of get a feel for the thing."

Monica Silles looked doubtful, but she put on a game smile. Anything for a sale, I guess. "I can call and ask."

"What are they like?"

"Frankly, I don't know. I've never dealt with them."

It looked as if I'd gotten as much out of Silles as I was going to. We walked down the stairs together. I looked at my watch. It was a little before three. I still had time to make it down to the County Clerk's Office. I told Silles I'd get back to her with my decision. She pressed her card into my hand and warned me not to wait too long. I told her I wouldn't and took off.

Parking around the County Courthouse was impossible—as per usual—and after circling three or four times, I pulled up in front of a fire hydrant and went inside. It took about half an hour to locate the information I'd come to find.

I stared down at the photocopy the clerk had handed me.

Brad and Dennis Richmond were listed as the president and vice president of The Maxwell Corporation.

Somehow I wasn't surprised.

Whichever way I turned, I seemed to bump up against the Richmond family.

Chapter 24

I absentmindedly folded up the pages I'd been given and stuffed them in my backpack, as I walked out the door. I clicked my tongue against my teeth while I thought.

So Amy had been staying in a place that the Richmond family owned.

Interesting.

I wondered if Brad Richmond knew about it.

Then I wondered if the Starter jacket was his. But I didn't think so. Try as I might, I couldn't picture him wearing it.

I checked my watch again. It was almost four. Maybe Brad Richmond was back in his office. I used one of the pay phones on the first floor of the courthouse to dial the factory and find out. According to the receptionist, he was in.

"Shall I connect you?" she asked.

I told her I'd changed my mind, I'd call again tomorrow, and hung up. I needed to speak to Richmond in person. Talking over the phone just wasn't going to do it. Then, before I realized what I was doing, I reached into my bag, got out my cigarettes, lit one, and inhaled. Last one for the day, I promised myself, and headed for the door.

It had gotten darker out since I'd been inside. And gustier. I buttoned my jacket and turned up my collar, but the wind still found a way in. It tugged at my hair and whispered in my ears as I hurried to the cab. While I unlocked the door, I noticed clouds were building up in the west. We were in for another storm. I drove quickly, weaving through the increasing late afternoon traffic. The cars had their lights on. Everyone was driving fast, anxious to get home after a day at work. The sky was banded with streaks of pale pink, light grey, charcoal, and black. Road, median, grass, and trees all looked smudged in the dusk.

Because of the traffic, it took me almost half an hour to get to the plant. I spent the time thinking of what I was going to say to Richmond, wondering what he was going to say to me, and smoking another cigarette. I was about to light a third one, but I tossed it and the pack out the window instead. Then I was sorry I'd done it, but it was too late. Even I realized it would be suicidal to try and retrieve them.

When I got to the lot, I parked in one of the spaces set aside for visitors and entered the building. The receptionist wasn't at her station, which was fine with me, because I didn't want to be announced. I just opened the door to the offices and went inside. As I walked down the corridor, I caught sight of her chatting with a coworker. I'm sure she would have stopped me if she'd seen me, but her head was half-turned and she was deep into her conversation. I nodded at the people I passed and they nodded back at me. No one asked me what I was doing there.

Luck was with me, because Elizabeth Walker wasn't at her desk either. She was probably getting ready to go home. I could see Brad Richmond from where I was standing. He was sitting at his desk. His head was bent. He was reading a computer printout and making notes on a yellow legal pad he had in front of him. His head shot up when I said hello.

"How did you get in without being announced?" he demanded. He looked annoyed at being interrupted, or perhaps he was just angry at being made to look foolish.

"I walked in. No one was at the front desk." I pulled over the leather chair from the side of the room and sat down.

That annoyed him even more. He placed his hands on the edge of his desk and pushed himself back. "Exactly what is it you want? Because I'm busy. I have things to do before I leave." He gestured at the papers on his desk.

"I just want to ask you about the house."

He did puzzled. "My house?"

"The one on Easton Avenue. The one that's held by The Maxwell Corporation."

"Oh that." He gave a small, little laugh. "We own a fair number of properties." He put his pen down. He tried looking bored, but he wasn't succeeding very well. "What about it?"

"I was driving by and I noticed it was for sale. I was thinking of buying it."

"Really?" Richmond raised an eyebrow to convey his disbelief.

"Yes, really. The realtor told me you had rented the place. I wanted to know how the arrangement worked out."

Richmond rolled his pen between the palms of his hands.

"I wouldn't know. You'd have to ask Gerri. She's the one that handles the rentals."

Now it was my turn to raise an eyebrow. "I didn't think she had anything to do with the company."

"Just this. It was Dennis's decision. Gave her something to do besides shopping." Richmond put his pen down. "Of course now that we're selling the properties, she's going to be out of a job." He gave a grim little smile of satisfaction.

"May I ask why you're selling?"

"I never liked the idea of diversifying in the first place. And since Dennis is no longer here, I'm going to put the money back where it belongs—in the business."

"Doesn't Gerri Richmond have a say?"

Brad's smile grew broader. "Not when it comes to something like this. Now, if that's all. I really have to catch someone before they leave for the day."

I thanked him for his time and got up to go. I was at the door when I turned around. "One last question."

"Yes?" he growled.

"Did you know that Amy was staying there?"

He opened his eyes a little wider. "Was she, now?"

"Yes."

"Imagine that." He shook his head in amazement.

I couldn't tell if he was lying about not knowing or not.

On the way out, I spotted Elizabeth Walker and Charlie Richmond talking together. Elizabeth seemed to be fascinated with what Charlie Richmond had to say, and I couldn't help thinking, as I watched her, that she was going to go far in life. She definitely had the ability to say one thing and do another. He made another comment and she laughed and strolled away. She was almost at the corridor when she saw me. She did a double take and came over.

"What are you doing here?" she blurted out, obviously surprised to see me.

"I just dropped in to have a little chat with your boss."

A worried expression crossed her face. "You didn't have an appointment, did you?" she asked.

"No."

"Because I didn't think you were marked down in the book."

"I wasn't," I assured her. "I just took a chance and walked in."

She sighed in relief and placed a hand across her chest. "Good, because Mr. Richmond would really be upset if I'd forgotten to let him know."

"So what did Charlie have to say?"

Elizabeth flushed and began to fidget. "He wants me to go out with him. It's tough," she continued, when I didn't say anything. "I can't be rude to him, but he doesn't take no for an answer."

"From where I was standing, it looked as if you were enjoying yourself."

Elizabeth's mouth crumpled. "He gets really mad if I act like I'm not interested in what he has to say. It's really hard. Usually I try and stay away from him. But once in awhile, he catches me." She gave a fatalistic shrug.

"Have you talked to anyone?"

"I don't want to make trouble. It's not like he has his hands all over me or anything like that."

"Maybe you should talk to your boss. I have a feeling he might like to do something about the situation."

"Thanks." She leaned over and gave me a quick hug. "Thanks a lot." She walked away, and I continued down the hallway. The office staff eddied and flowed around me. They were putting on their coats and chatting with each other as they got ready to go home. As I drove out of the lot, I called Gerri Richmond. I wanted to let her know about Amy staying at the house on Easton, but no one was home. I left a message on the machine and headed off to KFC.

"The least you could have done was call," Tim grumbled, when I walked in the door. "You're two hours late. I can't do all of this by myself." He gestured towards the boxes of cat products that needed to be unpacked and shelved.

I apologized and handed Tim his dinner. He accepted it grudgingly. "Did Manuel call?"

"Nope." Tim went in the back to eat. Zsa Zsa and Pickles followed behind him.

Actually I wasn't expecting Manuel to. I figured he'd roll in somewhere between three and four in the morning. But I was wrong. He was waiting for me when I got home from work. He must have been listening for the car, because he opened the door as I was about to put my key in the lock.

"Listen," Manuel began. "I know you must be really pissed and I'm really sorry about the way I've been acting for the last couple of days. If you'll just give me a chance to explain. . . ."

"You've got to be kidding." I stepped into the hall and put my backpack down on the table. "I want you out of here."

Manuel tugged his pants up. "You've been real nice to let me stay here and I've been a shmuck."

"No. You've been a liar. I spoke to TJ."

Manuel became absorbed in studying the cracks in the floor. He twisted the heel of his left foot back and forth. "I guess you want to hear what's been going on."

"Actually I don't give a shit." I walked into the kitchen.

"Come on Robin, don't be like that," Manuel pleaded, as he dogged my footsteps.

"How do you expect me to be?" I demanded. Then I stopped short. The counters were clean, the sink was gleaming, so was the floor.

"I did the upstairs too." Manuel went over to the refrigerator and opened the door. "See," he said, pointing to the pan sitting on the top shelf. "I even made us meatloaf. I figured we could talk while I heat it up." I didn't say anything, but I was wavering, and Manuel knew it. "Please Robin," he begged. "At least listen to me."

"All right," I conceded, sitting down. "But it had better be good."

Manuel's smile lit up his face. He turned on the oven, put in the meatloaf, along with some garlic bread, and sat down across from me. He proceeded to spin a long complicated story having to do with a friend named Jamal, his girlfriend, the girl's brother, hiding out, an abortion, money owed, a flat tire, and a fight out in the parking lot at Fay's.

"You believe me, don't you?" he asked when he was done. He looked at me anxiously, while he waited to hear what I was about to say.

"Yes." The story was too complicated and stupid for a lie.

"Good." Relieved, he leaned back in his chair.

"Why didn't you tell me this in the first place?"

He shrugged. "I don't know." James jumped up on the table and Manuel started to pet him. "I guess 'cause I didn't want you to think I was some kind of jerk. I mean these guys are my friends, right? What could I do?" He lapsed into silence.

I was about to say, "find some new ones" when the phone rang.

It was a collect call from Amy.

I told the operator I'd accept the charges. Amy got on a

moment later. Her speech was slurred. She sounded drunk. Or stoned. She was rambling, but I didn't want to interrupt her because I was afraid that if I did, she'd hang up on me.

"I dyed my hair," she told me. "Now it's black."

"It must look nice," I said, even though I was fairly sure it looked horrible. Black was the one color no one should ever dye their hair. It looked like shoe polish.

"No it doesn't. I hate it." She started to cry. "Everything is so complicated," she said, between sobs.

Manuel's head was practically resting on my shoulder, as he tried to hear what Amy was saying. I frowned and pushed him away.

"I didn't think it would be, but it is."

I picked my next words with care. "Things do tend to get out of control."

"People shouldn't lie."

"No they shouldn't," I agreed, looking at Manuel. He blushed and studied the ceiling.

There was a long pause on the other end of the line. I could hear Amy's breathing. It was heavy, almost feverish. "I'm sorry I involved you in this mess. I didn't mean to. You have to believe that."

"I do. You know your father's funeral is tomorrow."

Amy didn't say anything.

"Do you want to go?"

She didn't answer, which was an answer in itself.

"Amy?" I said, after a moment had gone by. "Are you still there?"

"Yes." Her voice sounded far away. "I need to talk to you," she told me. "Maybe we can meet."

One of my grandmother's sayings popped into my head.

Fool me once, shame on you. Fool me twice, shame on me. By those lights, I should feel ashamed indeed. "How do I know you're going to be there?" I demanded. "You've run out on me what? . . . Three times in a row?"

"I won't this time." Amy apologized again. "I really need your help. Please."

"This is the last time."

"Tomorrow at three o'clock. At Carousel. In front of the Halloween store." She hung up.

"I bet she doesn't show," Manuel said.

"Bet you're right."

I got a bottle of wine and two glasses out of the cabinet, went into the living room, turned the TV on, and slipped *The Shining* in the VCR. Manuel and I watched it together, while eating his meatloaf. Then I went to bed.

When I got up the next morning, I briefly entertained the idea of going to Dennis Richmond's funeral, but there didn't seem to be much point, so I went to work instead. Business was steady and, before I knew it, Tim arrived and it was time to take off for the mall. I got there ten minutes early. Around Christmas, it could take you half an hour to find a spot in the parking lot, but now I got one close to the entrance. The place was huge. It had all the usual national chain stores, a food court, several movie theaters, and a carousel that seemed out of place, its hurdy-gurdy music plaintive under the mall's relentlessly bright lights. A cathedral to the American spirit of acquisition, the place had done well, throwing the other malls in the area into a steep decline. The area's population was static, and new stores and restaurants took customers away from older establishments in a never ending game of retail roulette.

I rode the escalator to the second floor and sat on a bench in front of our appointed meeting place and studied the Halloween masks and costumes displayed in the window. The space had once housed a bookstore, but it had gone out of business. Now whoever rented it sold Halloween costumes up until the end of October, after which the space was given over to Christmas decorations. At the moment the place wasn't doing much business, but I was certain things would pick up, once the kids got out of school and dragged their mothers in to buy fake blood and fangs—two favorites that never seemed to go out of favor.

I was feeling restless, so I got up and walked inside. The store housed the usual array of monster masks and make-up. I walked out again and looked around. Amy wasn't there. I went over to Barney's, got myself a cup of coffee, and came back. She still hadn't arrived. She was now officially five minutes late. I decided to give her an hour. I spent it pacing, eating a Wendy's hamburger, drinking a second cup of coffee, and making another tour of the Halloween store. I left precisely at four and sped back to the store.

"Let me guess. Amy didn't come," Tim said when I walked in.

I was telling him he should get a job telling fortunes, when Manuel sauntered out from the back room. "I could have told you she wouldn't show," he said.

"You did last night," I reminded him. Pickles jumped on the counter and rubbed her head against my hand.

Manuel ran the palm of his hand across one of the cages. "Why did you go?"

"I guess because I wanted her to be there."

"I don't get it," he said.

"It's simple. At least I know I did the right thing. My conscience is clear."

And it was until the phone call came. Then everything changed.

Chapter 25

I was making room on the shelves for the new shipment of bird toys we were getting in tomorrow, when the phone rang.

Tim answered and handed me the receiver. "Who is it?" I asked.

He shrugged. "Some guy. He asked for you." He went back to fixing one of the filters.

I wedged the phone between my ear and shoulder. "How can I help you?" I enquired, as I kept on working.

"Is this Robin Light?" the person on the other end of the line asked.

I told him it was.

"Good." The voice was male, but it sounded muffled, as if he had wrapped a wool scarf around his mouth and was speaking through that. "Now listen carefully."

"Who is this?" I demanded.

He cut me off. "Just listen," he ordered. "We have Amy.

I want you to do exactly what I say. If you don't, she's going to get hurt."

I straightened up. "This is a joke, right?"

"Wrong."

And I heard a scream.

The scream rose in a crescendo of pain. It seemed to go on forever, even though it probably lasted thirty seconds at the most. Then there was silence, and the only sound I heard was the burbling of the water in the fish tanks. I became aware that my left hand was aching. I glanced down. I'd clenched it into a tight fist. My knuckles were white. I felt my nails digging into my palm. When I opened my fingers, I had four perfect half-moons incised in my palm.

"Now do you understand?" the man said.

My mouth was dry. My tongue seemed to be having trouble forming the word "yes." I said it anyway.

"Good."

A few seconds later, I heard Amy say, "Robin, do what he says" and a moan.

Then the man came back on. "Follow my instructions, and your little friend will be fine. If you don't, I'll ship pieces of her back to you, understand?"

"Yes," I whispered.

"Pay attention." He told me to write down his instructions.

My hand was shaking as I hung up the receiver.

"What's going on?" a voice asked in my ear.

I must have leaped at least a foot. It was Manuel. He was looking at me curiously. So was Tim. "Don't sneak up on me like that," I snapped.

"Bad news?" Tim asked.

I blurted it out. "Amy's been kidnapped."

"You're kidding, right?" he said, echoing my words.

"I wish I were."

Manuel sucked in his breath and tugged up his pants. "Why would anyone do something like that?"

A lot of answers came to mind, and I didn't like any of them.

Tim put his screwdriver down on the counter and shook his head. "Jesus," he said. "Jesus." He turned around in a circle and hit the counter with the flat of his hand. "God damn."

I walked over to where Tim was standing, removed my pack of cigarettes from my bag, extracted one, and tried to light it, but the flame from my lighter didn't seem to want to connect with the tip of the Camel. I managed on the third try.

"What does the caller want?" Tim asked.

"A small envelope that's supposed to be beneath my desk."

Tim stared at me. "Your desk?"

"That's what the man said." I bit my cuticle."Amy must have put it there when she ran out the door."

So I'd been right and George had been wrong, I thought, as I walked towards the back room. Manuel and Tim followed. Someone had been searching for something when they went through Dennis Richmond's apartment and my house and store. I wondered if that someone was Toon Town. And then I wondered why I'd let myself be talked out of my idea. It was a female thing, I decided. A facet of my personality I thought I had under control, but obviously didn't.

The macaw screeched as we went inside the room. Tim looked around.

"From what you said, I didn't think Amy had time to hide anything."

"The back door is right next to this room. She must have run in, tossed whatever she was carrying under the desk, and run out the door. That wouldn't have taken her more than a couple of seconds. I just hope it isn't drugs." I knelt down in front of the desk. Tim was so close to me, I could feel his breath on my neck. I worked the fingers of my right hand into the space between the desk and the floor. I didn't feel anything.

"So?" Tim said.

I stood up. My fingertips were covered with dust. I wiped them off on my jeans. "It looks as if we're going to have to move it," I said.

Manuel stood off a little, while Tim and I lifted the desk up. We carried it about half a foot and put it down. It was a lot heavier than I remembered it being.

"Look," Manuel cried, and he pointed to a three-by-five inch tan paper envelope lying on the floor amid the dust bunnies.

It was close to where the back of the desk would have been before we moved it.

"I see it." I bent down and picked the envelope up. It was sealed with Scotch tape. I felt it. Whatever was inside was hard and lumpy. My first thought was rock cocaine, but then I realized it couldn't be. The envelope was too small to be holding an amount worth any real money. Tim and Manuel crowded around me as I peeled the tape off and opened the flap. They gasped as I poured the contents into my palm.

The diamonds sparkled in my hand, passports to another world.

"How much do you think they're worth?" Manuel asked, in a hushed whisper, temporarily overcome by the sight.

"If they're perfect one carats, maybe two or three hundred thousand, maybe more."

Tim picked up one of the gems between his thumb and forefinger and held it up to the light. "Amazing. Really amazing."

I had relatives that were supposed to have bought their way out of Nazi Germany with stones like these. I wondered where Dennis had planned to go, as Tim handed the diamond to me. I put all of them back in the envelope and resealed it.

Tim shook his head. "Where did Amy ever get something like this?"

I thought of my last conversation with her. "From her father's apartment."

Tim snorted. "Boy, my father sure didn't keep things like this around our place."

"Maybe he wasn't planning on pulling a disappearing act."

"Even if he was, he could never have mustered together more than twenty extra bucks in cash. Twenty bucks doesn't take you very far. Maybe that's why he never left."

"Neither does two or three hundred grand. Not today—not if you're planning on disappearing for good." I weighed the packet in my hand. "I wonder what else Dennis had socked away?"

Tim sighed. "We're definitely in the wrong business."

"True." One thing about stealing stolen money: the person you steal it from can't very well complain. Who knew? Obviously Amy. Maybe Dennis's brother. Maybe his wife.

"So what do you have to do with that?" Manuel asked, pointing to the packet and interrupting my thoughts.

I glanced at my watch. "I'm supposed to leave it on the

water tower over by the Lincoln Square apartments in three hours.''

''How about Amy?'' Tim asked.

''After I drop the packet off, I'm to go to the phone booth on Plum Street and wait for a call that will tell me where to go to pick her up.''

''Wow.'' Manuel tugged on his goatee. ''This is intense. Really intense.'' He started drumming on the wall.

I told him to stop it.

''Sorry.'' He sat down. Two seconds later he was tapping his foot on the floor.

I found myself gritting my teeth. ''Manuel, cut it out.''

''Right.'' He gave me a sickly grin. ''This whole thing is getting to me. I think I'm gonna take a walk. You mind?''

I told him I didn't. Actually, I was glad to see him go. At the moment, he was just an annoying distraction.

''I'll be back in a little while.''

''Whatever.''

Manuel fingered the buttons on his shirt. ''If you promise someone you're going to do something, do you think you should?''

''That depends on what it is.''

For a second, I thought Manuel was going to say something else, but he didn't, he just turned and headed for the door. I walked toward the phone.

''What are you doing?'' Tim asked.

''Calling the police. They're better set up to cope with this kind of thing than I am.''

Tim swallowed. ''I hope that's the right thing to do.'' The doubt in his voice was palpable. His body was vibrating with tension.

''Believe me, so do I.'' I was reaching for the phone,

when it rang again. The sound pierced the silence. My heart started thudding. "It's probably just a customer," I said.

"Probably," Tim agreed, but he'd gone pale.

It rang again. The smallness of the room seemed to amplify the sound.

"Jesus," Tim murmured. "Aren't you going to get that?"

I picked up the next time it rang. "Yes?" I said. I could hear the catch in my voice.

"I'm not a customer," the voice on the phone informed me. I listened closely, but the voice was so muffled I couldn't identify it. "Modern electronics is a marvelous thing, isn't it?" the man continued. "All these cheap listening devices that you can buy through the catalogs. I can hear and see everything you and your employee say, so you follow my instructions to the letter, or your little friend gets hurt."

I knew who it was. The electronics stuff cinched it. It couldn't be anyone else. "Toon Town," I said.

"Just do what I said."

"This is you, isn't it?"

I heard a click. He'd hung up. "Fuckin' son of a bitch," I yelled into the receiver. "As long as you can hear me, I just want to let you know, I think you're a piece of pond scum." I kicked the desk.

"What's going on?" Tim demanded as I rubbed my foot.

"I'll spell it out for you." I reached for a pen and paper.

"But he was just here for a couple of minutes," he exclaimed, after he'd finished reading what I'd written.

"It was long enough." These days a listening device could be installed in seconds.

We searched the room, even though I knew it was a futile exercise. The devices Toon Town had planted could be anywhere. They could be hidden in anything: a pen, a wall plug, the bottom of a box. For all I knew, he could be standing outside and listening to what we were saying with an electronic ear. I dashed outside on the off chance that he was and I could spot him. I circled the block in the cab and looked in all the parked cars. But of course he wasn't there. That would have been too easy.

As I pulled up in front of the store, I debated about going to the police. I could drive down there right now. Toon Town wouldn't know. Unless he'd planted a bug in the cab too. The odds were against it. On the other hand, it never occurred to me that he would plant anything in the store. And my car had just been sitting out there. It was better not to take chances. I didn't want to upset him, even though I had a strong hunch that no matter what happened, he wasn't going to hurt Amy.

But I wasn't prepared to bet Amy's life on my intuition either.

I recalled the scream I'd heard.

It sure had sounded real.

But maybe it wasn't.

Maybe Amy had been faking.

Or maybe the scream had been prerecorded. You could get sound effect collections on CDs. I'd seen them on sale at Record Heaven. Which would mean she and Toon Town were in this together.

Maybe this was her way of getting me to give her the stones.

Of course she could have just asked.

Or come and gotten them herself.

So why hadn't she?

The most obvious reason was because she was afraid.

Of who?

Manuel had said she was scared she was being watched. I thought for a minute. And someone had gone through my house and ransacked my store. Maybe it wasn't a bunch of kids and Toon Town doing this stuff, after all. Maybe that's why Amy had staged this drama. If that were true, it would certainly make her behavior more understandable. On the other hand, she could be totally nuts.

Of course, Toon Town could actually *have* kidnapped her and be forcing her to tell where the stones were.

Maybe she hadn't met me at the mall because he'd grabbed her before she could.

Maybe she'd really been going to tell me everything.

And maybe I should go to circus school and learn to be a tightrope walker.

I rested my head on the back of the seat and closed my eyes. Suddenly I was seized by an overpowering desire to sleep. As I listened to the tree branches creaking in the wind, for some reason, I started thinking about the summer camp I'd gone to when I was seven and how much I'd hated it and how my mother had kept sending me back there anyway, even though I'd cried for two weeks before she put me on the train. And then I wondered if Amy had ever gone to camp and then I wondered why I was wondering. I yawned and opened my eyes. Even though I didn't want to, it was time to go back inside Noah's Ark. I got out of the car and crossed the sidewalk to the store. In the window, the cardboard witch, leaning against the stack of cat carriers, winked at me as I opened the door.

It was now eight o'clock. The next two hours took what seemed like ten to pass. Around eight thirty, Manuel came back to the store, spent ten minutes tapping his foot and jingling the change in his pocket, and left again, for which I was profoundly grateful. I was so keyed up that every sound he made grated on my nerves. Tim and I spent the rest of the time waiting on customers, rearranging the shelves, and mopping the floors. We didn't talk much. Given the circumstances, it was hard to think of anything to say.

"You better get going," Tim said, as the hands of the clock on the wall hit ten.

I nodded. "You have the key to my house?" He demonstrated he did by holding it up. He was supposed to drop Zsa Zsa off at home. "I'll call as soon as I can," I promised.

"I'll be waiting," Tim replied.

I buttoned up my jacket and went outside. A scimitar-shaped sliver of a new moon hung in the sky. Over to the left, I made out the Big Dipper. As I got in the cab, I heard a cat hiss and another one answer. It was a good night for prowling. I had half an hour to get to the water tower by the Lincoln Square apartments, which was more than enough time. For once, I drove slowly and scrupulously, obeying all the traffic laws. I didn't want to risk getting pulled over by a cop right now. As I turned into the complex, I thought that the choice of this locale for a drop site seemed to argue for Amy's involvement. After all, she was familiar with the place.

As I drove along, I had to admit it was a good choice. The parking lots were full. Most people were in for the night. If anyone saw me, they wouldn't remember. I'd just be another tenant coming home after a hard day's work.

As per instructions, I followed the road up to the water tower. It was an old, rusted structure—a hold over from the days when the area had contained factories and warehouses instead of apartments. I parked in the lot and followed an asphalt path the rest of the way. The groundkeepers obviously didn't tend this area of Lincoln Square. The gravel surrounding the tower was dotted with potato chip bags, soda cans, and pieces of broken glass.

I looked around when I got to the top. If Toon Town was

standing in the hedges down below—and I was positive he was—he would have a clear, unobstructed view of me, and there was no way I could see him. The wind was stronger here. It sent dry leaves skittering across the gravel and wrapped stray newspaper pages around the water tower's concrete base. I had to go around the tower twice before I found the girder that had a piece of duct tape stuck to it. Just as I had been told, there was a narrow space between where the steel girder and the concrete met. I wedged the packet in it and walked back down.

"I did what you told me to, you scum-sucking son of a bitch," I yelled, hoping that Toon Town would show himself.

He didn't and, after a minute, I got in my car, drove out of the development, and over to the public telephone on Plum Street. I parked right by it. Then I sat and waited for the phone to ring.

Chapter 26

Five minutes passed. Then ten. Then fifteen. I was supposed to have heard from Toon Town in five. I got out of the cab and checked to see if the phone was working. It was. I got back in the car and waited some more. I sat, suspended in an agony of anticipation, and chain smoked cigarette after cigarette, flicking the ashes out of the window as I watched a windblown beer can rolling around in the middle of the street, until it was crushed by a rap-blasting Caddy with tinted windows.

Forty-five minutes later, my throat was raw from all the cigarettes I'd smoked, and I was still waiting. It looked as if Amy was either dead or on the road with Toon Town, and I sure as hell hoped it was the latter. My legs ached, as I climbed out of the cab again—sometimes sitting too long makes my burn scars stiffen—and I limped a little as I walked towards the phone. I paused to rub my calves, then I fished a quarter out of my pocket, put it in the slot, and called Tim and told him what had happened.

"Jesus." He repeated the word a second time. "What are you going to do now?"

I had my answer ready. I ought to have. I'd spent the last forty-five minutes sitting in the car, trying to come up with a plan. "I'm going to check out the house on Easton Street. If they're not there, I'm going to the police."

"Why do you think they're going to go back there?" Tim asked.

"Because they seem to keep returning to it."

"Maybe you should go to the police first."

"Checking out the house won't take very long." I hung up before Tim could say anything else. Then I got in the cab and drove over to the water tower.

I just wanted to make sure the packet had been picked up. It had. I jumped back in the cab and sped down the road, surprising a fat sheltie and his owner on my way out. The sheltie's indignant bark followed me as I made a left onto the main road. I clicked on the radio, then clicked it off, as I headed for the house that the Richmonds were selling. I knew I was playing a long shot, but I was hoping that Amy and Toon Town had stopped there to get their stuff before taking off to wherever they were going. If I were lucky, they might still be there. If they weren't, I was going to have to call the police and tell them what had happened—a call I wasn't exactly anxious to make. I imagined the conversation. No matter how I put it, I looked bad in every version I came up with. I decided it was better to think about other things.

I could see the clouds coming in from the west as I drove. A wisp of grey obscured half, and then all, of the moon's sliver. As I waited for the light to change, I wondered who was chasing Amy and how they knew about the diamonds. Had she told someone? Had Dennis talked before he died? And how did Melanie fit into all of this? I could think of several possible answers, none of which made more sense than any other one. Of course, Amy would know. Maybe she would even tell me—if she were still alive.

I turned the radio back on and blasted 95.7 FM as loudly as I could, so I wouldn't have to consider the other possibility. Nevertheless, I could feel my heart fluttering in my chest, as I turned onto Easton. Small one-family houses. Ghosts and goblins in the windows. Jack-o'-lanterns on the porches. Carefully tended patches of lawn. Compact cars and minivans in the driveways. A place for everything, and everything in its place. Except for the house I was visiting. A jogger, his breath fogging the night air, passed me, as I turned off the radio. I didn't want to wake up the neighborhood.

I'd driven about twenty feet, when I saw it: Toon Town's Tracker. It was sitting in front of the house. Well, one thing lime-green has going for it: it's visible. I guess he hadn't figured on a life of crime when he'd chosen the color. Or maybe he just didn't care. I parked down the street so Toon Town wouldn't spot me, went around to the back, and opened the cab's trunk. I heard the sounds of television programs floating out into the night air, as I took out a baseball bat and a can of mace and, for a few seconds, I thought about the times Murphy and I had been a family. But that was in another lifetime. Now he was gone, and I was prowling around in the night. And even if I went back to that tight little world of couples and dinner parties and Sunday afternoon errands, it wouldn't be the same anymore. Too much had happened. I closed the trunk and concentrated on the task at hand.

I was glad for the clouds, as I cut across the adjacent

house's lawn. It made me less visible—not that anyone looking out the window couldn't see me—but since there wasn't much I could do about that, I just hoped they weren't looking. And they probably weren't. Down in New York City, where I grew up, no matter what time of the day or night it was, there was always someone sitting on the stoop or gazing out the window. Not here, though. Here people pulled into their garages, walked in their houses, shut the doors, pulled down the blinds, and minded their own business. Most times, I didn't like that. It made me feel isolated. But right now, I was thankful for their way of doing things.

Ducking down and keeping to the shrubbery, I walked around the house. All the lights were off. Maybe Toon Town and Amy had gone to sleep. Poor dears. They were probably suffering from post-kidnapping exhaustion. I went into the house the same way I had before—through the kitchen window. I took the storm off, set it aside, lifted up the frame, held onto my bat, and wiggled through. Every sound I made, every creak of the wood, every squeak, every breath I took seemed to fill the whole house. I was positive that Toon Town must have heard me—how could he not have?—and I moved against the wall and gripped my bat with two hands and waited. But he didn't come. After a minute of pretending I was a statue, I decided he wasn't coming down the stairs, and I moved away from the wall. I began to feel a strange sense of exhilaration, as I tiptoed through the kitchen into the living room. This is what a cat burglar feels like, I thought, as I looked around.

The room was exactly the way it was when the real estate agent had shown me around a couple of days ago. I walked into the dining room. Nothing had changed here, either. If Amy and Toon Town were here, they were probably asleep in the second bedroom. They had to be. It was the only room with a bed in it. I could hardly wait to see Amy's face when I clicked on the light. I was moving towards the stairs when I heard something—something so faint I couldn't make it out at first. It sounded like a mew, and then I thought maybe it was a groan, and then I wasn't sure what it was. I held the bat tightly as I went up the stairs. The carpet absorbed my footsteps. I kept my back to the wall, my eyes glued to the second floor landing, but I couldn't see anything up there. All the lights were off. The darkness was too dense. By the time I was halfway up the stairs, the mewing had subsided. When I got to the top step, I stopped and listened.

Nothing.

Then I heard a long drawn out groan. Then a moment of silence. Then a thud and another moan. Then more quiet. I cursed under my breath.

It was a person, a person who was hurt. Amy? It had to be. I heard one more thud. It sounded as if she were banging up against a door or a wall. Had Toon Town locked her up? Where was he? Why wasn't he responding? He had to be here. His car was parked outside. But then, why wasn't he saying anything? I bit my lip and tightened my grip on the bat. I didn't like this. I didn't like this at all. Nothing was adding up. Maybe I should have called the police. Unfortunately, it was too late to do that now. Especially if Amy was hurt. She might be dead by the time I got back.

I hugged the wall as I crossed the landing. If Toon Town *were* here, I certainly didn't want to let him know. The only thing I had going for me was the element of surprise. I'd just made it past the bathroom when I heard another moan. I cursed silently and quickly moved on to the first bedroom. I peered inside. By now my eyes had gotten used to the darkness. No one was there. I hurried on to the second bedroom, paused right outside the door, flattened my back against the wall, and listened. I heard a whistling noise. The sound of someone staggering. Then creaks. The sound of bedsprings groaning. Someone was sitting on the bed. Another moan. Softer this time.

I took a deep breath, counted to five, raised the bat, and stepped inside.

Chapter 27

The first thing I saw was a hunched-over shape sitting on the edge of the bed.

"Amy?"

But the moment the word left my mouth, I realized it couldn't be her. The shape was too big. And then I realized who it was. Toon Town. I moved a little closer and lifted the bat a little higher. I wanted to be ready for whatever was going to happen.

"Where is she?" I demanded.

"She's gone." Toon Town lifted up his head. His voice sounded wet. He was lisping his words.

When I turned on the light, I saw why. His mouth was full of blood. There were dark gaps where his front teeth should have been. His nose was mashed down. One eye was swollen shut. It was the size of an orange. He was wearing boxers and a tee shirt. His arms and legs were covered with purple bruises.

I lowered my bat and asked him what had happened.

He lifted his right hand. His pinky was hanging down. He coughed. A bubble of blood and phlegm dribbled down his chin. "I got into a fight with a truck."

"It must have been a big one. Did Amy do this?"

Toon Town made a gurgling noise I thought might have been a laugh. "What do you think?"

"I think someone beat the crap out of you." I pointed to the open closet door. "And locked you in there."

"Very good." He shifted his position. Then he grabbed his side and groaned. "Shit. I think I got some busted ribs."

"I wouldn't be surprised. Where did Amy go?"

He formed the next words carefully. "They took her."

"Who's they?"

"I didn't see. They came in when we were asleep."

"How many are we talking about here?"

"I don't know. I told you I was asleep."

"And they beat you up and stuffed you in the closet and took Amy?"

"Yes."

"Where are the diamonds?"

"They took them too."

"So why would they want Amy?"

Toon Town coughed. "They didn't tell me."

The wind was picking up outside. It rattled the windowpanes and tossed the cedar branches from side to side. "And you don't know anything."

"That's right."

I studied Toon Town's ruined face. "You're lying."

"Why should I do that?"

"I don't have the vaguest idea." I clicked my tongue against the roof of my mouth, while I thought. "Amy took more stuff from her father's apartment, didn't she?" It was the only explanation that made any sense.

Toon Town didn't answer. He didn't have to. The way his body stiffened up told me everything I wanted to know.

"How much money did Dennis Richmond have in his apartment?"

Toon Town didn't say anything.

"It must have been a lot."

Toon Town coughed again. A line of blood-colored saliva dripped onto his sleeve. He didn't notice.

"Amy knows where it is, right?"

Toon Town tried to shrug. He ended up clutching his ribs and groaning instead.

"This kidnap thing was a scam, wasn't it?"

Toon Town studied the wall in back of me.

"You guys thought you'd get me to give you the diamonds and then you'd leave town."

"We were gonna call and explain from the road." Toon Town's tone implied that that would have made everything all right.

"Why didn't you just come in and get them?"

"We were afraid we'd be spotted."

"By whom?"

Toon Town went back to studying the wall.

"The people who beat you up?"

Silence.

"You know, I get a better response from my cocker spaniel than I do from you."

Still nothing.

"Fine. I'm calling the cops."

"Don't," Toon Town rasped.

Something at last. "Why shouldn't I?"

"I know where Amy is."

"Where's that?"

He turned the corner of his mouth that could still move up. "Someplace where no one is going to find her."

"So why shouldn't I call the police?"

"Because I won't tell them."

"Why's that?"

"I want my money."

"I hate to tell you this, but you're in no position to get anything right now."

"I am if you drive me."

"You're crazy. You should be in a hospital."

He gestured towards his face. "I'll take care of this later."

"Do what you want. I'm phoning." I started to leave. I didn't have to worry about Toon Town going anywhere in the condition he was in.

"Don't waste your time. I won't tell the police where she is. I won't tell them anything."

I turned back. "They'll make you."

"How?" He managed a sneer. "I'll call my lawyer from the ER room. He'll be there before they read my X-rays."

"If anything happens to her, you'll be charged as an accessory."

"But it won't matter, will it? Because by then, it'll be too late for Amy."

"What do you mean?"

"You're not that stupid, are you?"

I tightened my hands around the bat's neck, then loosened them. Cracking Toon Town's head open was a luxury I couldn't afford. "You really are scum," I hissed.

He grimaced and clutched his side again. "Look, this is the deal. You drive me to where I want to go. You get Amy and I get the stuff."

"What about the people that took her? You think they'll just hand everything over to you?"

"I think that's something you don't have to worry about. Now, are you going to help me or not?"

I said yes, even though I knew Toon Town was lying through his teeth, because I figured I didn't have much of a choice.

"Good." Toon Town tried to stand up. He got an inch off the bed before he sat back down. His face was beaded with sweat from the effort. I didn't see how he was going to stand up, much less walk down the stairs.

"I don't think you're going to be able to do this," I told him.

"I don't care what the fuck you think," he growled. "Just help me get dressed."

It took me a good ten minutes to get his pants and shirt and shoes on. I inhaled his odor—acrid sweat, sour breath, and blood—as he leaned up against me. He was heavy, and I kept stumbling under his weight. The process of getting him out of the room and down the stairs seemed to go on forever. Progress was measured in inches. By the time we were halfway down the steps, my arms and legs were trembling with the effort of holding him up. His breathing sounded ragged. When we got out the front door, my shirt was soaked in sweat. I propped him against the wall, told him to wait, and ran to get the cab.

"Now what?" I asked, after I'd helped him into the front seat and settled myself behind the wheel.

"Now we go to Amy's house."

"She's there?"

"No. I have to get something." Toon Town put his head back on the seat and closed his eyes. A moment later, his jaw went slack. He'd fallen asleep. I studied his face. His skin was grey. His cheekbones jutted out. His mouth was a black hole. I could have been transporting a corpse.

It had started to rain. I turned on the windshield wipers and pulled away from the curb. Their swish formed a duet with the whistle Toon Town made every time he exhaled. I clicked on the radio, but I couldn't find anything I wanted to listen to, and I finally clicked it off. I spent part of the ride over trying to figure out what had happened and wondering if I were doing the right thing. Unfortunately, since I couldn't answer the second question without answering the first, I abandoned the effort as a waste of time. Except for an occasional semi lumbering along, 690 and 81 were deserted, and I made good time getting to Gerri Richmond's house.

"We're here," I told Toon Town, as I turned right at the stone pillars and threaded my way up the narrow, winding path to the cul de sac where Gerri Richmond's house sat. As I got close to it, I could see that the lights were off. The house was dark. There were two cars in the driveway, though. Maybe Gerri Richmond was out with a friend. Or maybe she was asleep, although it was early for that.

Toon Town grunted and opened his eye.

I pulled in behind the Mercedes. "Now what?"

"I need a list of the Richmond property holdings."

"Excuse me?" I couldn't believe what I was hearing.

Toon Town groaned as he sat up.

I turned towards him. "You're fishing. You don't know where the fuck Amy is, do you?"

A line of blood worked its way down his chin. He wiped it off with the back of his hand. "I know she's in one of the places on that list."

"I don't suppose you'd like to explain how you know?"

"No."

"So what are we supposed to do? Go to all of them?"

He glared at me. "You want to see her again, you'll stop asking questions and do what I tell you to."

Ordinarily, I would have told Toon Town to shove it, but this time I shut my mouth and did what he said.

"I'm just supposed to ask Gerri Richmond for the list?"

"That's right."

"And she's going to hand it over?"

"That's up to you."

"What happens if she calls the cops?"

"She won't, if you explain the situation to her correctly. After all, she has a stake in this, too." Toon Town closed his eyes again. He didn't open them when I got out of the cab.

I turned my jacket collar up, scurried for the door, and pressed the bell. The first bar of "Für Elise" floated out into the air. Gerri Richmond opened the door a moment later. Her eyes were unfocused. Her blond hair stood up in tangled clumps. Maybe it was my imagination, but I thought I saw glints of grey among the blond. Her makeup was smudged. Her silk shirt was stained with spots of something dark, but the double strand of pearls around her neck gleamed pure and unsullied.

"We buried Dennis today." She was slurring her words. She'd been drinking. "Did you know that?"

"Your stepson told me."

She waved her hand around. "Everyone came. Everyone who was anyone. We had a police escort to the cemetery."

I interrupted. "We need to talk about Amy," I told her. "She's in trouble."

"She's always been in trouble." Gerri turned and walked away. "From the day she was born."

I closed the door and followed her. She wobbled as she walked. We went through the darken hall into the den. The light from the street lamp threw our shadows on the walls.

"Serious trouble," I emphasized.

She stopped and turned around. "The police think she killed Dennis. Do you?"

"No."

"Well, I'm not so sure." I could hear the rain pattering on the roof and the windows. Gerri Richmond cocked her head and listened to it for a minute before speaking. "They never got along. Even when she was little, they never got along." She shook her head. "Have you ever made a mistake?"

"Lots of them," I answered impatiently. Time was short. I could hear the clock ticking away inside my head.

"A really big mistake that you couldn't take back? That you couldn't undo?"

"Yes."

"Well, Amy is mine."

Maybe that explained why Amy turned out the way she had. If my mother felt that way about me, I sure wouldn't want to stick around—actually she had and I hadn't. The window blinds were up in the house across the way. Someone was in the kitchen stirring something on the stove. I wondered what the meals in the Richmond family must have been like. Not pleasant, I was willing to wager. I regarded the room. The white, overstuffed sofas seemed to float in the dark. Gerri Richmond collapsed on the nearest one. I sat next to her. The coffee table in front hosted a bottle of

Stoli, a glass, and a large number of wadded up Kleenexes. It looked as if Gerri had been sitting here for awhile.

She was reaching for her glass, when I told her that Amy had been kidnapped.

She froze. "I don't understand."

When I told her why she began to laugh.

Chapter 28

I was so stunned I couldn't think of anything to say.

Gerri Richmond's laughter broke over me like waves. "Here I've spent all this time looking for the money Dennis stole, and my own daughter has it. Perfect. Absolutely perfect." She went into another laughing fit. "And you don't know where she is."

"Toon Town thinks he does." I explained about the list.

"How does he know that?"

It was the obvious question. The one I'd asked. The one Toon Town wouldn't answer. I could have told her that. But I wanted the information instead of a debate, so I lied. "Amy told him she'd hidden the rest of the stuff in one of your places. He figures they'll go there." Maybe I was even right.

"I'll get the list." Gerri Richmond levered herself up and staggered out of the room.

I sat and watched the second hand of my watch revolve.

After one minute, I got up and walked over to the mantel. It was crammed with family photographs. They'd been arranged chronologically over what I'd guess to be a fifteen-year period. In the beginning, we had the quintessential American family. Two children. Two parents. Everyone smiling. The Richmonds at a picnic. The Richmonds at the beach. The Richmonds at Disney Land. Midway, things had changed. The Richmonds were still smiling, but the smiles looked forced. Everyone was leaning away from, instead of towards, one another. Another couple of photos later, Charlie and Amy were scowling. She'd cut her hair very short. Almost buzzed it. A homemade job, by the look of it. How old was she? I guessed eleven or twelve.

I studied the next snapshot. This one had been taken somewhere in the Bahamas. On the beach. Everyone was wearing bathing suits—except for Amy who was wearing all black. She'd pierced her nose. I ran my eye over the last photographs. Amy wasn't in them. Neither was Charlie. If I were going to do an art show with the pictures on the mantel, I'd title it "Portrait of Family Disintegration." I was wondering what had happened, when I heard Toon Town beeping. I glanced at my watch. Another minute had gone by. Time to get going. I went to find Gerri. I heard her voice rising and falling, as I walked out of the den. The sound formed a thread and I followed it into the kitchen. The room could have been a magazine ad in *Better Homes and Gardens*. It had all the amenities. Jen-Air grill. Center island. The wall stove built into a brick alcove. Glass refrigerator. The only thing lacking was the family.

Gerri was leaning against the counter. She was curling the phone cord around her hand as she talked. When she saw me, she hung up. "I was talking to Charlie," she said. "I thought he had a right to know what was going on."

"I think maybe you should tell him after you give me the list."

"Are you saying I don't care about my daughter?" she demanded.

"I'm saying I need the list," I reiterated.

She brushed by me. "It's in my bedroom."

"I'll go with you." As I followed her down the hall, I wondered if she were telling me the truth about talking to Charlie. She hadn't shown any need to keep him apprised of things before. Our footsteps echoed on the floor, as we headed for the stairs. Toon Town sounded the horn again. We were running out of time. I followed Gerri Richmond up the stairs and into the master bedroom. The smell of Le Dix lingered in the air. Gerri flicked on the light. I took a look around. The carpet was white. The bed was king-sized and canopied, the dressers and nightstands were painted white with a gold overlay. A large, rectangular mirror in a gilt frame decorated the space over the double dresser. Other than that, the walls were bare. Several cartons stood near a large treadmill.

Gerri followed my gaze. "Dennis's things," she explained, as she headed for the desk on the far side of the room.

Well, she was more efficient than I'd been, that was for sure. It had taken me six months to tackle Murphy's belongings. Either that, or she was anxious to get all reminders of him out of her life.

I watched her open and close drawers and go through papers. "It's here somewhere," she muttered. "I know it is." She took the three drawers out and dumped them on the floor. Then she got down on her knees and started pawing through the mess she'd created.

I got down with her. I saw invitations. Notices from Amy's school. Notices from the superintendent's office talking about disciplinary hearings. Letters from the Richmonds to the only private school in town asking about admission for their daughter.

"Here it is." Gerri lifted a piece of paper up and waved it in the air.

I snatched it out of her hand and scanned the list. There were five addresses all together. Not as many as I feared. "I'll call the moment I have her," I told Gerri, as I got up.

She nodded. I waited for her to say something else, but she didn't. Instead, her hands went to her pearls. She fingered the smooth white beads as if they were her rosary. I watched her for a few seconds more, before heading for the door.

Just as I reached it, I heard her whisper, "Tell Amy I'm sorry."

I wanted to turn back and ask her if she were sorry for anything in particular or for everything in general, but there was no time to listen to her confession. I ran down the stairs and out the hallway. The front door slammed shut behind me, and I walked out into the rain.

Toon Town opened his good eye as I slipped inside my car. The other eye had turned a deeper shade of purple. "Did you get it?" he asked. I could detect a quaver in his voice that hadn't been there earlier. He was getting weaker. I wondered how long he'd been able to hold out, as I handed him the list.

"Here it is."

"Good." His hands were shaking as he took it. He held it up to the street lamp. His lips moved as he read. "All right." He tore up the list, rolled the window down a crack, and threw the pieces out into the rain.

I guess he wasn't taking any chances. Then he told me to get on 690 and get off at West Street.

I did what he said.

I watched him out of the corner of my eye as I drove. He was gripping his knees with his hands. Every once in a while his head would drop down, then he would snap to and bring it up. He was having trouble staying awake, or maybe he was having trouble staying conscious. I couldn't decide which. When we got to West Street, he told me to keep straight. After five blocks, he directed me to make a left.

The houses in this part of town ranged from the small but adequate to the tumbled down. Windows were frequently covered with plastic. The lawns were festooned with "For Sale" signs. Piles of old furniture dotted the curbs. It was like Appalachia. Everyone who could move out already had. The only ones left were the old, the young, the sick, and the unemployable. Recently I'd read an article by a professor of sociology asking whether drug dealers had caused this type of urban exodus or had merely taken advantage of it.

Naturally, though, he hadn't asked the people who were still living there—like the men standing outside. No matter what the weather, they were always there, clustered in convenience store parking lots or lounging on street corners, talking and passing bottles wrapped in brown paper bags back and forth. They followed me with their eyes, as I drove by. Condemned to idleness, I had the feeling they'd still be there if I came back the next day, the next month, or the next year.

When we hit North Street, Toon Town told me to follow it.

"I have a question," I said to him.

"What?"

"Did you trash my store?"

"No. Why are asking me something like that?" His voice rose a little.

"Then what did you mean when you said you were going to get back at me?"

"I was gonna bug your store and your house." He gave me a sickly grin. "Shake you up a little. But I never got around to your house. The store is what gave me the kidnap idea." Toon Town's voice trailed off. He looked spent. Talking seemed to tire him out.

I kept driving. The street was four miles long and twisted and turned through several residential areas. Two miles later, we came to a commerical block, and Toon Town ordered me to slow down.

"This is it," he said, when he came to the middle of the block.

The building he was pointing to was three stories high. Judging from the number of "For Sale," "Reduced Price," and "For Rent" signs tacked on the wall, it had been vacant for awhile. Its pseudo-modern style—glass, metal strips, and colored panels, a style popularized twenty years ago—hadn't worn well. Almost a third of the windows were broken, and the panels, once pink, were greyed-over with dirt. As I tried to read the faded sign hanging over the main entrance, I thought about why the Richmonds didn't just abandon the place and throw it back at the bank. Maybe they were using it as a tax write-off.

"You know what this place was?" Toon Town asked me. Under the streetlight, his face was a technicolor kaleidoscope of purple, black, and red.

"No."

"The Evan's School for Mortuary Science."

Somehow, given the players in this little drama, I wasn't surprised.

Death seemed to be the subject, the verb, and the modifier of their universe.

Toon Town brought his hand up and pointed to an empty spot. "You can park here."

I pulled over to the curb and took my phone out of the glove compartment.

"What are you doing?" he croaked.

"I'm calling the cops."

"Don't." He was pleading now.

"How are you going to stop me?"

"You said you cared about Amy."

"That's why I'm doing it. I'm not compromising her life by going in there and getting everyone upset." Not to mention getting myself killed.

He coughed. A spasm of pain crossed his face. "Amy is the only one in there."

"Come again?"

"You heard me. Don't act so surprised. You knew I was conning you back there. I could see it."

I was surprised, though, surprised he'd been able to read my reactions. If I were in his condition, I wouldn't be doing character readings. Of course if I were in his condition, I'd be unconscious. "But now you're going to tell me the truth?"

"Yes."

"I'm listening." I got a cigarette out of my backpack, lit it, and waited.

Toon Town began. His voice was so low I had to move forward to hear. "Amy was in the basement looking for a clean towel when he came in."

"At the house you said 'they.' Which is it: he or they?"

"He."

"Does he have a name?"

"You want to hear this or not?"

I told him yes and shut up. I'd ask my questions when he was through.

"Amy must have heard what was going on upstairs and snuck out the back door."

"How can you be so sure he didn't grab her?"

"I could hear him as he went through the rooms. He was looking for her. She wasn't there." He closed his eyes and opened them again. His face was beaded with sweat. "I knew she'd come here. She gabbed about it all the time, about how cool it was that her family owned a building like this. But I couldn't remember the address. I figured once I saw the list, I'd know which one it was. And I was right. I did. All you have to do is get Amy. Just tell her I'm waiting for her. She'll come right out."

I studied his face. He was leaning against the door. His will was the only thing keeping him going. I didn't think he had the energy to lie. "Then what?"

"Then you drive me to my mother's house and drop me off. I keep the diamonds and you keep Amy."

"You really have this planned." I rolled down my window and flicked my half-smoked Camel into the street. "And she's just going to go with me?"

Toon Town coughed. His face looked more swollen than it had earlier. His chin was covered with dried blood. "I'm sure you'll find a way to make her."

"I don't think so." I activated the phone.

"Wait," Toon Town cried. "I think she's got some stuff she was gonna sell to Justin on her. I don't think she ever got rid of it."

I clicked the off switch. I'd forgotten about that. "How much?"

"Enough that if the cops come, they're going to put her away. Ten hits of acid can get you a five-year minimum."

"She'll walk. She's only fifteen."

"They could still put her in juvie. You never know what's going to happen these days," Toon Town whispered. He was fading fast.

What Toon Town said was true. You never did know. I rubbed my temples. And then there was the fact that if I called the cops and Amy saw them, she'd probably run—something she was very good at—and then things could go bad real fast. She was just stupid enough to keep going when they told her to stop and get herself shot for her pains. If I went in myself, I'd collect Amy, drive Toon Town to a hospital, call my lawyer, then call the police. It was time everything got straightened out—it was past time. I was tired of chasing Amy. Tired of the Richmond family in general. I wanted my life back. Such as it was. Which is why I told Toon Town I'd do what he asked.

"Good. This way everyone's happy." He closed his good eye again. It seemed to me his breathing had gotten shallower. Or maybe it was my imagination.

I wanted to get as close to the building as possible, so I made a U-turn and parked behind a grey Plymouth. When I told Toon Town I was going, he moved his head slightly to acknowledge he'd heard me.

As I closed the door, I wondered if he'd be conscious when I returned. I was actually hoping he wouldn't be, because it would make things easier if he were out cold. I moved around to the back of the cab, opened the trunk, and got out a flashlight and my baseball bat. Of course I already had my box cutter. If I'd had an Uzi, I'd have taken that too. Then I trotted down the alley to the back of the building. It turned out to be your basic, run-down, rubble-strewn, bad neighborhood, who-gives-a-shit back lot. I tried to avoid the broken beer bottles, fast-food wrappers, crack vials, and used condoms, as I walked to the service entrance. Fast sex. Fast drugs. Fast food. Welcome to the mid-nineties. The triumph of form over content.

The back door was locked, but since five out of eight bottom windows were broken, it didn't make a whole lot of difference. As I knocked the remaining shards of glass out of the second window to the left with the end of my flashlight, I tried to suppress my growing sense of unease. I mean, why should I be nervous? Could it be because the last time I'd gone into a deserted building looking for Amy, I'd almost gotten blown into tiny little pieces? Or maybe it was because I was about to voluntarily walk into a place where you learned how to embalm people? If this were a movie and I were in the audience, I'd be telling my character, "Don't go. Turn back." And when my character went in, I'd turn to my friend and say, "how can she be such a moron?"

Simple. My impatience was getting the better of me.

I just wanted to wrap this up.

Besides, I thought I had everything covered.

Fat chance. The truth is, no one ever does—unless you're God. And even he has trouble on some days.

Oh well.

I took a deep breath and climbed through the window. Welcome to the funhouse. I turned on the flashlight the moment my feet hit the floor and moved it in a semicircle. I was in a large room. It smelled musty. And something else. Something acrid, something chemical. My light caught chairs over by one wall. A large blackboard took up another wall. Wooden shelves laden with large jars full of dark liquids—that I had a feeling I didn't want to know about—lined a third. Four stainless steel tables sat in the room's center. I heard a rustling noise. Mice, I told myself, but I shivered anyway.

My sense of foreboding grew.

I couldn't imagine Amy voluntarily hiding out here.

In the dark.

Alone.

I couldn't even imagine doing it with a friend.

This made no sense.

None at all. And in the past couple of years, I've grown not to like things that don't make sense.

I grasped the flashlight and bat with my knees, cupped my hands, and yelled out for Amy.

Her name echoed in the dark, as if I were in a canyon in some unnameable country.

I stood there with my head cocked, listening for an answer.

From far away, I heard the unmistakable sound of a door slamming shut.

The front door.

It had to be.

I cursed and started to run.

The door to the next room was slightly ajar. I crashed through it. And that was the last thing I remember.

Chapter 29

The first thing I did, when I came to, was sit up. Which was a mistake. My head started pounding, the room started spinning, and I threw up. Great. I have a concussion, I thought, while I puked. By now I recognized the symptoms. I should, I've had enough experience—not that this was an area I'd ever wanted to acquire expertise in. When I was done, I gingerly explored the back of my head. It was very tender, I could feel a bump, but my fingers came away dry. No blood. For a change. I wondered who had hit me. Amy? Then who had I heard down at the other end of the building. Who else had been here?

I groaned, as I picked up my flashlight—thank God I'd put in new batteries. Otherwise it would have probably gone out by now—and started to get up. I was moving my hands to give myself better leverage, when I felt something hard under my fingers. I brought the light around. It was a brick. Then I noticed two more lying on the floor close by. I had an idea. I got up and dragged a chair that was standing nearby over to the door. I had to wait for a second for the new wave of dizziness to pass, but when it did, I climbed up and shined my light on the top of the door. It was dusty, except for three clearly defined spaces—spaces I was positive the bricks had occupied.

I climbed back down before I fell off. Cute. No one had been waiting. I'd walked into a booby trap. And I was pretty sure I knew who'd set it: Amy. It was the kind of thing she'd do. Amateurish, but effective. Just like the mousetrap she'd put in her desk drawer. I wondered if she'd ever read the Hardy Boys when she was growing up. Another wave of dizziness hit me, and I leaned against the wall and closed my eyes. Knowing Amy, she hadn't meant to kill anyone or even injure them that badly, just to slow them down. Which she'd certainly done. When I could, I opened my eyes and shined my flashlight on my watch face. Twenty minutes had passed since I'd first come in. Amy was long gone by now. I wondered if Toon Town had known about Amy's little surprise when he'd sent me in. Or was this something she'd thought up on her own?

I promised myself I'd ask her, if I ever got the chance. Which was seeming less and less likely.

I followed the same route going out of the building I had coming in.

I'd had my share of surprises for the evening. I wasn't anxious for any more.

I'd taken five steps, when I groaned. God, I couldn't believe it. I'd left my keys in the ignition. I'd been so fixated on getting Amy that I'd turned the motor off and just walked away. I checked my pockets anyway and then, just to be sure, I checked them again. The only things I found were some pennies and a stick of gum.

As I climbed out the window, I told myself maybe Toon Town and Amy hadn't taken off.

Maybe Amy had just run away and left Toon Town collapsed in the cab. But I didn't think so.

And then I thought about Amy driving. She had to be. Toon Town certainly couldn't.

The thought hurt worse than my head did.

I started to pray that I was wrong.

But I wasn't.

The spot where my cab had sat was empty. It was gone. Along with my backpack and my phone. And the worst part of the whole thing was that I couldn't blame anyone but myself.

I started looking for a phone booth. All the stores were shuttered for the night. There were no houses and, even if there were, I would have hesitated to knock. This was the sort of neighborhood where people were apt to answer with a knife in one hand and a gun in the other. I kept going. The rain was lighter now, but it was cold, the drops numbing my skin. I turned up my collar, hunched my shoulders, put my hands in my pockets, and tried to keep to the wall as much as possible. A dog yipped off in the distance. The humming of the streetlights kept time with my steps. Half a block later I spotted an AM-PM Mini-Mart and headed towards it.

A pay phone sat off to one side of the parking lot, well out of the way of the two gas pumps. I accidentally kicked a Snapple bottle as I walked towards it. It rolled down the tarmac, stopping just short of the street. I sneezed, as I dug some quarters out of my jacket pocket. I called my house first. No one answered. I called Tim's house next, hoping he'd gone back there. But he hadn't. Which left me with one choice.

I took a deep breath and dialed George's number. I'd been going to call him anyway. This just wasn't the way I wanted to do it. He picked up immediately—he'd probably been studying or working on his paper.

"I'm glad you phoned," he began. "I've been thinking about the other night. I was out of line."

"So was I." I was surprised at how happy I was to hear his voice. "I had no call to say what I did."

"You want me to come over? I'm about ready to take a study break."

"Good." I gave him an extremely abbreviated version of what had happened.

"That wasn't what I had in mind."

"I know."

He sighed. "All right. Give me the address. I'll be right there."

I went into the store after I hung up. It was small, its merchandise shoehorned into several shelves, most of which were filled with snack foods of various kinds. The black-and-white checkered linoleum floor needed to be washed and one of the overhead neon lights flickered in a way that indicated it was going to have to be changed soon. The clerk glanced up when I came in, then went back to reading a book. He was maybe eighteen or nineteen and had the look of a college student. During the time that George took to arrive, which was twenty minutes, he didn't do anything to indicate he was aware of my presence.

Which was okay with me, because I wasn't in the mood to make polite chitchat. I wasn't even in the mood to say hello. I spent the time watching the rain falling, wishing my headache would go away, thumbing through yesterday's edition of the *Herald Journal,* and trying to piece together what had happened.

I was still trying to do that when George roared up. As I walked out, he leaned over and opened the Taurus's door. I got in. The seat was soft. The air smelled faintly of George's aftershave. I could feel my muscles start to unknot. Why were we always fighting? I wondered. Why couldn't we just talk things through?

"Let's go," I said, and closed the door.

"Not until I know what's going on." George turned off the engine and waited.

"Fine." Since I had a pretty good idea where Amy was going, fifteen minutes really weren't going to matter much, one way or the other. I settled into my seat and told George about the kidnapping ploy and finding Toon Town and how we went to Gerri Richmond's and then to the embalming school building. I told him about the booby-trapped door and how I'd gone in one end of the building and Amy had gone out the other and driven off with my car.

"How'd she'd get the cab started?" George asked. He'd been silent until that point.

I was going to say Amy had hot-wired it, but I was too tired to lie, so I told him the truth. George started laughing before I'd even finished. At another time I would have joined in, but not now. Now all I felt was an irrational anger. Anger at George for laughing. Anger at Amy for doing what she'd done—making a fool out of me. But most of all, what I felt was anger at myself. Then, as quickly as it had come, the rage subsided and I began to smile. The situation really was pretty funny. I looked over at George. He'd stopped laughing and had begun making soft popping noises with his lips—a sign that he was thinking.

"Where do you think Toon Town would have gotten his hands on a bugging device like the one you described?" he asked.

"Remember, he installs security systems for a living. He probably has access to lots of stuff."

George shook his head in disgust at himself. "That's right. I forget. And even if he didn't, he could get it through the mail." He followed a man walking into the mini-mart with his eyes. "It's amazing what you can get through catalogs."

"Isn't it," I observed, as a car drove down the street, rap music blaring out its window, the sound waves echoing in the night like the wake of a boat.

George waited until it was quiet before he continued talking. "So at the moment," he said, "as far as you know, Amy and Toon Town have the diamonds."

"Yes."

"And Amy took them from her father's apartment?"

I nodded.

"And someone's been chasing her ever since."

I nodded.

"I guess you were right, after all."

"I wasn't going to say it."

"At least not tonight."

I shrugged and smiled.

George drummed his fingers on the dashboard. "What I'd like to know is, where this guy came from and how come whoever is following Amy knew she'd taken them."

I could think of three possibilities. I ticked them off. "He either saw her coming out of her father's apartment, or Amy told someone, or he figured it out."

"Those three possibilities all depend on the fact that this person already knew the diamonds were there," George observed.

"I know."

George shook his head. "Dennis was a moron. He should have just transferred the money to the Cayman Islands like everyone else. It would have been a hell of a lot easier. On him."

"Well, his wife said the funeral was nice."

"Let's hope he found that thought comforting." George started drumming his fingers on the dashboard again. "The question is: where did the money come from?"

I thought about Frank and Charlie arguing over the balance sheet. Then I thought back to when my family had run a business and what had happened there. "He was skimming off the family business. He had to be. It's the only thing that makes sense."

George nodded his head in agreement and turned the key in the ignition.

"All right," he said. "Where do you want to go?"

I brushed a strand of hair out of my eyes before I answered. "I figure, given Toon Town's condition and the fact that Amy's probably behind the wheel, they're going to go to the ER room at St. Ann's, the house on Easton, or Toon Town's home."

"Which one do you want to start with?"

"St Ann's. It's the closest."

"What if they're not in any of those places?"

"I guess I'll have to call it in."

George put the Taurus in reverse and backed up onto the street. "Boy, Connelly's gonna love this when he hears about it." He took a left.

"Maybe he won't."

"And maybe jellybeans won't melt in the rain."

We were passing the school when I saw my cab.

It was parked right where I'd left it when I'd gone in the building.

Chapter 30

George raised an eyebrow. "I guess they didn't get very far," he observed.

"I guess not."

George parked a little way down the street, and we got out and started towards the cab. Both of us were silent. Both of us were uneasy. George liked the unexplained even less than I did. When we reached it, I hesitated for a few seconds before opening the door to the driver's side.

"Here goes," I said, afraid of what I was going to find.

But everything looked the same. I checked the rear seat. My backpack and cell phone were still there.

George zipped up his Windbreaker. "Why do you think they came back?" he asked.

"Maybe Amy left something inside." It was the only answer I could come up with, but it wasn't very satisfying. Where was Toon Town? Unless he'd had a miraculous recovery, I couldn't imagine him walking across the street, let alone through the building. And I sure as hell couldn't imagine Amy carrying him.

"So what do you want to do?" George enquired, as I closed the cab door. A small smile played around the corners of his mouth. I could tell he knew what I was going to say. I didn't disappoint him either.

"You have a flashlight in your trunk?" I asked. I would use mine if I had to, but the beam was weak, and I would have preferred something of a better quality.

"We could wait until they come out," George suggested. "It might be easier."

"Not for me." I was cold, I was tired, I was hungry, and I didn't want to spend the rest of my night in a car—even if I were with George.

"I figured." He walked back to the Taurus.

He returned a minute later carrying two substantial-looking metal flashlights. He handed one to me and we walked across the street. This time I made a full circuit of the building. There were three exits, not two, as I'd previously thought. One in back. One in front. And one on the right side of the building. I checked each of them. The one in the back and the one on the side were locked, but the one in front wasn't.

"They must have come in this way," I observed, and pushed the door open with the flashlight handle. Nothing fell down. Amy had missed an opportunity—or maybe she just had something else waiting for us inside. George played the beam of his flashlight up, down, and around. It caught squares of linoleum floor tile, bulletin boards, and a covered radiator, but no trip wires.

We looked at each other and stepped inside. Nothing happened. George made as little noise as possible shutting the door, but the click seemed to reverberate throughout the hall. I sniffed the air. It smelled old, as if it had been there for fifty years or more. I took a step. The linoleum groaned. George took a step. The linoleum groaned louder.

"Forget about trying to surprise them," he whispered. His breath was hot on my ear.

"I know," I whispered back.

But just the same, we tried to make as little noise as possible, as we moved across the hall. I'd taken about ten steps, when we came to another door. It was open. I inspected the floor with my flashlight. Its beam picked up drops of something dark. I nudged George to show him. Then I squatted down and touched one of the spots with my finger. It was wet. I brought my finger up to my nose and sniffed.

"Blood." I wiped my hand on my jeans. If I had to bet, I'd say it was Toon Town's. I was surprised he'd gotten as far as he had.

George grunted and focused his beam of light in front of him. There seemed to be more spots, but then some of them scuttled away and I realized they were roaches. I repressed a shiver. I hate those things. Probably a holdover from all my years in New York.

"I guess the trick is to follow the spots that stay still," George said, as he moved ahead.

I didn't reply. The dark disoriented me, and I was glad that the Windbreaker George was wearing was fluorescent. It stood out in the dark like a beacon, tethering me to him. I kept listening for sounds, but the only noises I heard were rats scuttling out of the way and the sound of my heart beating in my chest. George and I seemed to be in the main reception area now. The space felt bigger. A large kiosk squatted in the center. I caught glimpses of a stairway with a bannister off to the left. Three doors loomed up in front of us.

George and I both stopped. A car roared by outside and the noise made us jump.

"You see any more spots?" George asked. He was still whispering, even though Amy and Toon Town had to have heard us by now.

I fanned my flashlight in a half circle. My beam picked up something I thought might be a spot about three feet in front of me and off to the right a little. I walked over and, when it didn't move, I squatted down and touched it with the tip of my finger. It was wet. Then I saw more blood splatters. They led to the middle door. I stood up and indicated the path with my flashlight. I caught a whiff of George's cologne as he brushed by me. I followed. He paused in front of the door. I heard him swallow. I heard him take a deep breath. Then he raised his leg and kicked the door open. I felt a movement in the air, as the door flew back and crashed into the wall. The dark amplified the crash and it reverberated through the room. For a second, before George and I lifted our flashlights, the door framed a rectangle of blackness that seemed absolute, the definition of nothingness. Then I heard a moan.

George turned back to me. "Did you hear that?" he asked.

"Yes."

We heard the moan again. It was fainter this time. And it was coming from inside the room. Our lights picked up desks and chairs, a piece of crumpled paper on the floor, a blackboard with writing still on it, and then a figure huddled on the floor in the far right corner. George checked the doorway for traps. There weren't any, and we went through. The air smelled of chalk dust and fresh urine.

"Toon Town?" I asked, as I walked towards the figure in the corner. I was positive it would be him.

He groaned, then answered yes in a voice so low I wouldn't have heard it if I weren't almost next to him.

George and I squatted down beside him. He turned towards us and I heard the intake of George's breath as he looked at Toon Town's ruined face. His eye and his mouth had swollen even more since I'd seen him last. In the light, his injuries seemed grotesque. He was barely recognizable.

His mouth moved. He was forming words, but they were garbled, and I couldn't understand what he was saying. "I'm sorry," I said. "Can you say that again."

He tried. I could see his face contorting with the effort. "I'm shot," he finally managed to get out.

George played his flashlight's beam over Toon Town. The midsection of his shirt was saturated with blood. George picked up its edge, looked, then put it back down.

"He's been shot in the stomach," he said. I couldn't read the expression on his face. It was too dark. Then he rested a finger on the side of Toon Town's neck. "His pulse is low." He unzipped his Windbreaker and draped it over Toon Town. I did the same with my jacket. I touched his hand. It was cold and clammy. I wondered if he would live.

George bent over Toon Town. "Can you hear me?"

"Yes."

"I'm going to call someone to help you right away, but I have to know: is Amy hurt, too?"

Toon Town groaned. "I don't know. They took her."

"Who is they?"

Toon Town closed his good eye.

"Please tell us," I begged. "I know you don't want anything to happen to her."

A spasm crossed Toon Town's face. "I don't know where

they took her," he said, when it had passed. "I didn't see. They shot me. Then they left."

George sighed. "I'm going to call for an ambulance now."

Toon Town said something I couldn't catch.

"They'll be right here. You'll be fine." George patted Toon Town's hand, trying to reassure him. But I could hear the lie in George's voice. I wondered if Toon Town heard it too. Then George stood up. "I'll be back as soon as I make the call," he said to me. He started walking towards the main entrance. I could hear his footsteps echoing through the room as he went.

Toon Town pulled on my sleeve. I leaned down. He pulled some more. I leaned closer. My ear was just a couple of inches away from his mouth. His breath was sour. "I didn't mean for it to happen this way," he told me. He made a strange mewling sound. It took me a few seconds to realize he was crying. "I thought Amy would be all right. I wouldn't have called if I didn't. You believe me, don't you?"

"Yes."

"I just wanted a little candy. That wasn't so wrong, was it?" Toon Town made a rasping sound and grabbed my hand with his. It felt as if I were shaking hands with the iceman. A few seconds later, he slackened his grip. His hand fell back down. He began to ramble. "Families. You can't trust them at all. You think you can, but you can't."

I leaned closer. "Are you talking about Amy's family?"

"Worse than mine," Toon Town mumbled. "Mine might hit me, but at least you know where you stand. Not like hers. Double-dealing sons-of–bitches."

"Who are you talking about?"

"I was gonna go down to Mexico and live on the beach. Why should they have all the fun just because they were born better than me?"

"Do you mean her brother? Her cousin? Her uncle? Her mother? Who?"

But Toon Town didn't answer my question. I don't think he even heard it. "I'm smarter than they are. Just because I couldn't afford no college education." And then he stopped talking.

"Come on," I said. "Tell me." I leaned even closer.

But he didn't. He shoulders arched up. He made a gargling noise. Then his head fell to one side. I realized I couldn't feel his breath on my face anymore. I sat back and rested one of my fingers on his neck. I couldn't feel any pulse at all. Nothing. Toon Town was dead. I closed his eyes and stood up, wishing that I felt sorrier about his death than I did and wondering who it was that Toon Town had been talking about.

I gave him one last look and headed for the door. There was no point in sticking around. Toon Town didn't need me now. I held the flashlight to my watch. George had been gone five minutes at the most. It seemed like fifteen, though. I walked through the room quickly. I wanted to get out as soon as possible. I didn't like this place. I wouldn't have liked it in the daylight, and I sure as hell didn't like it now in the dark. I was walking through the reception area when I thought I heard something. I stopped and listened. There it was again. It was a song. I made out the first stanza to "Three Blind Mice." Then I heard a giggle. The sound seemed to drift out of nowhere. I wondered if that was because the dark had affected my spatial perception, or because the acoustics in the building were strange.

Then the same person—it sounded liked a young girl—started singing "Old MacDonald Had A Farm." She was slurring the words as though she were either very drunk or very stoned.

Amy?

But that didn't make any sense.

Given what Toon Town had said before he died and the way he looked, I would have expected her to be dead, not stoned or drunk off her ass.

But if it wasn't her, who the hell else was it?

By now, whoever was singing had gone on to "London Bridge." She'd gotten to "take a key and lock her up," when I realized the sounds were coming from the direction of the stairs.

I briefly entertained the notion of going out and getting George, but I decided against it. If the person singing was Amy, I wasn't going to need him and, if it were someone else, I didn't want them slipping out the side or back doors while I went out the front. As a possible witness to what had happened here, I wanted to make sure they didn't go away.

I walked towards the stairs, aimed the beam up, grabbed the bannister, and started to climb. I'd gotten to the fourth step when I heard a crunch. I'd stepped on something. I hoped it wasn't a giant roach. I lowered the beam and looked. I'd stepped on a small bone. The roach would have been better. I shone the beam up the next couple of stairs and saw more bones. Little ones. A small pile of them. I swallowed. My heart was pounding, as I went up to inspect them. I lifted one up and the others came with it. They were all attached.

I saw the clasp and started to laugh. I was holding Amy's bracelet. So it *was* Amy upstairs. The girl was amazing. Nothing seemed to touch her. As I slipped her bracelet in my pocket, I wondered who her guardian angel was and if maybe he could care for me, too.

I redoubled my pace. Amy was singing "Row, Row, Row Your Boat" when I got to the second floor. By the time I got to the third floor, she'd just finished. I swung my flashlight around. There was nowhere else to go. I couldn't go any higher. Amy had stopped singing now. I couldn't hear anything. Everything was quiet. I stood absolutely still and listened as hard as I could. Then I heard footsteps.

Above me.

Amy was on the roof.

Jesus, I thought, as I walked from room to room swinging my flashlight this way and that to make sure there were no booby traps, this girl doesn't make anything easy for anyone. I was in too much of a hurry to watch where I was going, and I kept crashing into things. Rats scurried out of the way. I started shouting out Amy's name. I don't know if she heard me or not, but she started singing again. Finally, in the fourth room, I found the way up to the roof. It was one of those pull-down metal staircases that you could raise and lower. As I climbed up, I realized that even though it was night, it was lighter outside than it had been inside.

The first thing I did when I clambered out onto the roof was to take a deep breath of fresh air. God, it was good to be outside, away from the must and the mold. The sky was still grey, although the clouds had thinned enough for me to see the moon behind them.

The roof looked bigger than I thought it would. Enclosed by a small wall that was a couple of feet high and maybe six inches wide, the roof's surface was tarred, just like the one on my old apartment building in New York City. A smokestack stood in one corner.

"Amy," I yelled, while I looked around.

"Yes?" Her voice was high and light.

I turned towards it.

I gasped when I saw where she was.

Chapter 31

Amy was standing on the wall of the building. Her head was cocked. The wind was ruffling her hair. She was watching me as if I were some odd, wonderous thing. Then she spread her arms and picked up one leg holding it out into the air, as she balanced on the other. " 'Bet you can't do this," she cried, a little girl again, walking a fence in the country. Only this wasn't the country and she wasn't on a fence.

"I bet you're right." She was teetering now. Any mistake on her part would send her plunging over the edge and, while a fall from a three story building might not kill her—if she were lucky—it sure wasn't something she'd walk away from unscathed. "Just stay right there," I told her.

"You want to see what else I can do?" She giggled again.

"You'll show me in a minute." I walked towards her quickly. I didn't want to run. I was afraid I might scare her. "Put your leg down."

She pouted, but she did what I asked.

"How about getting back on the roof?"

"No." She stamped her foot. "I like it up here."

"That's okay." I did soothing.

"It's fun." Then she went into her pocket and took out a small piece of bunched up tin foil. "You wanna hit? I have lots."

Well, Toon Town had apparently been telling the truth about the acid. "When we get downstairs."

I was almost next to her. "But I'm not giving any to Wally." It took me a minute to realize Amy was talking about Toon Town. "Because he did a bad thing."

"What was that?"

"He told Shep where I was. He promised he wouldn't, but he did."

"Who is Shep?" I asked, as I closed my hand around Amy's wrist. It was tiny. I hadn't realized how fragile Amy was. I was pulling her towards me, when I picked up a faint sound in back of me. It was, I realized, the sound of someone running, someone running towards me. Amy was staring behind me.

I heard her say, "oh oh," as I told myself to move to the side. But it was too late to do anything except brace myself. A second later I felt a hand between my shoulder blades, I smelled a strong whiff of cologne, and then I was being propelled forward. I bumped into Amy. She yelled, tottered, and fell off the roof.

Because I still had one hand around her wrist, I began to go over too. I fell to my knees and leaned backwards, while I tightened my grip on Amy. I was dragged another foot before I stopped moving. I turned to look and see if whoever had pushed me were still there, but the roof was empty. He'd gone back down the stairs. I was aware of the pain in my shoulder, as I turned back. I had to get Amy on the roof now, because I couldn't hold her this way for long. I knew she couldn't weigh more than ninety pounds, but right now she felt like a thousand.

I leaned forward. "Give me your other hand," I yelled, as I reached for it. My left shoulder felt as though it was about to be wrenched out of its socket.

Amy began to laugh.

"Give it to me now," I screamed.

"I'm Peter Pan," she cried. "Let's fly off to Never-Never Land."

Oh God. From what I could see, we were already there. As I bent over the wall and grabbed Amy's jacket collar, my eyes fastened on the ground below. I hadn't realized that three stories was so high off the ground. My stomach turned over. Just don't look down, I told myself. I closed my eyes, braced myself, and yanked. Sweat was pouring down my face. My arms felt as if they were on fire. They were beginning to shake from the strain. I could feel the veins in the side of my neck twitching and my face flushing. I pulled harder. Now I could see the top of Amy's head above the wall. Her laughter floated around me, surrounding me with its sound. I moved back a little, worked myself to a standing position, gritted my teeth, and pulled harder. I heard the sound of ripping material, but the top part of her chest appeared above the roof wall. I pulled some more. She was halfway up.

"Help me," I pleaded.

She giggled.

I moved back two steps and pulled with all the remaining strength that I had left. Amy flopped onto the roof, as if she were a fish I'd just landed.

She got on to her hands and knees, then sat up and

crossed her legs. "That was fun," she said. "Let's do it again."

"Let's not." Even though my hands were shaking, I managed to take off my belt, which I'd doubled up because it was too long, put it through one of Amy's belt loops, and wound the end around my hand. It was something I did when I couldn't find Zsa Zsa's leash. I figured the principle was the same. Then I collapsed.

"Why you'd do that?" Amy asked.

"Because I'm old and I'm tired of running."

I expected an argument, but all she said was, "Cool." Then she sat back, rested her head against the wall, and closed her eyes, no doubt enjoying her version of home movies.

I just sat there, wondering when I'd get the energy to move, watching the clouds drift across the moon's face, and wondering where the person was who'd tried to push me off the roof. He was probably far away by now. He obviously hadn't waited around to see what happened. Why? I wondered. Didn't he care? Or maybe he just had a weak stomach. Then I realized I'd smelled that cologne before. I just couldn't remember where.

I was beginning to shiver. I looked down. My skin was covered with goose bumps. I didn't have a jacket on, and the cold from the ground was seeping into my legs. "Come on," I told Amy. I forced myself up and went to pick up the flashlight I'd dropped.

She came along with me. She didn't have any other choice. "Where are we going?"

"Home. We're going home." And I pushed her in front of me.

We walked down the stairs into the building. The darkness closed over us. I heard a rat scurrying by. I quickened my pace. We had gotten down the last flight of stairs, when I caught the sound of George's voice calling for me.

"I'm here. In the reception area," I yelled, and I moved towards his voice.

He was standing in the main entrance way. He must have just come in, because the front door was still slightly ajar. "Sorry, I took so long," he said, as I walked towards him. Amy lagged behind. George's voice seemed to frighten her, and I had to pull on my belt to keep her moving. "But your cell phone was dead. I had to go back to the mini-mart. Then I got put on hold. How's Toon Town?"

"Not very well. He didn't make it."

George made a popping noise with his mouth. "I had a feeling he wasn't going to."

Amy moved behind me. "I want to go," she complained, sounding like a bored little girl.

"Is that who I think it is?" George demanded, narrowing his eyes so he could see into the dark.

"I found her on the roof."

"Unfucking believable." He shook his head. "The police are . . ."

"Blue people," Amy cried, and she began to clap.

Suddenly I could hear sirens in the distance. The police would be here soon.

"She's stoned, isn't she?" George asked.

"Off her ass. And she's got a lot of hits on her, too."

"Fucking great. How many?"

"I'm about to find out." I began going through her pockets. I pulled out ten small tin foil packages plus an unwrapped pane. "She's got enough stuff in this pocket alone to send her away for a couple of years."

George shook his head. "Amazing. Like father like daughter."

"We could get rid of it before everyone gets here."

"No good. Not in her condition. First thing they're gonna ask her is what's she's carrying. God only knows what she's gonna say." George went in his pocket and handed me his car keys. "My car's down the street. Get her out of here."

"What are you going to do?"

"I'll wait. Don't worry. It'll be okay." The sirens were getting closer. "Go now."

"Thanks." I leaned over and kissed him.

He kissed me back. "Just go."

I grabbed Amy and hustled her through the door.

"But I want to see the blue men," she protested. "I want to see the pretty lights."

"Don't worry, you will." I dragged her down the street. She kept looking back. By now the sirens were loud. The cops were going to be here any second. When we got to the Taurus, I opened the door and pushed Amy in. She started to get out. "Stay," I said, depressing the lock button. Then I slammed the door shut, ran around to my side and got in. I'd just pulled out and made a U-turn when the cops rounded the other corner.

I drove away slowly. I didn't want to do anything that would arouse suspicion.

I could see three squad cars lined up by the curb. George was standing outside, with his arms crossed over his chest, waiting.

I wondered what he was going to say.

Chapter 32

It took me about twenty minutes to drive to Amy's house. Along the way, I stopped and dropped the acid I'd taken off her down a sewer grate. Amy thought that was funny and began laughing hysterically, but after a minute, her laughter turned to tears. She wouldn't tell me why she was crying: she probably didn't know herself. I couldn't get her to stop and, after about five minutes, the sound of her sobbing tore at my sympathy and shredded it to pieces. I was glad when I saw the stone pillars that marked the turnoff into Elysian Fields and even gladder to be ringing the bell on Gerri Richmond's door. When no one answered, I started banging and yelling—actually it was a miracle one of the neighbors didn't call the police—and kept at it until I heard "I'm coming" over the din I'd created.

"Who is it?" Gerri Richmond's voice was thick with sleep. "What do you want?"

"Robin Light. I've got Amy with me."

"Oh my God. Wait a minute. I have to shut off the alarm." I heard a beep beep and the click of locks being undone. Then Gerri Richmond flung the door open and rushed out. She was wearing a white silk nightgown and robe. She hadn't bothered to belt the robe and it billowed behind her in the night air. "Where's my daughter?"

I pointed to the front seat of the Taurus. "In there. She doesn't want to come out." Amy had curled herself into a ball and put her thumb in her mouth when I'd stopped in front of her house. "She's taken some acid and she's really not in good shape." Gerri Richmond's hand flew to her mouth. "I think you'd better call a doctor."

Gerri ran over and opened the car door. If the ground were cold on her bare feet, she gave no indication of it. "Amy," she cried. She began stroking her hair. "Amy, can you hear me?"

Amy didn't move.

I touched Gerri on the shoulder. "It would be better if she were under a doctor's care as soon as possible." I told her about what had just happened and about how it would just be a matter of time before the police showed up at her door.

Gerri Richmond's face became even more drawn as I talked. When I was done, she told me to stay with Amy. Then she turned and rushed into the house. She was back a few minutes later. "They're coming," she announced. Then she got in the car and put her arms around her daughter.

Amy didn't respond. Gerri Richmond began to cry. I started to say something, but she said, "don't," so I turned my head away and watched the white cat cleaning itself in the window of the house across the way. Listening to Gerri Richmond's quiet sobs depressed me, so I tried to think about other things instead. Like who had killed Toon Town and what was happening to George and where I had smelled the cologne I'd smelled up on the roof before, and who the hell Shep was.

I was still trying to come up with some answers, when I heard a car coming up the road. A minute later, I saw its lights cutting through the dark. I held my breath, hoping it was Amy's doctor instead of the cops. It was. No flashing lights. I stepped into the road and waved it down. The car screeched to a stop under the streetlight. It was a BMW. I guess the rehab business was booming. Who said drugs don't pay? The only people who don't get rich are the kids that use and the kids that sell. Everyone else makes a bundle—one way or another.

"Where is she?" the doctor asked, after he'd gotten out of his car. Like his car, he looked expensive. Maybe it was the leather trench coat or the five-hundred-dollar-a-pair Japanese glasses or the Rolex on his wrist.

I pointed to the Taurus. "Inside there. She's curled up in a ball." I told him what had happened and what was probably going to happen.

He nodded as I talked. Then, when I was done, he went over to confer with Gerri Richmond. They talked for about five minutes, after which he gave Amy a cursory examination and a shot. She didn't flinch when the needle went in. She was doing a good imitation of catatonic. Finally, I ended up having to help him carry her over to his car and put her inside.

"She'll be all right," he assured me.

"I hope so." Amy was sprawled on the seat like a rag doll. Her eyes were vacant. Her mouth had dropped open.

"She was like this the last time, too." He got in his car and roared off.

As I watched the taillights disappearing around the curve, I realized I was very cold. I turned towards Gerri Richmond. She was shivering.

"I guess I ought to thank you," she said.

I didn't say anything.

"Do you want to come in and have a drink?"

"Yes." I was suddenly aware that I wanted one very badly, so I followed Gerri Richmond inside.

She went straight to the coffee table in the den, grabbed the bottle of vodka, and poured two big shots. "Here's yours," she said, handing me one. She finished hers before I was halfway done with mine and poured herself another. "What do you think is going to happen now?" she asked.

"I think the police will be here soon. I think they're going to want to talk to Amy." (And me, I added silently.)

"She's not going to be able to tell them anything."

"She will eventually."

"I know." Gerri downed her second shot.

I took another sip of vodka and put the glass down. "The money Dennis took?"

"What about it?"

"Where did it come from?"

"Where do you think?" She poured herself another shot and started talking about herself. I didn't interrupt. I figured she'd work her way back to answering my question sooner or later. "I grew up in the Bronx. My mom worked as a sales clerk at Alexander's. We never had extra money for anything. Ever. Then Dennis came along. He was my ticket out." Gerri shook her head. "It was funny. He married me because I was pregnant."

"Too bad Amy wasn't his."

Gerri gulped down her third shot. "It should have worked. There was no reason it shouldn't have."

"But it didn't."

"In the beginning, it was all right. But then, I don't know. We stopped liking each other. Or maybe we stopped trying. And Amy just got worse and worse." She rolled the shot glass between the palms of her hands. "And Brad and Dennis started fighting. And that got worse, too. When Dennis came home, he'd be in a horrible mood. He was afraid Brad was going to take the business away from him and give it to Frank."

"How could he do that?"

"Dennis always thought Brad was smarter, even though he really wasn't. He kept thinking he was going to come up with something." Gerri put the glass down and leaned back on the sofa.

I could guess the next part of the story. "So Dennis began to build himself a little retirement fund, a fund no one was supposed to know about."

"That's right."

"Only things didn't quite work out that way."

"No."

"Did Brad suspect?"

"He did, but he couldn't prove it."

"Why didn't he bring the auditors in?"

Gerri picked up her glass and put it back down. "Frank was involved in an . . ." she hesitated, "an accident at the plant about three years ago. He was stoned. Someone was seriously injured and subsequently died. Frank could have been charged with manslaughter. Brad paid a lot of money to hush it up. I think he was afraid if he brought the auditors in, Dennis would go to the police. Anyway, this was family business. They both liked to keep things private."

"So how did you find out about the money?"

Gerri snorted. "He wanted to buy a Range Rover. I knew

we didn't have the money, but he told me not to worry about it. That wasn't like Dennis. I knew something was up. I started searching. It took me awhile, but I found the records—and some cash. He'd made a safe in his closet between two floorboards."

"So what happened when you told him?"

"He laughed and told me he was planning to tell me anyway. He said it was for our old age."

"And you believed him?"

"Yes, I did. I guess I shouldn't have." Gerri poured herself another shot of vodka and gulped it down. "That money was mine too. I wanted it." She touched her pearls. "Amy must have heard us talking about it. I bet that's why she followed him. She thought she could make him give her the money so she could go to New York."

"That's what she said to me." I toyed with my glass. "One thing bothers me, though."

"What's that?"

"You must have been out looking for Dennis, too. If Amy found him, why couldn't you?"

Gerri shrugged, knocked back her fourth shot—at this rate she was going to be horizontal soon—and poured herself a fifth. "I wasn't really looking for him. I didn't care."

"Why's that?"

"I was glad to see him go."

"You didn't care about the money? You just told me you did."

Gerri Richmond drank her fifth shot down. "He drove Amy off. He told her to get out of the house. I should have protected her."

I studied Gerri Richmond for a minute. She wasn't the kind of woman to just let things go. I leaned forward. "You did find him, didn't you?" I said softly.

Gerri looked away.

"Did you tell Amy where he was?"

She snapped her head around.

"It would be an interesting way of telling him you knew where he was," I observed.

Gerri put her face in her hands. Her voice was muffled when she spoke. "I wanted what was best for her. She's talented. She deserves to go to art school."

"You could have afforded to send her."

"No, I couldn't. I don't have any money of my own. Dennis wrote all the checks."

"So really, you're better off with him dead. You get the house, possibly part of the business."

She brought her hands down. "I didn't kill him."

"Then who did?"

"I don't know."

"I think you do."

"Why can't you just leave everything alone?" she cried.

"Because it's gone past that point."

She got up and stumbled out to the living room. I followed. She stopped in front of the mantel and studied the photographs. "I'm glad I have these," she said, and she picked up an early photograph of her family and hugged it to her breasts.

I came up behind her. "Who is Shep?" I asked. Gerri's back stiffened. She didn't say anything. "He almost killed your daughter tonight," I continued. "He's the one that's been supplying her with LSD." Gerri remained silent. "If you don't tell me who he is, you might as well just put a gun to Amy's head now." I listened to the silence. "You owe her that much," I insisted.

"I know," she said softly. After another minute, she gave me the name.

Chapter 33

It was Frank Richmond. Once I heard the name, everything fell into place. Shep was his nickname. It derived from his middle name, Shepard, Gerri informed me. Which, I couldn't help reflecting, was probably a corruption of the word Shepherd—now there was a misnomer if ever there was one—I shook my head. Now I remembered where I'd smelled the cologne before. A wave of Aramis had washed over me when I'd introduced myself to Frank Richmond in the hallway the first time I'd gone out to the plant. He'd had enough of the stuff on to make me sneeze.

"Nobody calls him that anymore," Gerri remarked. She was still standing in front of the mantel, staring straight ahead at nothing. "They haven't for years."

"Amy still does," I replied. I went into the kitchen and dialed the number Connelly had given me.

He answered with a growled, "Yes?" on the fourth ring.

"Did I wake you?"

"What the fuck do you expect me to be doing at four thirty in the morning?" he roared. "Cooking a four-course dinner?"

"How about earning your salary?" I told him about this evening.

"So you want me to go down and pull this guy in for questioning on the strength of the testimony of a doped up girl and your powers of olfactory remembrance?"

"Meaning, you're not going to talk to him?"

"No. I will. On the off chance you're right."

I ran my finger over the edge of the cabinet. "Aren't you going to thank me?"

"For what? Disturbing my sleep? You should be happy I'm not arresting you." He hung up.

Oh well. I hadn't really expected anything else.

I went back to the living room and asked Gerri for Frank's address. She was still cradling the picture, lost in the contemplation of her past. She gave me the street and house number without turning around.

I don't think she heard me say good-bye.

I saw myself standing there, stranded in my history. The thought made me hurry out.

I closed the door softly, as I left.

Leaving her alone in her big, empty house.

I saw the Sundance out of the corner of my eye, as I turned onto the street Frank Richmond lived on. There was something familiar about the car, though I couldn't put my finger on what it was and, after a few seconds, I let the thought go. I had too many other things to think about.

I knew I should have gone home, but I couldn't—not until I had the satisfaction of seeing Frank being driven away in Connelly's car. Of course Connelly wouldn't like my being here—but that was too bad. He owed me. After all, I had solved a case for him—even if there were a lot of loose ends. Too many, really. I was thinking about them as I parked behind a blue pickup truck about thirty feet down from where Frank lived, turned off the engine, and waited for Connelly. I figured it would probably be twenty minutes before he showed up. I'd gotten there as fast as I had, because Frank Richmond lived only five minutes away from Elysian Fields.

The apartment he occupied turned out to be located on top of a shabby beauty salon called Short Cuts. It was within walking distance of Gerri's house. I couldn't help thinking that Amy had probably snuck over here to buy her stuff, and I wondered if her father had found out what she was doing and threatened Frank, and he had retaliated by killing Dennis. The other two deaths had followed from that act. I guess I'd find out soon enough. As I rubbed my arms and stamped my feet to keep warm, I noticed the lights were on in Frank's apartment. Either the guy had insomnia, or he was an early riser, or he was cleaning up from his earlier activities. Probably it was a combination of the first and third items on the list. I would imagine that after a night like Frank had had, it would take more than a warm cup of milk to settle you down enough so you could fall asleep.

I was just thinking that I wasn't going to have that problem when I finally crawled into bed, when I saw the door to Frank's apartment open. I scrunched down. Frank walked outside and looked around suspiciously, checking out the street. Satisfied that no one was out, he turned and headed towards the back of the apartment. He was carrying a plastic garbage bag in his hand. When he returned a few minutes later, his hands were empty. Then he went inside. A few minutes later, the light in his apartment went out. I was just getting out of the Taurus to investigate when Connelly pulled up. He'd made better time than I thought he would.

"I should have known," he said, when he saw me. "Is he in there?"

I nodded. "And I'd check the dumpster in the back if I were you. He just threw something out."

"Probably yesterday's pizza."

"Or the gun Toon Town was shot with."

Connelly grunted. He wasn't going to give me anything if he didn't have to. "Stay here," he ordered. Then he drove up in front of Frank Richmond's door and got out. He moved stiffly, as if his joints hadn't had time to adjust to being awake yet. I followed, taking care to keep a good ten feet or so behind.

Connelly turned and frowned at me. "Don't come any closer," he warned. Then he turned and knocked on the door.

Startled by the noise, a rail of a cat dove under a car. The light upstairs went on. Connelly knocked again and identified himself. A few minutes later, the door opened, spilling a stream of light out onto the pavement. Connelly stepped in and closed the door behind him. I did the only thing I could do: wait. Ten minutes later, he and Frank Richmond stepped outside.

Richmond's gait was smooth, his shoulders were erect, he looked tired but confident. Then he caught sight of me. The color drained out of his face.

"You should wear less cologne," I said.

"I don't know what you're talking about," he stammered.

Connelly motioned for him to get in the car. Frank Richmond did as he was told. Connelly slammed the door shut, got in on his side, and drove away. Maybe it was because I was so tired, but the sight of Frank Richmond being brought in for questioning wasn't nearly as satisfying as I thought it would be.

On the way home, I kept thinking about Amy and what was going to happen to her, and I couldn't let go of the thought that there was something I had missed. Something important. It was right there, but I couldn't get hold of it. It kept sliding away from me. I hit the steering wheel in frustration and got a sore hand for my troubles.

Except for two other cars, Genesee Street was deserted at four thirty in the morning. Houses were dark and stores were closed. When I was in my twenties, I liked being up at this hour. I enjoyed eating breakfast and watching the city wake up. But now all I wanted to do was go home and go to bed. As I pulled into my driveway, one of my neighbor's kids was getting into his car. He had an early morning paper route and had to arrive at the collection place by five at the latest, if he wanted to get people their papers by six thirty. He waved at me and I waved back. As I got out of my cab, I could hear him trying to start his Plymouth. It was a rusted out piece of junk that groaned and wheezed every time the kid turned on the ignition. Finally, he got the thing started and pulled out into the street, and I went into my house.

Zsa Zsa came running down the stairs to greet me. She was hysterical with delight at seeing me, and I petted her and told her what a marvelous girl she was for a good five minutes before I went up to my bedroom. By now, I was so tired that my bones were aching. I went past Manuel's room on the way to mine. His door was ajar, and I could see he was sleeping—something I hoped I was going to be doing very soon. The moment I got in my room, I shucked off my shoes and headed straight for my bed. I sighed with pleasure, as I lay down. Zsa Zsa hopped up next to me and snuggled into my side. I gave her a quick belly rub and called George, but he wasn't home. He was probably still downtown. I hung up and looked out the window. With the leaves off the trees, I could see some of the houses built on top of the hill above me. As I watched, the lights came on in two of them. I was just closing my eyes, when the phone rang. I reached over and got it.

"About the diamonds," Connelly began. I guess he didn't do preliminaries.

"What about them?"

"Richmond said you have them."

"I wish."

"That's what I figured."

"Did he say anything else?"

"He's confessed to the three homicides."

"That was short."

"Sometimes it goes like that. I'm getting ready to take his statement. You're going to need to come down later. Let's say around two." Connelly hung up.

I replaced the receiver and went back to staring out the window. I could hear the roar of a garbage truck climbing up the hill. Today was garbage day. I should have taken mine out, but I was too tired to move. I turned on my side, hugged Zsa Zsa to me, and closed my eyes. A car that sounded like my neighbor's kid's Plymouth clunked by. A moment later, another car honked, and I heard a door slam. I put my pillow over my head. The neighborhood was getting ready for the day, and I was trying to end mine. But every time I closed my eyes, I started replaying scenes from last night. I couldn't seem to get them out of my mind.

I kept seeing Amy tottering on the edge of the roof, Amy curled up in a ball crying, the doctor getting out of his car, Connelly taking Frank Richmond away. Then all of a sudden, I knew what was bothering me. It was the Plymouth Sundance that I'd passed on the way to Richmond's house. I'd seen that car two other times. It had been parked in front of the Mortuary School. And Manuel had gotten into it in front of Noah's Ark. I jumped out of bed and ran into Manuel's room. Suddenly I wasn't tired anymore.

"Manuel, Manuel," I cried, as I shook him awake. "Get up."

He groaned and opened one eye. "What time is it?"

"Early. Listen, the other day someone picked you up from the store in a Sundance. Who was it?"

"You're angry. I'll replace the Scotch we drank."

"Manuel, I don't give a fuck about the Scotch. What's his name?"

"Her name."

"Fine. Her name."

"It's Dee."

"Dee?" I blinked. "What kind of name is that?"

"That's her nickname." Manuel yawned. "It's short for Doodlebug."

"What's her real name?"

"Lisa."

"Lisa what?"

"You got me. Why do you want to know?"

I swear, Manuel and his friends could be poster children for the War On Drugs. "Where does she live?" I demanded, impatiently.

"On Oak Street. Right off of Lodi."

"What's the number?"

"I don't know. It's the pink house in the middle of the street. She lives downstairs. You're not going to talk to her, are you?" Manuel demanded, panicking. "Because I don't want to get her in trouble."

"You haven't. Go back to sleep."

"What's this about?"

"Nothing important," I lied, and I headed down the stairs before Manuel could ask me any more questions. Then I grabbed a jacket, told Zsa Zsa to guard the house, and headed out the door.

The sky had lightened. Bands of grey and pink and pale yellow showed in the east. The grass, stiff with frost, crunched under my feet, as I hurried to my car. People were out now. Some of my neighbors were setting out their trash and others were pulling out of their driveways.

Dee. I'd heard that name before. Where? Amy had scribbled UB in her notebook. Those letters had stood for Brad Richmond. It wasn't him. But they had to do with him in some way. I lit a cigarette and backed out of my driveway. Manuel had said her real name was Lisa. As I turned onto East Genesee, it hit me. Of course. Brad Richmond had called his secretary Dee. Lisa. Elizabeth Walker. She'd been so helpful. She'd told me all about Charlie. She'd even hugged me when I suggested she go speak to Brad Richmond about Charlie harassing her. Unbelievable. As I drove by a phone, it occurred to me that I should let Connelly know where the diamonds were. I stopped and dialed his beeper, but he didn't reply and, after a few minutes, I gave up.

Maybe I should have waited to get in touch with him, but I was pretty sure that if I did, Elizabeth Walker wouldn't be around for Connelly to find. She had the money, she had her ticket to Cancun, if she were smart—and she was—she would be gone very soon. In fact she might be already. I got back in George's car and sped off. As I drove, it occurred to me that with Elizabeth Walker in the picture, all the loose ends fit quite nicely. She was the circle that linked all the strands.

I wondered, why hadn't Frank given her up?

I wondered, what would make him take the fall for her?

Ten minutes later, I was on Oak. I spotted the house Manuel had described immediately. Unfortunately, the Sundance wasn't in the driveway. I parked, walked up to the apartment, and rang the bell. No one answered. I tried the door. It was locked. The living room blinds were up, so I cupped my hands over my eyes and looked inside. I couldn't see anyone moving. I straightened up and listened for footsteps or a radio going or some sign that someone was home, but I couldn't hear anything. It looked as if I were too late. Elizabeth Walker had left. I stopped at the nearest phone and left a message for Connelly. Then I went home.

Manuel was waiting for me.

He didn't look happy.

Chapter 34

Manuel was standing framed in the kitchen door when I came in. "I'm sorry," he wailed.

"You should be." I was about to say something else, when Elizabeth Walker stepped out from behind Manuel. She must have been hiding in back of the kitchen door. I caught my breath.

Manuel appeared ready to cry. "She's got a gun."

"You called and told her I was coming?" I could hear my voice. It was incredulous.

"I didn't know," Manuel cried. "I thought you were going to yell at her because of what we were doing. I wanted to warn her."

I guess all those articles about how communication is important between two people are right, after all.

"You have any rope in this house?" Elizabeth demanded. She sure didn't look sweet anymore. I wondered why I thought she had. It was the way she dressed, I decided. The flowered print dress and the pink nail polish.

"I think I have some in the basement."

"Let's go get it." Elizabeth motioned for Manuel to move.

He took a couple of steps and I could see the gun she was holding to his back. I heard muffled barking as I opened the basement door. I looked around. "Where's Zsa Zsa?"

"Locked in the downstairs bathroom," Elizabeth Walker said. "Let's go."

The three of us went down the stairs slowly. I tried to think of something I could do, but I couldn't. By the time I got to Walker, she would have shot Manuel.

"I'm really sorry," he whispered to me, as I clicked the basement light on. "I thought she liked me because I'm a good dancer."

I remembered the woman I'd seen him dancing with at the club. It had been Elizabeth Walker. Then I thought about the empty pizza boxes, the crushed cushions, Manuel's unexplained absences, the telephone conversations that had been cut short when I went out of the room.

"You've been seeing her all this time, haven't you?" Manuel hung his head. "And you've been telling her what I've been doing." He didn't look up. He couldn't bear to meet my eyes. I glanced over at Elizabeth Walker. Her smile told me everything I had to know. "You know," I said to her, "they have Frank in custody down at the PSB. He's already confessed to the three murders."

Elizabeth shrugged. We could have been talking about a problem with her carburetor.

"So that isn't going to do you any good."

"He won't say anything about me. He couldn't stand the thought of my being in prison."

"How chivalrous."

"Frank's a chivalrous guy. Now get the rope." She pressed the gun muzzle into Manuel's back to make sure I got the message. As I looked at Elizabeth Walker, there wasn't a doubt in my mind that she'd pull the trigger.

I did what she asked. Then she told me to tie Manuel's hands behind his back, and I did that, too.

"Tighter," she snapped, after she tested what I'd done.

"Any tighter and his circulation is going to be cut off."

"It's not going to matter."

Manuel blanched as I drew the rope in. What was about to happen to us was finally penetrating. Then we all went back upstairs.

"You really are a piece of work," I said to Elizabeth Walker, as we trooped into the hallway.

Elizabeth turned up the corners of her mouth. "My grandmother used to say that."

"I take it she didn't mean it as a compliment." I know mine never had.

"She worked as a maid in a motel all her life. Why should I care about what she thought?" She opened the door and glanced out to see if anyone was outside. Evidently no one was, because she told us to get in the Taurus. "You drive," she told me. "And I'll sit next to Manuel."

I stole a look at him. He was biting his lip to keep from crying. I wanted to tell him it was going to be all right, but I couldn't. Instead, I asked Elizabeth Walker where her car was.

"In your garage." She prodded Manuel along. He stumbled slightly as he walked and banged his head getting into the car. Walker got in next. "What are you waiting for?" she asked.

"Nothing." I looked around, hoping that one of my

neighbors hadn't left for work yet and was phoning the police, but I knew that they had left already. Then I got in.

The front seat was cramped with the three of us sitting in it—not that that was going to matter much. I had a feeling we weren't going to go very far. Elizabeth Walker told me where she wanted me to go. The area she indicated was about ten minutes outside of Syracuse. It was mostly marsh and I couldn't help reflecting, as I pulled out of the driveway and headed down East Genesee for possibly the last time, that it might be awhile before anyone found our bodies. It was going to be a perfect late fall day, I decided. The sky was cloudless, the temperature felt about fifty, everything was bathed in a golden light. I thought, if I'm going to die, I'd rather do it when it's grey and cloudy. Then I tried not to think about that.

"What about Amy?" I asked Elizabeth Walker.

"What about her?"

"She knows about you."

"Not really. She knows about Frank. Frank's her supplier. Frank beat up her boyfriend."

"Why did he do that?"

"Because he thought Toon Town was sleeping with me."

"Was he?"

"Not really. I used to go down on him once in awhile. That's not really sex."

Right. It was one of those distinctions I'd never quite understood. What had he said to me? I just want a little candy. Elizabeth Walker was the candy. "When he called, he thought you'd show up."

Elizabeth nodded.

"But you sent Frank."

She smiled. "I had to do my laundry and pay my bills. I hate paying late fees on my credit cards, don't you?"

"Absolutely. And it was Frank who shot Toon Town and shoved some acid down Amy's throat and put her on the roof."

"If I had both hands free, I'd clap. Amy's never seen me do anything and, even if she had, her head is so screwed up I don't think any court in the universe would listen to anything she has to say. No prosecutor would risk putting her up on the stand."

Unfortunately I had a feeling that what Elizabeth was saying was true.

"Get on Thompson," she ordered.

I snuck a look at Walker as I drove by The Springfield Garden Apartments. She was thin. A little too thin, really. Except for a slight overbite, her features were regular. She was okay looking. But not remarkable. Average would be the word I would use, certainly not a woman men would kill for. Not by any stretch of the imagination.

"How do you do it?" I asked.

"Do what?"

"Get men to do what you want?"

I'd never been able to get Murphy to do the dishes, let alone anything else.

Elizabeth laughed. "The usual way. I tell them what they want to hear. I make them think they're the most important thing in the world to me. I pretend they're the greatest thing in bed ever. I ask them for their advice. I let them think that I can't do anything without them, isn't that true Manuel?" she cooed.

He cringed and looked down at the floor. Even though I shouldn't have, I felt bad for him. Dying is bad enough. Dying because you've been a moron is terrible. I turned on to Thompson. The road was filled with people going to work. Right now I wished I were one of them.

"Did you plan this whole thing out?" I asked Elizabeth Walker, as I sailed through another green light. It was incredible. Today I was making every single light. Usually I never make any.

"No."

"At least tell me what happened."

"Why should I?"

"To satisfy my curiosity." But Walker didn't say anything. I guess she didn't care. "All right. Let me see if I can figure it out."

She curved her lips up in that thing she did that was supposed to be a smile. "Go ahead. Be my guest."

I turned onto James Street. "Let's see. Dennis and you had a thing going." She nodded slightly, to show I was on track. "How'd you find out he was stealing money from the company?"

"He told me. Actually Brad wanted me to see if I could find out anything for him. That's how this whole thing got started."

"And then you suggested that he chuck everything and that you and he run away together."

"He wanted a change."

"Well he certainly got that." We were getting closer to our destination. It was not a comforting thought, and I tried to put it out of my mind. "Who suggested the apartment?"

"I told Dennis we'd have more fun there than in a hotel. He had that place a week later. It was a sublet. It came with all the furniture and everything."

"Convenient."

Elizabeth didn't say anything.

"I guess you must have been seeing Frank too."

Elizabeth nodded her head briefly.

"And you decided to use one to get rid of the other."

Here was this man who was hiding out with a lot of cash. Walker must have figured no one would miss him. It could be weeks before his body was discovered. By that time, she would be far away. For a woman like Elizabeth Walker, it was an irresistible setup. And everything would have worked, if it hadn't been for Amy taking the diamonds.

"Dennis must have had other money, too," I observed. "Why didn't you just let the stones go?"

"Dennis lied to me," Elizabeth Walker said, indignantly. It was the first time I'd heard real emotion in her voice. "He told me he'd taken a million, but he hadn't. I couldn't find anything else. Those diamonds were it."

"Why didn't you and Frank go and get them yourselves?"

"We were going to, but then I ran into Toon Town. Once I realized he was seeing Amy, I figured it was easier for him to do it for me." She pointed. "Take a left here."

I took the turn wide and Manuel was thrown up against me.

"Slow down," Elizabeth Walker ordered.

I did. "How did you know Toon Town was seeing Amy?"

"He told me. He was buying some stuff from Frank, and we got to talking, and he told me about this rich, crazy, whacked out bitch he was seeing who'd just got out of Cedar View. Then he described her, and of course I knew who it was instantly. How many other people walking around Syracuse look like her?"

"Why the kidnapping?"

"We were afraid the cops were watching your place. So Toon Town came up with this plan. Which would have worked, if Frank hadn't gone off into one of his paranoid fits."

"So where are the diamonds?"

"In my flat." Walker told me to turn right. We were getting nearer the marshes.

"One more question."

"Yes?"

"How did Melanie fit into this?"

"Amy told her about what was going on. She went and told Toon Town she wanted a little traveling cash."

"And he told you and you told Frank."

Elizabeth smiled. "You got it."

"So the story Amy had told me about Melanie owing Toon Town drug money was hype."

"No. It was true. Toon Town had fronted Melanie some money for some grass. She just figured that under the circumstances, she didn't have to pay it."

"So tell me? Has this been worth it?"

"It will be after I leave."

"All the people you've killed?"

"I didn't kill them. They killed themselves."

"How do you figure that?"

"If Dennis hadn't stolen the money, he'd be here today. Melanie shouldn't have tried blackmailing Toon Town."

"Okay. How do you rationalize him?"

"He was a sleaze. Always sniffing around me. He had a girlfriend. He should have stuck with her."

"And what about Manuel?"

"He should have been smarter."

Manuel didn't even argue. I think he was too scared to say anything at all.

"And me?"

"You should have minded your own business."

I glanced over at Walker. "You're serious, aren't you?"

"Bad attracts bad. It's a well known fact."

"Given that premise, I can hardly wait to see what happens to you."

"Nothing is going to happen to me. I didn't do anything wrong. I just took advantage of the situation. I didn't set it in motion."

By now we were driving along a deserted stretch of road. The sky was a brilliant blue. Each cattail was outlined in the light. I could hear crows cawing off in the distance. It was now or never. I put my foot on the gas, turned the wheel to the right, and drove straight into the marsh.

"What are you doing?" Walker screamed, as she was thrown against the door.

"You did say you wanted to get away from it all, didn't you?" I pressed down even harder on the accelerator.

"I'm going to shoot your friend, if you don't stop," she threatened.

"Go ahead. You're going to shoot him anyway." We were bumping up and down. I heard the sound of metal tearing down below. We'd hit something. I wondered what it was, as I leaned over Manuel and grabbed Walker's wrist. She fired the gun. Manuel screamed. The smell of gunpowder filled the car.

"Oh my God," Manuel moaned.

I kept my hand on Walker's wrist. I was turning towards her when, out of the corner of my eye, I saw a rusted-out car in front of us. We hit it head on. The next thing I knew, I was on the ground lying in about an inch of water and staring at the sky.

I jumped up and began looking for Elizabeth. It took me a minute to spot her. She was on the other side of the car, crawling around on her hands and knees searching for her gun. She had her hand on it by the time I ran over.

She raised it, aimed at my chest and fired. I could hear

something whizz by my ear as I ducked. I kicked out at the gun. It flew out of her hand and I leaped for her. We rolled over in the mud. I could feel her nails clawing at my face. Then she put her head down and bit my shoulder. I screamed and punched her head. She let go of me and started crawling towards the gun.

"Don't bother," I told her, as I dragged her back by her leg. Then I punched her in the face and she fell back down.

I ran back to the car. Manuel was lying across the seat moaning. There was blood all over the place. "Thanks a lot," he said, when he saw me.

"I'm sorry Manuel."

"I guess you really were pissed at me, after all."

I started to laugh. I couldn't help it. "Where'd she shoot you?"

"My shoulder."

I tore the sleeve of his shirt off and looked at the wound. It wasn't as bad as I thought it was going to be. Walker had clipped him as I pulled her wrist up.

"What happened?"

I told him, as I helped him up and untied his hands.

"You know what?" he said.

"What?"

"From now on, I think I'm going to stick to females my own age."

"Good idea." And I hugged him.

Chapter 35

There were a couple of inches of snow on the ground, as George, Manuel, Gerri, Amy, Mr. Bones, and I walked down the path to Murphy's grave. We'd all managed to squeeze ourselves into my cab, since George's car was still in the shop. It would be another week before it was fixed. Fortunately, insurance was picking up the tab, but, even so, George told me he'd never let me get behind the wheel of a car of his again, even though he allowed that he would have done the same thing himself.

I snuck a look at Amy as she chatted with her mother. She was out on a day pass from Cedar View. Two weeks had made an enormous difference. She'd dyed her hair reddish brown and gotten rid of the heavy black eye makeup and the white lipstick. It looked as though the old Amy—the one I'd seen in the early photographs—was re-emerging. She caught me looking at her and smiled.

"I want to thank you," she said.

"It's okay."

"My mom said I should do something to make up for all the trouble I caused." She fidgeted. "I was thinking, maybe I could work in your store a couple of days a week when I get out of Cedar View."

I nodded. "It sounds like a good plan."

By now Gerri was talking to George and Manuel. Amy drifted over to my side. "So how's Mr. Bones getting on with your mother?" I asked. Gerri had come to the store and picked him up a couple of days after I'd delivered Amy to her.

Amy grinned. "Go figure. She thinks he's cute."

"Well he is."

"She just doesn't want him running around the house and pooping everywhere."

"That seems fair." I leaned over and stroked Mr. Bones. "He looks very dapper." Amy had put his harness on for the occasion.

"I'm going back to school in a couple of weeks."

"What about art classes?"

"I'm going to take those at night at the university. Then, when I graduate, I'll have a portfolio."

I broached what I was going to say next carefully. "Listen, if this upsets you, you don't have to talk about it, but if you want to, I'd really like to know how you found out about your father's diamonds."

"No, I don't mind." Amy kicked at the snow with her boot. The flakes flying up glittered like mica in the sun. "The first time I went up there, Dad was in the middle of shaving. He was really surprised to see me, let me tell you." She laughed as she recalled the expression on his face. "Anyway, he let me in and told me he'd be right back. And there was this little packet on the coffee table in the living room. I figured maybe it was drugs—Dad had been taking tranqs and sleeping pills—so I opened it. To see what was inside." She looked sheepish. "I thought, what the hell, maybe I'd take a few. Only it was diamonds. I don't know, I just put them in my pocket and ran out the door." She shrugged. "I guess that wasn't very nice, was it?"

"It certainly wasn't very smart." But then at her age, I hadn't been very smart, either.

Amy kicked up another clump of snow. "Maybe I was feeling guilt, or maybe I was smoking some bad weed, but I kept on thinking my dad was gonna find me and have me put in jail, and then I remembered what Murphy had said to me about you. I thought maybe you could get in contact with him, or something. I was working up my nerve to tell you, when I saw those cops waiting outside of your store and I freaked. The door to your office was open. I saw the desk and threw the package under it and ran."

"Then what happened?"

"I decided I'd better talk to my dad, so I called him and he told me to come on up. But when I got there he . . . was," her voice dropped, "gone. I didn't know what to do."

"So you called me," I finished.

She nodded.

"Why did you keep running away?"

"I don't know. I wanted to talk to you, but everytime I was going to, I kept getting this idea in my head that you were going to call the police and turn me in. I thought they'd arrest me for Dad's murder. I didn't think they'd listen to anything I had to say. At least that's what Toon Town kept telling me."

"Well, there you go." By now we were almost at Murphy's grave.

"He wasn't a very good person to listen to, was he?"

"I think it's safe to say that when a twenty-five-year-old man starts hanging around with a fifteen-year-old girl, he has a few problems."

"Tell me about it," Manuel grumped. I'd been so involved talking to Amy that I hadn't realized that Manuel had drifted back to join us. His gunshot wound was almost healed and, although he'd have to go to physical therapy for a couple of months, he was going to have complete mobility in his arm. "I'm definitely sticking to women my own age." He turned up the collar on his ski parka.

"Nice jacket," I commented. I think it was the first weather-appropriate piece of apparel I'd ever seen him wear.

"My mother made me put it on," Manuel said. "Walter bought it for me. I think it makes me look like a jerk."

"No. It's okay," Amy said.

"Really?" Manuel straightened his shoulders. "You're not shucking me?"

"No," Amy answered. "I'm working on not lying so much anymore."

I moved up in front of Murphy's tombstone and joined Gerri and George. George took out a couple of bottles of Sam Adams out of the bag he was carrying and opened them up.

"He did try," I said, indicating the tombstone.

Gerri nodded. "I think he meant well." She pulled her sheepskin jacket around her.

I nodded back in Amy's direction. "Are you going to tell her?"

"I've been toying with the idea."

"I think you should."

"When she's stronger." Then Manuel and Amy came up and Gerri fell silent.

They continued whispering to each other, while George

poured the two bottles of beer over the grave. He made a short speech, and I did the same, and we both promised Murphy we'd come and visit him at least twice a year. Maybe if he had more company, he'd cause less trouble. On the way back to the cab, George pulled me aside.

"When are you going to pay me my twenty-five dollars?" he said.

I did wide-eyed innocence. If it worked for Elizabeth Walker, maybe it would work for me. "I don't know what you're talking about."

"You lost the bet." He put his hands on his hips. "Didn't you think I'd be able to smell it?"

"Actually I was hoping you wouldn't."

"Don't you have any standards at all?"

"A few. But I'm working on getting rid of them, too."